The Evolution
of NIKKI
Blue

MONIKA M. PICKETT

The Evolution of NIKKI Blue

MONIKA M. PICKETT

ACKNOWLEDGMENTS

Thank you to my amazing editorial team, Janine Coveney, Clarence Haynes and Shona McCarthy. I am beyond grateful for your patience and expertise. Thank you to my siblings, Felicia Porter and Isreal Born. You are my biggest cheerleaders.

To my granddaughter, Cruz Paolucci, may you have the courage to stand tall in your own light. You, your brother and sister are my legacies.

I dedicate this novel to myself. It is my turn to shine.

- Monika M. Pickett

CHAPTER ONE

I was taken aback by the face staring back at me from the car window.

"It's you...the lady from the escalator."

Mona's dimples caved in as she smiled and opened the car door. I melted as she spread her arms and beckoned me toward her.

"It's me." Her strong arms enveloped me.

"What are you doing here?" I asked.

"I came to see you."

"How long are you here?"

"Just the weekend. We can do whatever you want. I know you have Karlos, so just let me know and I will work around your schedule." Her words ran together as I gazed at her. She was more stunning than her pictures.

"I would love to hang out," I said. "I just have to find a babysitter."

"Good. I couldn't go back to New York without seeing you. We better go. I know you have to get back to work. Call me later."

"Um, I will."

My mind raced in a million different directions as I walked back to my office. I couldn't wrap my brain around the fact that she was single. Had she really come all the way from New York just to see me? She was probably full of shit, like everyone else. But what if she wasn't? We often fell asleep on the phone every night, not wanting to let each other go. My eyebrows furrowed when I remembered I'd bought a two-hundred-dollar ticket to the Breast Cancer Survivors Gala for that night.

While grieving over leaving Valencia, I realized that I too was a survivor. Although I physically didn't have breast cancer, I walked that journey with her. I changed my life for her. I changed my son's life, only to have her want a life that didn't include us. I snapped back to reality and called my sister, Ce, on the way to pick up Karlos from school.

"What are you doing tonight?" I asked.

"Not a damned thing. Why?"

"I have a date."

"With who?" I could hear the excitement in her voice.

"Mona, from Chicago. Girl, if you don't watch your nephew tonight, I'm leaving him at the fire station."

"I thought you were going to the breast cancer event tonight."

"I was but she's only here for the weekend."

"Of course, I'll watch my nephew. Anything to get you out of the house."

Still, I felt guilty about spending two hundred dollars on a ticket and not going to the gala. I rationalized it away as a donation. I anxiously dialed Mona's number.

"Hi," I said.

"I thought you were going to stand me up like you did nineteen years ago."

"I learned my lesson."

"What do you want to do tonight?"

"I'm open."

"Shelly couldn't stop talking about you when we stopped by your office. He's an amazing cook. I thought maybe you could have dinner with us. He lives in Alexandria. Is that far from you?"

"I live in Maryland, but Karlos is spending the night at my sister's. She lives in Arlington, about fifteen minutes away from Alexandria."

"How does seven o'clock sound?

"Perfect!"

I felt so many emotions as I drove to Shelly's house. Was I ready to date someone so soon? It had been six months since I'd left Valencia, but our relationship had ended a long time ago. My heart said one thing, but my head said another.

I nervously rang Shelly's doorbell.

"Hi, Nikki."

"Hi, Mona." She motioned me in.

"It smells so good in here," I said.

"Shelly has been cooking all day to impress you." His face lit up when I walked into the kitchen.

"Hi, Shelly," I said.

He hugged me gently. "You're so lovely."

"Thank you. I was thinking the same thing."

"Would you like a drink? I have white and red wine."

"I'll take white. Thank you."

"So, Mona mentioned you have a little one. How old is he?"

"He'll be ten in November…"

Mona motioned me to sit at Shelly's counter. We spent the next hour listening to him sing as he cooked.

"Your voice is amazing," I said. He bowed dramatically.

"Shelly is a songwriter. He needs to sing his own songs instead of writing for other people."

The night wore on and eventually Shelly made a graceful exit upstairs. I relaxed as Mona poured us another glass of wine.

"I just realized that I hijacked your evening. Did you have any other plans?"

"I did. I was going to a breast cancer survivor's gala. I decided not to go because I wanted to see you."

Mona tilted her head. "You decided to spend time with me instead?"

"Yup. The ticket will be a donation and I can wear the dress some other time."

"I'm glad you chose me," she said.

I lost track of time as we listened to music. I couldn't stop staring at her as she talked. I couldn't help but interrupt her.

"You're so beautiful. Now, tell me again why you're single?"

She sipped her wine. "Well, the last woman I dated was still in love with her ex-boyfriend. Then, I was seeing this married guy I told you about."

"The NBA player?"

"Yeah, but of course that didn't last. I didn't feel good about myself when I was with him."

"Because he was married?" I asked.

She nodded. "That, and because I would always want a woman. I moved from Atlanta to be with a man, but I always had affairs with women. But enough about me." Mona placed her hand over mine and I didn't move it. "I couldn't wait to see you," she said.

"Why?"

"You seem so different, like a good girl."

"I'm a good girl...sometimes."

She grasped my hand and led me to a futon. She sat down and I straddled her. We looked deep into each other's eyes as we held hands. I leaned in and kissed her, my tongue tracing her full lips. She opened her mouth as we kissed slowly. I began to flow as I cradled her face in my hands. Our mouths never parted as I guided her onto her back. I sat on top of her as she reached under my shirt.

Nikki, what are you doing? You just met this woman. But I've poured my heart out to her, night after night. I need someone to want me.

Those thoughts went out the window as she began to unbutton my jeans. I sat up and removed them.

"I want you." Her voice was deep with desire as she sat up and removed her clothes. I exhaled at the sight of her nipple ring. After she lay on her back, I slowly traced it with my tongue. I wanted her to want me even more, so I made her wait. I lay down and placed the full weight of my body on top of hers. We fit together like a puzzle as I parted her legs with mine. She moved against me, our breasts pressing together. Suddenly, she pushed my breasts together and licked my nipples at the same time.

I felt delirious. Her moans invited me to go further. I tried not to climax too fast, but it was too late. I moved her hands, gripped her shoulders, and climaxed as she pulled me deeper into her.

She whispered, "I want you to eat me."

I kissed her before moving down her body. I opened her legs and laid down between them, my head resting in her hair. I began to inhale her scent. My mouth devoured her as she guided my head with her hands. My tongue played cat and mouse with her clitoris. I tasted her before I felt her climax. I held her ass in my hands until she let out a deep moan. I rubbed my face in her wetness as we caught our breath.

"You *are* nasty," she proclaimed.

We burst into laughter before drifting off to sleep.

I woke up the next morning, my body pressed against hers. Was I finally over Valencia? But Mona was bisexual. I had convinced myself that a bisexual woman would always want a man. Besides, how would that work? I just bought a house a house in Maryland, and she rented a place in New York but owned a home in Chicago. I had to stay focused. I had one year before earning my MBA from Johns Hopkins.

Mona shifted as if she felt my energy.

"Good morning." She rolled over onto her back.

"Good morning," I said. "What time is it? I promised to take Karlos and my nephew Ahmad to the medieval festival today."

She pulled me closer. "I would like to meet Karlos while I'm here."

I sat up on one elbow. "I want you to meet him, but I don't know if I'm comfortable with that. You said you've never dated someone with children."

"I understand."

I had been hurt so much that I was afraid to open my heart again, but over the past few months, she made me feel safe. I leaned over and kissed her on the lips.

"The festival is in Maryland. I could pick them up after I go home to change and swing back to get you."

"I don't want you to go out of your way. You can pick them up and I'll have Shelly drop me off at the festival. He can pick me up afterward." It was nice to have someone who thought of me for a change. Besides, if things got weird, I could always leave.

I couldn't stop thinking about Mona as I drove to pick the boys up from my sister's house. I laughed as she raised her eyebrow at the sight of me.

"Girl!" I said. "I have to call you later, but me and the boys have a date at the castle." It was the perfect opportunity to tell Karlos about my Mona. Although he was just nine years old, I never wanted to blindside him.

"Breezy, one of Mommy's friends is visiting from Chicago. She's going to meet us here. Is that okay?"

"Does she have a son, too?"

"No, she doesn't. She just wanted to hang out with us, but do you mind? This was supposed to be a special day just for you and Ahmad."

"It's okay, Mom."

I called Mona and gave her directions.

The boys chatted constantly as we drove to Maryland. Karlos's eyes lit up as we approached the festival gates.

"Are there kings in there?" he asked.

"Yes! Kings, queens, and horses," I exclaimed.

My phone vibrated as we heard the roar of the crowd as the festival commenced. I called Mona and gave her our seat numbers. She looked sporty and chic in wide-leg jeans and a Bob Marley T-shirt. Her chunky silver jewelry glistened in the sunlight. I motioned for the boys to move down a seat.

"You made it."

"I wouldn't have missed it for the world," she said.

I leaned forward and yelled to the kids over the cannonballs. "Karlos, Ahmad, this is my friend, Miss Mona." Ahmad waved as Karlos offered a faint smile.

"They're handsome and look so much alike."

"Thank you. They look so much alike because me and my sister look like twins. She's just taller and more chocolate."

Mona surprised me by buying the boys turkey legs and drinks. She was comfortable for someone who didn't have children. Then I remembered that she said her students at the academy were her babies. That explained her ease.

We walked around the park and laughed while the boys had their faces painted. I couldn't remember a time when I'd spent quality time with Karlos and Valencia. I always felt torn. We aimlessly followed Karlos and Ahmad as they ran from ride to ride.

"Thank you for hanging out with us today."

"I had to see if what I was feeling was real," Mona said. "I haven't felt this way in a long time. Will you come visit me in Chicago?"

Before I could answer, Shelly pulled up beside us. I promised to call Mona when I got home and put the boys to bed. We hugged goodbye and I daydreamed on the way back home. What was I feeling? She seemed so different from anyone else. I tried not to think of her as the boys showered and watched a movie before bed. I took a deep breath before dialing her number.

"Hi, I'm sorry if it's too late but I just put the boys down."

"No need to apologize. They come first. So…have you thought about visiting me in Chicago?"

I hesitated.

"I would love to, but I don't know if I can take off. To be honest with you, I can't afford it. You know I recently bought a house."

"I invited you, lady. So, I'll pay for your round-trip ticket. Are you having second thoughts?"

"Perhaps."

She laughed. "Perhaps?"

"Can I think about it and let you know?"

"Of course. I'm not going anywhere."

I thought about Mona's departure the next day and called Dean. From the age of seventeen, I could still count on her to lift my spirits.

"Hmm mm…wassup, trick? I was wondering when you'd call."

"You knew she was coming?"

"I was trying not to slip up and tell you."

"She canceled her plans to see me?"

"Plans? *You're* her plans. I'm sick of that dimple-faced bitch talking about you."

"Do you think she likes me?"

"She flew all the way here to see your silly ass. She really likes you."

"I don't know, Dean. We've been talking every night for three months. I didn't tell her that I left Valencia just six months ago."

"You better catch it, honey. Miss Thing has a fabulous villa in Chicago. She just opened an after-school arts program in Harlem. She's back and forth, studying and replicating performing arts schools. She's building a school and a performing arts academy in Chicago. You better hear me when I say she takes care of bitches."

"I don't need nobody to take care of me. I want someone to love me."

"Oh, bitch…you always want to be married."

CHAPTER TWO

Mona consumed my thoughts more than I cared to admit. I reminded myself to focus. I was determined to graduate from business school. I never wanted to depend on a woman. I continued to guard my heart, or so I thought. Still, I was fascinated as she shared her hopes and dreams. I revisited our conversation regarding her affair with a married NBA player. She said she wasn't proud of those indiscretions and that her heart would always be with a woman. I felt assured when she stated that he wasn't an issue because she couldn't stop thinking about me.

And yet, I pressed the issue further by asking her about Melissa.

"That has been over for a long time, but she doesn't want anyone else to have me," she said.

"But what do you want?"

"I want you."

"I don't know if I even believe in love anymore."

"Why don't we take one day at a time? I want to get to know all of you, and that includes Karlos. I know you're a package."

I thought about how different she was than any woman I had ever dated. Her consideration of Karlos tugged at my heart. Valencia had wanted me, but not Karlos. Danielle had wanted Karlos, but not me. Could this time be different?

I threw myself into work and school. Being a single working mother while juggling grad school was beginning to take its toll. Karlos's father, Christian Calabrese, helped as much as possible while climbing to the rank of army company commander. Life threw me a curve ball when I realized the owner at my new job didn't want to pay me the agreed-upon commission. He never expected me to reach my sales goals so quickly.

Ivan Nikoli was a heavyset Croatian who looked to be in his late fifties. His stated plans for hiring additional staff for the IT start-up never transpired. It was awkward being the only staff member in the small Arlington office. He was rarely in the office as he worked remotely from his Fairfax home office.

During my fourth month of employment, he began to come into the office more often. There were only two desks in the tiny office. One day, I realized he was listening in on my sales calls. I tried to maintain my composure as he awkwardly critiqued one of my calls. I was incensed as he stood over my desk, his voice bellowing through the small office. "He bluffs! You don't close him!"

I scolded myself for taking a job solely for the money. A twenty-four-thousand-dollar-plus commission position allowed me to pay for my half of Karlos's tuition. Mona calmed my nerves that evening.

"The blessing is you didn't need a down payment for your house. I'm sure you were able to save some money. I wish *I* had a VA Loan."

"I'm sure you do, but the things I saw over there…you wouldn't want to experience. VA Loan or not."

"You're absolutely right. I can't imagine the things you saw. Never mind."

"Was it more difficult buying a building versus a house?"

She hesitated. "Not really. Doug gave me one hundred thousand dollars and I bought the building at an auction. I wasn't making enough money when I was at BEAT, so I accepted his gift. It took me five years to renovate it. I couldn't keep taking money from Doug when I knew I couldn't give him want he wanted."

"Must be nice."

"What was I going to do? Say no?"

"I guess you had to do what you had to do."

I ended the call, caring more than I wanted to.

I was happy that Karlos was with Christian that weekend. I had two semesters to go before earning my MBA. I was exhausted yet determined to graduate. I could finally be proud of myself. I would forever be able to write MBA behind my name. Knowledge was power and no one would ever be able to take that away.

My patience began to wane at work. Ivan began cutting my hours as he questioned my revenue reports. He said his contract with his supplier had been renegotiated at a lower rate. I didn't believe him, so I tried to close as many new accounts as possible.

I couldn't wait to call Mona.

"Hi, are you still at work?"

"Yes, but I always have time for you. Have you thought about coming to see me?"

"My schedule is so crazy with school and work…"

"You don't want to see me?" She sounded sad.

"You know I want to see you. I know you said you would pay for my ticket but…I'm embarrassed to accept it."

"You never have to be embarrassed with me."

"You want to see me that bad?"

"Yes." I went to bed and prayed that I wasn't wrong about what I was feeling. I drifted off to sleep thinking about what could be.

My spirit felt lighter as I waited in the drive lane for Karlos after school.

"Hey, Breezy."

"Hi, Mom. Guess what?"

"What?"

"I made you something in art today."

"You did? Buckle your seatbelt and then you can show me."

"Close your eyes and hold out your hand," he said. I reached behind me and held my hand out. I felt something cold and hard. "Open your eyes!"

I slowly pulled my hand forward. My eyes welled with tears when I opened them.

"You made this for Mommy?"

"Yes, you like it?" I tried not to cry as I held a smiling ceramic mouse with a graduation cap and scrolled degree.

"I love it! Are you sure you made this, or are you tricking me?"

He giggled. "I made it because he's in school like you."

"I love it."

CHAPTER THREE

I was surprised when Dean called out of the blue. "I heard you bought a new house."

"Hey, Dean. Girl, I gotta find another job. Shit…I wish I had the body to dance again."

"We should go to the Playground this weekend."

"Girl, please. Karlos is home this weekend and I have a case study due on Monday." I hung up and continued to unpack while Karlos watched a movie. I got up early the next morning and reviewed my case study. I was surprised when Dean called again. She wouldn't take no for an answer.

"Where are you?"

"I'm home, studying, why?"

"What's your address?" she asked.

I exhaled. "Dean, I really need to finish this case study."

"I'm trying to bring you a housewarming gift." I reluctantly gave her the address. Thirty minutes later, there was a knock at the door.

"Somebody's at the door, Mom," Karlos yelled.

"I know, honey. It's Dean." He followed me downstairs.

"Open the door, woman! It's me."

I was speechless when I opened the door and saw Dean and Mona standing at the door with boxes full of groceries. Mona and I blushed as we gazed at each other.

Dean's sigh was exaggerated. "Oh? To hell with me! Help me with all this shit."

Karlos inched around my legs and squealed. "This is so much stuff!"

I grabbed a box from Dean and leaned in to kiss Mona on the cheek. "What are you doing here? And what is all this stuff?"

They followed me up to the kitchen. Karlos began to rifle through the boxes as Dean leaned against the counter and looked from me to Mona.

"I love y'all together."

I looked at Mona. "When did you get here? We just talked this morning."

She began unloading the groceries. "Dean had just picked me up. I took the first flight out. I wanted to help you get settled."

"She thought you could use some groceries since you're a starving graduate student. We went straight to LotsCo from the airport."

I shook my head as Karlos raced to his room with a Pop Tart. "This is so thoughtful."

There was an awkward silence as Dean dramatically looked at her watch.

"I love you bitches, but I got a gig in DC. Mona, call me when you're ready for me to pick you up."

I tried not to look disappointed. "You're not staying?"

Suddenly, I remembered that, although Karlos's room was fully decorated, after four months of being in my new home I still only had an air mattress in my room.

"I would love to stay, but is it okay? Would Karlos be okay?"

"He should be okay. We can watch a family movie after dinner."

We finished putting the groceries away and I gave her a tour of the house. I was embarrassed as we walked upstairs to my room. I stopped and turned to face her at the landing. "I should've told you before I invited you to stay, but I didn't want you to leave."

"What?"

I lowered my head. "I only have an air mattress."

She stepped up into my bedroom. "It's fine, honey. I slept on an air mattress for so long when I got my first apartment that I had to go to the hospital because of back spasms. I'm so proud of you. You bought this house all by yourself. That is major."

I tried not to look at my make-shift desk that held an old desktop computer and printer. She must have read my mind because she leaned in and kissed me.

"How about you pick out a bed you want. That'll be my house-warming gift."

I pulled away. "Mmm...I don't know about that. You've already been so kind, buying us groceries. That had to be at least two hundred dollars."

She lay down on the air mattress with her hands behind her head. "It's the least I can do since I plan to be in it."

The weekend flew by as I watched Mona interact with Karlos. I was cautious about bringing another woman into our lives so soon after Valencia. Karlos seemed to be comfortable with her as he tried to teach her to master his new video game while I studied.

That Monday morning, I was sad as I drove her to the airport after dropping Karlos off to school.

"Thank you for letting me spend time with Karlos. He's a good kid."

"Thank you for being so kind. I wish you could stay longer. I like having you around."

"I like being around."

We kissed, said our goodbyes, and promised to talk later that evening.

I couldn't stop smiling on the way to work. I was lost in a dream that I didn't want to wake up from. I walked into the office to find an envelope on my desk with my name typed on it. My throat tightened as I opened it and read that I was being laid off. What a coward Ivan was not to face me. What was I going to do now? I felt sick to my stomach, but the nausea subsided when a check fell from beneath the letter. There was a three-thousand-dollar commission check. Thank you, Father God. I could pay my mortgage for two months. But what about Karlos's tuition?

My head began to pound as I grabbed my purse and closed the door. I was grateful that Christian was picking up Karlos from school.

I got undressed and collapsed on my air mattress as soon as I got home. I pulled the covers over my head and wondered how strong God wanted me to be. The next morning, my eyes felt swollen as the sunlight beckoned me to open them. The shrilling of the phone jolted me back to reality. I smiled at the sound of Mona's voice.

"Well, hello. I was worried about you and Karlos when I didn't hear from you last night. I called twice."

I burst into tears.

"What's wrong?"

"I got laid off yesterday. What am I going to do? I just bought this damned house. What an asshole! He didn't want to pay my commissions even though I was meeting my sales goals." I wiped the snot from my nose.

"Oh, honey. Try to relax before you make yourself sick."

I exhaled. "I have to find another job. My tuition is paid with my student loans. I have enough money to pay my mortgage for two months. I need to apply for unemployment as soon as possible. I just want to run away."

"Shhh…don't cry. We will figure it out."

"I can't catch a fuckin' break."

"I have an idea. Why don't you come to Chicago and clear your head? I know you're going through a lot right now, but maybe a change of scenery will help."

"I wouldn't be great company. I have so much to figure out."

"We can figure it out together. Do you think Karlos can stay with your sister?"

"I don't know. I'm sure she would keep him, but…"

"I'll check for a roundtrip flight, and you can let me know when you can leave."

I fell back to sleep, wondering how fast I could find a job.

I pulled myself together before Christian dropped Karlos off. His smile made everything better as he raced to his room. I waited for Christian to bring in his bags.

"Damn, girl! Had a rough night?"

I ran my fingers through my hair. "I got laid off." I looked at the ceiling to keep from looking at him.

"Holy shit! What are you going to do? You just bought this house."

"Thanks a lot, Christian. I'm aware of that."

He leaned against the door. "Look, I'm sorry. You've had a rough couple of years. Karlos is just getting settled from moving from your mom's. Now you have to move again?"

"No one said anything about moving, Christian. I'll figure it out. I always do."

My heart was heavy as I drove Karlos to school that morning. He had no idea how our lives were about to change and neither did I. Later on, I broke the news to my mother. As usual, she went into full panic mode.

"What are you going to do?" she asked. "Will Karlos have to go to a new school? You can't move him again."

I rolled my eyes out of sheer exhaustion. "I know, Mom. I filed for unemployment this morning. I got my last commission check so that gives me some time."

Next, I frantically called my sister. She was my biggest cheerleader.

"Are you fuckin' kidding me? Damn it! We're just going to pray that you find something soon."

"I can't even think straight. Oh, that reminds me. You know I've been seeing Mona. We talk every night. It was nice seeing how she was with Karlos when she surprised me last weekend. She invited me to Chicago."

"I know that's right! Are you going? Maybe this trip will help you catch your breath."

"I don't know, Ce. I'm overwhelmed. I really like her, but I'm scared. What if she's like everyone else? You know, saying she wants one thing but does another."

"Well, just give it a chance. You never know. She could be the one."

"Do you have any plans this weekend? I may decide to visit her this weekend. If so, can Karlos spend the night?"

"No plans that my nephew can't be a part of."

I was relieved when I called Mona.

"Who is this?"

"It's me, lady. You still at work?"

"Where else would I be? Melissa is getting on my damned nerves. I had to fix some shit I know she did on purpose. I wish her ass would quit."

I tried not to think about the fact that Mona's ex-girlfriend worked for her. She sounded annoyed whenever they interacted. I made a mental note and changed the subject.

"Maybe I can change your mood," I said. "My sister said she would keep Karlos for a few days. So, if you still want to see me…"

"If? You just want to hear me say it."

I giggled. "Say what?"

"I want to see you."

"Do you…still want to see me?"

"You know I do. I can't wait to hold you and make everything better. I may need it more than you." I felt inspired as she shared her plans to open a multi-million-dollar performing arts facility on the South Side of Chicago. It felt good to be a shoulder for her to lean on. My mind drifted as the stress left my body.

Please, God…let her be different.

CHAPTER FOUR

I couldn't concentrate that week as I prepared to leave for Chicago. I was surprised when Mona called the night before to say that one of her male friends would pick me up from the airport. She had to attend a fundraiser and would leave once I arrived.

"Are you sure this is a good weekend to visit?"

"You'll give me a reason to duck out early. I circle the room once, see who I need to see, and I'm out. I'd rather be home painting." She said her friend Tommy would be picking me up and dropping me off at the fundraiser.

A fundraiser? What would I wear? She was so stylish that I didn't want to disappoint her. I packed Karlos's bag for the weekend before rifling through my closet. I settled on a pair of tall black leather boots. I felt sexy as I pulled out a zebra print mini-skirt suit and a red silk shirt with a draped neckline was the pop of color I needed.

I hugged Karlos tight when I dropped him off at my sister's. Hopefully, I would be in a better head space when I returned. My sister pumped me up as usual.

"Yes, girl! You better remind these hoes! Have fun and let her spoil you. You deserve it. Call me when you board." I hugged her tightly and left for the airport. My spirit felt light as I daydreamed on the plane. I decided to reach out to Stew from National Society of Black Anesthesiologist when I returned home to see if he knew of any sales opportunities. He'd left NSBA but he was well connected and respected in the advertising industry.

I stared out the window and allowed myself to get lost in the city lights as the plane circled over Chicago. What was this journey about? Where would it take me? I smiled and decided to go with the flow as I walked to baggage claim. I grabbed my bag and before I could turn around a tall handsome man placed his hand over mine.

"Nikki?" His bald head shone almost as brightly as his teeth.

"Tommy?"

"Your chariot awaits you."

"How'd you know it was me?"

He grabbed my bag with one hand and guided me with the other. "Mona said I would know you when I saw you. She told me about you, Miss Nikki."

I blushed. "Oh, Lord. What did she tell you?"

He looked at me and batted his lashes. "Enough…"

I listened intently as he pointed out landmarks as we drove to the fund-raiser. We pulled up to a grand building with a breathtaking entrance.

"I'm going to call her and let her know we're here."

I was caught off guard when he said, "She wants you to come in. She's almost ready. I'll wait out here for you ladies."

I looked down at my outfit and smoothed out my skirt. I felt like an overdressed stripper as a few tuxedo-clad guests walked in. A stern-looking white man opened the door for me. *Great! I'm underdressed.* But none of those feelings mattered when I locked eyes with Mona. It was as if we were walking in slow motion,…like we were the only people in the room. She seemed taller as she sauntered toward me. She was dressed in all black. Her neckline was draped with an exquisite silver necklace.

"I'm here," I said. She hugged me and I wanted to pass out from inhaling her perfume.

"Yes, you are. Was Tommy on time?"

"Yes, he's hilarious." I followed her as she guided me to the bar.

"I'm almost finished. Why don't you have a drink, give me about fifteen minutes, and we can get out of here."

I watched her walk away, greeting important looking people as she worked the room.

We held hands in the back seat as Tommy drove us to his house.

"Ladies, this is where I bid you adieu."

I thanked him before moving to the front seat. I waited as they kissed goodbye and Mona slid into the driver's seat.

"I can never eat at those events. Are you hungry?"

"A little."

We drove to her favorite sushi restaurant up North. I was in awe as she pointed out landmarks I'd only read about. Two hours felt like twenty as we talked about our hopes and dreams. I could feel myself falling for her. I was determined to fight it, but I was slowly losing the battle.

Her four-level Greystone was dark when we entered. I was in awe when she turned on the lights. We had walked into the first floor where she had her office. Huge paintings hung on the walls for as far as I could see.

"I know you're tired, so I'll give you a tour in the morning. I took my security guard, Misty, to the doggy hotel in case you weren't comfortable around dogs."

"Yeah, I need to jump in the shower. Thank you for being so considerate. I wasn't raised around dogs. I think I've always been afraid of them."

"You'll meet her next time you visit." She grabbed my bag and I followed her up the steps to her residence. We walked through the kitchen and up a wrought-iron spiral staircase.

The moonlight glistened through the floor-to-ceiling windows. We entered a bedroom, and she sat my bag down.

"Let me get you a fresh towel and washcloth. The bathroom is right there. Let me know if you need anything else. I'm going to check my messages."

I thought of how safe she made me feel as the water from the shower cascaded over my body. I heard music drifting from another room as I changed into my pajama short set and dabbed perfume behind my ears. She was sitting on the bed when I came out of the bathroom.

"That shower felt so good."

She stood up and extended her hand. "Come on. I made something for you. I want you to listen to it while I jump in the shower."

"You made something for me? When did you have time? You're always so busy."

"I always have time for you."

We walked hand-in-hand down a long hallway and entered a room with rounded walls. There were two chairs and a table in front of a marble fireplace. Our shadows danced on the walls from the flickering candles. We sat in the chairs.

"It looks like an artist lives here," I said.

"It took me several years to make it into what it is. I didn't have any money, so I watched and learned as the contractors tore it down, floor by floor. Now, I can do everything from hang drywall to run electricity. I didn't have an income until two years after I started the after-school arts program out of my basement. But enough about me. I want you to listen to something I made for you."

She walked over to her sound system and stuck in a cassette. "I was thinking of you when I made this," she said. "I hope you like it." She walked down the hall and I sat back in the chair and listened to Brenda Russell sing "So Good, So Right." The sweet melody played over and over in my head as I thought to myself. *Could it be that we were feeling the same thing? Afraid to be hurt, yet still believing in love. What if we could be everything I've always dreamed of?*

I was lost in my thoughts when the second song began. I smelled her perfume before she walked into the room and sat down beside me.

"You...made that for me?"

She grasped my hand. "That's how I feel about you. I want you to know that you are not alone. This...feels so right."

"I have to listen to the whole cassette. Thank you. I love it." I barely finished my sentence when she leaned in and kissed me. She pulled me to my feet and guided me to an iron canopy bed. She sat at the foot of the bed and pulled me between her legs. We held each other for what seemed like forever.

I nuzzled her neck and whispered in her ear. "You smell so good."

She pulled me deeper into her. She lay back on the bed as I climbed onto her lap. She slowly pulled my shorts down. I raised my hips to help her. I caught my breath as she removed her tank top and sweatpants. I wanted to faint as she covered my body with hers. We kissed as she positioned herself between my legs. I wanted her to control me...own me. I couldn't let her get away. Not this one. I had to make her forget about anyone that came before me.

We slid in our wetness as I spread my legs into a Chinese Split. She raised up and looked from one leg to the other. I smirked as her eyebrows furrowed in disbelief. I wanted her to stay there forever. Her thrusts became faster as we looked into each other's eyes.

"Tell me you love me," she whispered.

"I love you." With one final thrust she came all over me. We were drenched as she collapsed on top of me. I caressed the back of her head and we held hands as we drifted off to sleep.

"I love you, Nikki."

We woke up the next morning and I realized that we were making love versus having sex. It was two o'clock in the afternoon when we dragged ourselves downstairs to the kitchen. I smiled as she slowly shook her head.

"What?" I said.

"You're something else."

"Why do you say that?"

"I can't explain it. It's like I finally feel wanted."

"I love hard and I *know* what I want," I said.

She gazed at me as she scrambled the eggs. "I know what I want, too, and it's you."

"I'm a single mother, in grad school, bought a house, and just got laid off. Why me? Why me, when you've dated actresses, singers...?"

She slid my plate across the counter.

"Money and fame don't make you happy. I've dated women you've probably seen on television, but some of them are miserable. I love the way you make me feel and I hope you feel the same way."

We made love again before getting showered and dressed. Then we spent the day sightseeing. I didn't want to leave as we lay in each other's arms once more on my last night before returning home.

"What are you thinking about?" she asked, pulling me closer.

Don't do it, Nikki. Don't ruin this moment.

Before I knew it, I was leaning on my elbow. "Can I ask you a question?"

"Yes, babe."

"I know we've only been seeing each other for six months but…can you not sleep with anyone else?"

She turned over and lay beside me.

"That's a lot to ask, but tell me why? Why is who I sleep with important?"

"I don't want to share you with anyone, especially a man."

"I don't want a man or another woman," Mona said. "I want you, and…"

"How can we get to know one another if we're seeing other people? Every time you lay down with someone, or I lay down with someone, we leave a piece of ourselves. I don't want that anymore. I need more than that."

She hesitated before leaning over and kissing me. "I can do that…for us."

CHAPTER FIVE

I tried not to cry when Mona dropped me off at the airport.

"Thank you for coming to see me. I enjoyed you."

I gently squeezed her hand. "No...thank you. I needed to get away. I have so much to do. I'll call you when I board."

Tine flew even faster than the plane as I daydreamed about a life with Mona. Would she keep her word? Was that too much to ask?

My spirits were lifted when I recalled my conversation with Stew. He asked me to call him back about a potential job opportunity. I put Karlos to bed before returning his call.

"Yeah, I got your message," Stew said. "I don't know if you remember Lonnie, he's the publisher of *Today's Anesthesiologists*. He has a small team, but everyone works remotely. I know you're in school, so that may work for you."

"Is it full-time or part-time?"

"It's whatever you need it to be. The caveat is that it's straight commission. You would have to grind, but he has the same target market as NSBA. You could do this shit in your sleep. Take his number. He said to hit him up this week."

I felt encouraged as I wrote Lonnie's number down. *Please God, let this be an open door.* After studying that night, I called Mona to share the good news.

"I was thinking about you," I said. "I wanted to hear your voice before I went to bed."

"Thank you for thinking of me."

I spent the next hour telling her about my plans to graduate.

"Do you see yourself staying in that area?"

"You mean Maryland?"

"I mean the East Coast."

"I never really thought about it, but yeah. Christian is here and I always want him to be in Karlos's life."

"What if we decided to be together? Would you and Karlos move to Chicago?"

I paused. "I don't know. I love you, but…what if I uprooted Karlos and left my family and things don't work out between us?"

"But what if things did work out?"

"You're all I think about," I said. "It has to work out."

"I feel the same way. I want a family and I don't want to settle anymore. I would rather be alone than to think we want the same thing only to find out we don't. We can travel between Maryland and Chicago until you graduate. You and Karlos can move here. They have great schools here."

"You have it all figured out, huh?"

"No, but I was hoping you want the same thing."

"I do…but what about my house?"

"I'll buy you another house."

I laughed. "I see it's going to be hard saying no to you."

"Promise me you'll think about it."

"I promise."

I was anxious as I dialed Lonnie's number that morning.

"Hey, Lonnie. This is Nikki Blue. I was referred to you by Stew."

"Nikki, of course. Stew said you'd be calling. So, you're the rep who stole a few of our clients."

"Sorry about that, but you know Stew was a taskmaster."

Lonnie said he needed someone to hit the ground running. The fact that I worked for Stew was more than enough for him to offer me the position. He asked me to take until the end of the week to decide. I wouldn't have benefits but, thank God, Karlos was covered under Christian's insurance.

I accepted Lonnie's offer at the end of the week. The thought of selling advertising again lit a fire within me. Maybe the plans Mona and I had made could work after all. But what if Christian fought me about moving Karlos across the country? Just the thought gave me a headache. I shook my head and decided to cross that bridge when I got to it.

I dared not tell anyone I was thinking of picking up and moving across the country. I had to tell my best friends, but, due to school and work, I couldn't remember the last time I'd seen them. I would have to tell Ce and my mother before I told anyone.

Mona was thrilled when I called to tell her about my new position.

"I knew you would find something."

"Thank God, he was looking for a sales rep with experience in his target market."

"Target market? You *are* a real salesperson."

"I guess I am if I sold you."

"Speaking of sales. What are you doing next weekend?"

"Studying. Why?"

"I was thinking. I could come for the weekend and we can go shopping for a bed. That will be your housewarming and congratulations gift for your new position."

I hesitated because I wasn't comfortable having someone buy me such a costly gift. "I feel so poor. I can't even afford to buy my own bed."

"Don't feel like that. Karlos is in private school, and you just bought a house. Besides, it will be our bed."

The excitement I felt carried over to my new position. Lonnie was kind enough to turn over some existing accounts. I closed a repeat advertiser by the end of my first week. I knew that was his attempt to motivate me.

My mood shifted when I called Mona. She sounded irritated.

"Is everything okay?"

"I'm sick of this nut! I wish she would resign and stay out my damned business."

"Who?"

"Melissa! She knows I'm seeing someone. She brought the invoices into my office and asked me about your number. It's listed every day and night."

"So what? Y'all separated two years ago."

"I think she knows this is different."

"Why do you care?"

"Babe, she has access to all my business. Most importantly, my financials. She's done crazy shit before whenever I started seeing someone. I can't afford to have her fuck up my business."

"You sound so angry. Do you still have feelings for her?"

"No, but she still has feelings for me. She asked me if I was seeing someone."

"What did you tell her?"

"I told her no," Mona said.

"No? Why are you hiding our relationship, or whatever it is we're doing?"

"Whatever it is we're doing? Where did that come from? This is my business and until I can get her crazy ass out, I have to keep her out of my personal life."

"Do what you need to do, Mona. Let me go. I have to study." I hung up the phone before she could respond. She immediately called back.

"Did you just hang up on me?"

"I said I have to study."

"Let me say this to you. If you ever hang up on me again, you won't have to worry about hearing my voice again. I've been through that shit before and it's not cute."

"I'm sorry. Your relationship with her brings back bad memories."

"I don't have a relationship with her. She happens to be my ex who works for me."

I began to cry.

"Why are you crying?"

"I don't like how I'm feeling."

"How are you feeling?"

"Insecure."

She exhaled. "You have nothing to be insecure about. I love you and only you. I just haven't figured out how to get her out of my life."

"I'm sorry."

"Me, too. Just give me some time to figure this out. But please, don't ever hang up on me again. I, too, have bad memories."

I woke up the next morning, determined to focus on my goals. Spending time alone with Karlos made everything better. We stopped for ice cream after an indoor soccer game.

"Your left foot is wicked, Breezy. They were expecting you to shoot with your right."

"I know, Mom. They don't know I can shoot with both. What about Saturday's game? Olney has a fast left mid and I won't be there to help the team."

"Why won't you be there? It's your dad's weekend so he'll take you."

"He said I can't go because he's not driving that far."

"When did he say that?"

"When he picked me up from school the other time."

"Well, Mommy doesn't have class this weekend and Mona is coming to visit. I'll ask your dad if we can switch weekends so I can take you to your game. This is a big game, and your team needs you."

I could barely get Karlos in bed that night before calling Christian.

"Hey, Christian. I'm calling you to talk about this weekend. Karlos has a big game on Saturday. They're playing Olney and he told me you said you're not driving that far so he can't play."

"Look Nikki, I didn't sign him up for soccer, you did. My weekends will not revolve around a nine-year-old's soccer schedule."

"Really, Christian? Playing soccer keeps him busy while I'm in school," I replied. "Most importantly, it teaches him discipline and keeps him out of trouble."

"You're in grad school, not me! You act like he's playing professional soccer. Good, Lord!"

I tried to remain calm. "Me being in grad school will benefit both me and Karlos. The better my life is, the better his life is."

"Yeah, well, I'm not driving all over Virginia and Maryland for a kid's soccer game."

"What if I pick him up from school Friday, take him to his game on Saturday, and meet you halfway after his game?"

"You don't give up, do you?"

Before I could stop myself, the words slipped out. "Look Christian, I may not always live this close to you. One day, you're going to wish he were here."

"What do you mean by that?"

"I'm just saying. What if I landed a job in another state that I couldn't turn down after graduation?"

"You're not taking my son to another state."

"Oh, please. You barely spend time with him. You act like you can't do anything without Jill's permission. She makes you choose between her and your son."

"What the hell are you talking about? I see my son. And you're not taking him anywhere!"

"Whatever, Christian."

I was relieved by finally putting the energy of moving to Chicago in the universe. It helped knowing that Christian would prevent me from taking Karlos with me. That was the beginning of the battle, but I had to prepare for war.

CHAPTER SIX

My relationship with Mona began to progress quickly. A couple of weeks after she met Karlos, she invited us to meet her in New York. I was excited that morning as we headed up 95 North. I kept him out of school so we could beat rush-hour traffic. Mona's assistant, Yani, gave me her conference itinerary for the boutique hotel in Manhattan. Nothing could prepare me for driving in New York City on a Friday afternoon. My Honda Accord felt tiny as cabs cut me off and honked because I was driving too slowly. I panicked when I realized I was lost. I turned the radio off to concentrate.

"Are we lost, Mom?"

"No, honey. Why do you think that?"

"Because you always put your hand over your mouth when we get lost."

I laughed. "I think I missed our turn, but we're almost there." I was relieved when I saw the Q Hotel. The venue's purple awning was framed with billowing drapes.

Karlos's eyes widened. "Gosh, Mom. Is Miss Mona rich?"

"I don't know, honey, but she works very hard and her job pays for this. She's the boss."

I was exhausted by the time we got to Mona's room. Karlos knocked on the door and stepped back. Mona opened the door and playfully peeked through the crack.

"Miss Mona, it's Karlos and Mommy."

"Are you sure it's Karlos?"

He giggled. "Yes! It's me and Mommy."

She threw the door open wide. "You finally got here," Mona said. "I've been waiting for you."

Karlos hugged her and raced into the room. Her embrace was comforting.

"I thought you'd changed your mind."

"I got too excited and got lost."

Karlos squeezed between us. "Mom, we have two rooms!" I turned to see there was an adjoining room.

"I booked an adjoining room so Karlos would be comfortable," Mona said.

My heart melted. She had only stayed at the house once when Karlos was home. I never let him see us in bed together. I was grateful she was considerate enough to think of him.

Mona managed to integrate activities for Karlos around her work schedule. We all watched a movie together after dinner that night. Karlos thought we were at a theater as he continuously ate snacks from the bar.

"Breezy, that's not free. Miss Mona has to pay for that."

He lowered his head as Mona grabbed two Twizzlers out of his hand. "You can eat whatever you want. Just save me some."

We were on our second movie when Karlos fell asleep between us. I shook him gently.

"Come on, Breezy. You're going to sleep in your own room. Mommy will keep the door open."

"Goodnight, Miss Mona," Karlos said groggily.

"Goodnight, Karlos," she replied. I kissed him and tucked him in before joining her in the middle of the bed.

"Thank you for thinking of his feelings and booking two rooms," I said. "I hadn't thought of that."

She held my hands in hers. "I'll always think of what's best for him."

Karlos was exhausted by the time we ended the weekend at the FAO Schwarz toy store. A feeling of sadness came over me as I got dressed that morning.

Mona sat on the edge of the bed while Karlos busied himself with his new comic book.

"I don't want to go," I said.

"And I don't want you to go," Mona replied. "When am I going to see you again?"

"When do you want to see me?"

"Every day. When is your winter break?"

I stood between her legs and kissed her. "Mid-December to mid-January. Why?"

"A group of my friends go to Key West every year. I thought it would be nice for us to go."

"I've always wanted to go to Key West. I would have to see if Christian can keep Karlos."

"Well, let me know so I can book our flights. We'll all be staying at Opal's. It's a women's only resort."

She walked us downstairs and hugged Karlos first.

"Thank you for coming to hang out with me, Breezy. Maybe you and your mom can visit me in Chicago soon."

"Can we, Mom?"

"Maybe," I said.

I felt confident as I prepared for fall midterms, but those feelings were quickly shattered. After two months of working for Lonnie, he informed me that the company was being dissolved. The numbness I felt wouldn't allow me to break down.

My mother's voice echoed in my head: *God is not going to give you more than you can handle.* I barely had any savings left. I was ashamed to tell anyone that, once again, I'd been laid off. I mustered up the courage to tell Mona.

"I keep running into a brick wall."

"Don't worry," she said. "We'll figure it out. You graduate in six months, and I know you won't have a problem finding a new position."

"I feel like I can't breathe."

"I wish I were there to hold you."

"Me too."

She paused. "But…"

"But what?"

"If you lived here, I could hold you every night."

I remained silent.

"Hello?" she said.

"I'm here."

"I want you with me all the time. What if you sell your house, focus on graduating, and you and Karlos move to Chicago?"

"Is that what you really want?"

"Yes, but what do you want?"

"I love you but I'm afraid of uprooting Karlos, again. I have no family, friends…no support system in Chicago. What if I move to Chicago and you change your mind?"

"I'm not going to change my mind. I want us to be a family. I can help you find a job and we have great schools."

"Great private schools? It's important that I keep him in a private school," I said. "It's just so much. Picking up and moving across the country with no support? I've never made such a major life decision when it comes to a relationship. I want us to be a family, too, but I'm just…"

"Don't be afraid. I love you and we'll figure this out together. I want you and Karlos here with me."

I couldn't believe what I was contemplating as we hung up the phone. Could I move across the country without any support? I envisioned us having a life together. I drifted off to sleep, wondering how I would tell my mother and sister. More importantly, how would I prepare for the war that would ensue with Christian?

I threw myself into my classes. I was determined to graduate with honors. I was fueled by anxiety as the winter break approached. Karlos was spending the break with Christian, and I decided to take Mona up on her offer to go to Key West. Christian didn't seem happy for me when I told him of my plans.

"What do you have planned while he's on break?"

"I'll be in Key West."

He chuckled. "How can you afford that and you aren't working?"

I continued packing Karlos's bag. "Don't worry about all that."

"I'm just saying, Key West is expensive."

"Someone is taking me."

"This must be serious."

"I'm seeing someone, but she lives in Chicago."

"Has Karlos met her?"

"A few times. We were with her when we went to New York."

"Good for you. I hope it works out this time."

Mona and I had planned to meet in Miami before catching a commuter plane to Key West. My sister was happy for me when I gave her my itinerary. And yet, I sensed some hesitancy.

"She seems nice, but I want you to be with someone who deserves you."

"I know, Ce. We are taking one day at a time, but she's good to me and for me."

I heard the excitement in Mona's voice when I called before boarding. "I'll see you in an hour!"

I was nervous, as this was the first time we would be out as a couple in a group of lesbians. I tried not to look too excited as I scanned the airport's baggage claim area for her face. She looked radiant in all white linen.

"Hi!"

"Hey, babe," she said.

"You look like a fucking million dollars!"

She blushed. "Thank you, babe, but you just love me."

We grabbed our bags and headed toward our connecting gate.

"How long is this flight?"

"It's short, about forty-five minutes. I think everyone arrived yesterday or this morning. You'll get to meet Robin and a few of her girlfriends."

I was shocked when we walked out to the smallest plane I'd ever seen.

"Is this the plane?"

"Yup," Mona was calm as she buckled her seat belt.

"This shit looks like a toy plane."

She placed her hand on my thigh. "We'll be there before you know it."

I closed my eyes and braced myself for takeoff. A short time later, the flight attendant's voice startled me from my sleep as she announced our arrival into Key West.

The quaint restaurants and shops were bustling with vacationers as the cab driver pointed out popular attractions.

"Oh, look," I said. "I'd like to get a manicure and pedicure before the lingerie party tomorrow."

I was looking forward to spending quality time with Mona, but Robin had planned a full week of themed parties. I had packed different outfits in case we participated each day.

Opal's was a small, women-only resort. There was an older butch woman at the front desk who beckoned us with a hearty welcome.

"Well, aren't you ladies dazzling! Welcome to Opal's." I looked around the lobby as Mona checked us in. The décor reminded me of the 1986 movie *Desert Hearts*. We walked down the hall to a white stucco room with vintage furniture. I opened the French doors.

"Every room on the first floor opens up to the pool," Mona said. I held her from behind.

"How many couples are here?"

"I'm not sure, but at least seven couples and a few single women."

We unpacked our bags, ordered room service, and took a nap. Mona kissed me on the lips as I opened my eyes.

"I have to make a few calls for work, so why don't you get your nails done while I'm working? We can get ready for the party when you get back." She gave me money for the cab ride and my nails. The nail tech had just started my toes when my cellphone rang.

"Hi, some of the girls are having drinks by the pool before the party. So, come to the pool when you finish."

"Okay. Are there a lot of women there already?"

"Just a few. but some of them are juiced up already."

"Already? Are we dressing up for the lingerie party?"

"You know I'm not doing that."

"I'll just throw on some shorts and meet you at the pool."

She chuckled and said, "Hurry!"

"They after you?"

"A few women keep asking me where my girlfriend is," she whispered into her phone.

"What'd you tell them?"

"I told them that you were getting your nails done and they looked at me crazy. I think they're assuming you're butch."

"I'll be there shortly. Have fun." I hung up the phone knowing what I was about to walk into. Based on their reactions, these were women who were stuck in the old-school norms of labels. I'm sure they couldn't imagine two feminine women together. I was going to confuse them even more. I felt sexy as I jumped in the cab back to Opal's. I took a quick shower and got dressed. I lightly dusted my face with a bronzer. It was too hot for a full face of makeup. My lashes and freshly arched eyebrows were just enough.

I could hear the music from the room. My yellow toenail polish glistened as I stepped into a pair of clear plastic heels. I lathered up my thighs with baby oil before slipping into my cut-off jean shorts and white V-neck T-shirt. The humidity hit me as soon as I opened the door.

I could hear laughter over the music as I rounded the stone columns. There were at least twenty women in the pool. I scanned the pool chairs for Mona. She was too shy to wear a bathing suit in front of strangers. I recall her telling me early in our relationship that being in an exclusive lesbian setting made her nervous.

"Why does that make you nervous? Like, the lesbians are going to get you?" We laughed.

"I don't know, but it does."

Her voice brought me back to reality.

"Honey..." She was seated with a group of women. I felt the stares as my heels clicked on the concrete.

"Hey, babe," I said. She stood up and kissed me on the lips.

"Your toes are hot! Let me see your nails."

I spread my fingers dramatically.

"Ladies, this is my honey, Nikki," she called out.

"Oh, I like her, Mona. I'm Robin. What you drinking, baby girl?"

I sat down beside Mona. "Thank you, any cold beer will do."

"Aw shit, a beer drinker."

Mona looked mischievous as she leaned over. "They're confused," she whispered.

"Why?"

"They were looking crazy when I told them you were getting your nails done. Then you walk up in here looking like a sex kitten."

I scanned the pool as a few women eyed us.

"They don't know I'm a boy for real."

"They really don't."

Women began changing into their lingerie as the night wore on. Several of them had been drinking most of the day. Coupled with the heat, it was a recipe for disaster. Robin began a game of Truth or Dare. Mona and I bowed out and settled for being spectators. We laughed until our stomachs hurt at their drunk antics. That was the day I realized you have to be very secure when you have a beautiful girlfriend. I slowly sipped my beer as a white couple made their way over to us. There were teetering on the edge of the pool as they drunkenly danced offbeat. The brunette slipped out of her cover-up and danced over to Mona.

"I think this would look better on you, Miss Mona," she said.

I sensed Mona's discomfort. "No, you got it."

I watched as the brunette grabbed another drink from the passing bar girl and draped her cover-up over Mona's breasts.

"Babe…" I said. Mona glanced at me and gently pushed the woman away. Robin and her girlfriend Kat looked amused.

My voice was louder this time. "Babe! You better handle this before I do."

Again, she nervously pushed the brunette away before turning to the woman's girlfriend. "Get your girl."

"Yeah," I said, "'cause this bitch about to be in the pool!"

Mona turned toward me. "Babe!"

"I ain't playing. She 'bout to get it."

Kat stood up. "I got your back, Nikki. This bitch is out of pocket."

Tension filled the air until the brunette's girlfriend touched her shoulder.

"Come on, baby. They don't want to play."

Everyone then burst into laughter.

"I know that's right, Nikki. Baby…you ain't the one!" Robin handed me another beer.

"No, I'm not."

That was the moment I realized the difference in our personalities. Mona didn't like scenes and I didn't mind causing one.

CHAPTER SEVEN

Ireturned home with a newfound determination. But how could I tell Karlos that we were moving again? I dreaded having that conversation with Christian, but why should everyone be happy but me? I deserved happiness, too.

I had to pass my corporate finance class that first semester in order to take Finance II the second semester. If I didn't pass both classes, I wouldn't graduate. I was passing my marketing classes effortlessly, but corporate finance was the bane of my existence. There were many Saturdays when I took Karlos with me to class because I didn't have a babysitter. I remember bracing myself when I walked into my first Corporate Finance I class. Professor Will just smiled and continued his lecture as Karlos and I sat in the back of the class.

"Okay, Breezy, Mommy wants you to do your homework while Mommy does hers."

"Your class is big, Mom."

"Shhh…" I finally got the nerve to look at Professor Will. He was a stocky man with chocolate skin. His salt-and-pepper hair framed keen features. He nodded at me as one of my classmates stood at the board.

"Great job!" He walked midway through the classroom and looked at the board.

"Miss Blue, how about you take a crack at number two?"

I froze. Why was he calling on me? Was this punishment for being late and bringing Karlos to class? I stood up and walked to the board. I was halfway through the equation when I got stuck. It felt as though everyone was staring at me, knowing I didn't have the answer. I turned to face my classmates as Professor Will's voice bellowed from the back of the classroom.

"What do you think, young man?" I looked up and he was kneeling beside Karlos. "What is the dividend payout ratio?"

"Um…I think…I think that one is too hard for my age," my son squeaked out. My classmates burst into laughter as Professor Will ruffled Karlos's hair.

"I agree. Your mom tried but that's a hard one."

I was relieved when Professor Will completed the equation. I helped Karlos pack his book bag as my classmates filed out of the class.

"I'm sorry, Professor Will. I didn't have a babysitter and I couldn't miss class."

He continued to pack his briefcase. "That's quite all right. Some of your classmates miss class and they don't have the responsibility of being a parent. I'm glad you didn't miss the class. We have four more classes before finals. How are you feeling about the class?"

"I'm struggling," I admitted. "I know I can't take Corporate Finance II without passing this class."

He placed his hand on my shoulder. "Don't be so hard on yourself. You're almost there. I can email you some extra problems that you can prac-tice on in preparation for finals. I think you have a B right now. If you pass the final with at least a C, you'll be fine. It won't be easy, but you can do it."

The day I walked into my final Corporate Finance I exam, I felt nause-ated. I closed my eyes and prayed before picking up my pencil. I felt confi-dent about the first half and took educated guesses on the difficult questions. I did the best I could and that is all I could ask of myself.

My shoulders relaxed when I saw Karlos's gap-toothed grin as he ran across the school yard.

"I thought dad was picking me up."

"Nope. Mommy just finished a big test and I thought we deserved some ice cream."

I tried not to think about my exam as we drove home. The ride seemed longer that night. I thought about Mona to distract myself. Before opening my email from Professor Will, I called her.

"I'm nervous. I can't take Finance II without passing this class. If I don't pass, I won't graduate and all my…"

She stopped me. "I feel like you passed it. Then you can take your last class, graduate, and move home."

"Home?"

"This will be you and Karlos's home, too."

I took a deep breath. "Okay. I'm going to open this email."

I opened the email and my eyes focused on the bottom of the page. The "C+" jumped off the page.

"I passed!"

"I told you."

I exhaled. "I barely passed with a C-plus."

"We have to celebrate. Is Karlos with you or Christian next weekend?"

"We switched weekends. He's taking Karlos with him to visit his grandmother. Why?"

"I'm going to book your ticket to come home."

"Why do you keep saying home?"

"I want to make sure you don't change your mind," Mona said.

"I won't."

I couldn't wait to tell my sister about my plans for that weekend.

"I know that's right! What does she do again?"

"She founded a performing arts organization."

"This is your second visit. When are we going to meet her?"

"Maybe next month." It hadn't occurred to me that my mother and sister hadn't met Mona in the six months we'd dated. I either met her somewhere or we stayed in a bed all weekend when Karlos was with Christian. Everything was happening so fast, but it felt so right.

I'd fallen deeper in love when she showed me that she would do anything to make me happy. On our four-month anniversary, she said she needed to get away from Chicago. The quaint bed and breakfast was tucked away in the small beach town of Three Oaks, Michigan. The anonymity was refreshing as we walked through town without her being recognized. I didn't have to share her with anyone as I breathed in the crisp air.

"I want to live here," I said.

She chuckled. "I haven't been up here in years. One of my friends had an aunt who let us use her house during the summers when she was out of town. The parties were crazy."

"No,...really honey. I want to live here."

She looked incredulous when I picked up a local newspaper and dreamily began scouring the real estate section.

Two months later, I knew she was falling just as hard. She refinanced her home in Chicago and purchased our vacation home an hour outside of Chicago. The loan was in her name but, to show me she loved me, she added my name to the deed. We didn't tell anyone for fear they would think we had lost our minds.

I began to spend more time in Chicago whenever Karlos was with Christian. During one of those weekend trips to Chicago, I almost ran to the car as Mona waited outside the airport. She looked stunning as she sat in a vintage Alfa Romeo.

"You're here."

"I'm here. This is beautiful. I thought you only had the truck."

"I just got it out of the shop, but I gotta have a truck for these Chicago winters."

She'd barely finished her sentence when her phone rang. I gazed out the window as she hissed into the phone. "Why would you make that decision without speaking with me first? That requires my signature and I'm not coming all the way back into the office. Leave it on my desk!"

"How long are you going to deal with this?" I asked.

Mona shook her head. "Don't do this."

"Every time you talk to her your whole mood changes."

"I'll fix it. I just don't know how yet."

We spent that weekend running errands as she showed me around Chicago. It hit me that I was really going to step out on faith and move across the country with no support system. I began to feel comfortable as I washed her clothes and cleaned the house. Getting to know her dog, Misty, was another story. I remember when I walked into the house and saw her: Misty was a grey Weimaraner with blue eyes. Her growl was ferocious as I backed out of the door until Mona handed me a treat to win her over. I gingerly coaxed her with treats until she got used to me.

I had almost forgotten how beautiful her home was. A white baby grand piano stood in the center of the living room. I sat at the bench, gazing at the fireplace and the art on the brick walls. This was a bachelorette pad. No, this was a "pussy-pad." I could only imagine the things that had happened within these walls. I walked downstairs to her office and sat in the chair in front of her desk. Oh, yeah. The pussy-pad days were over. We were going to make this a home. I thought of the women who'd come before me. I needed to leave my mark. The voice of one of my gay friends from high school rang in my ear: *Miss Thing, you better sling the coochie and the booty to get her off the market!*

While Mona was out, I spent the rest of the day pampering myself until I thought Mona would be home. I ran a bubble bath in her claw-foot tub. I sat on the bed in her guest room and slowly lathered my body with lotion. I put on some heels and looked around the room until I found a pen and a piece of paper. I closed my eyes and relished the moment before writing. My note directed her to strap up with the dildo we purchased and to meet me in her office. I left the note on the living room table where I knew she would see it.

I lit some candles and placed them in the hallway to her office. Anxiety set in as I sat on her desk, my legs crossed with anticipation. I was starting to think she was working late when I heard the alarm sensor. I listened as her heels clicked on the hard wood floor above. I leaned back on her desk as the sound of her heels became louder...closer.

Our eyes locked as soon as she rounded the corner.

"Where does she sit?" I asked. Mona looked confused as I repeated myself. "Where does she sit?"

Without saying a word, she entered the office and sat in the chair directly in front of me. We sat in silence as I opened my legs. Instinctively, she got up and stood between them. I wrapped my legs around her ass, pulling her closer. Her scent was intoxicating as I nuzzled her jawline. I wanted to make her wait...make her want me. I gently pushed her away and I guided her onto the chair.

I slowly bit her lip before plunging inside her mouth. My heart raced as she cupped my breasts, releasing them from my lace top. I tore my lips from hers and placed her head between my breasts. The sensation of her lips on my skin was tortuous. I gently pulled away and unzipped her pants. She stood up as I leaned over her desk and spread my legs. She began to fondle my ass. I stretched out further across her desk as she slowly eased the dildo inside of me. She began to stroke…in and out. Her moans became melodic as I met each thrust. They became faster and faster as she gripped my shoulders. The sound of my wetness echoed off the walls of her office.

I thought of how that bitch stressed her out in this very space. The more I thought of her being stressed the harder I rode the dildo. Without warning, I reached behind me and grabbed the dildo. She gasped when I pulled it out and slowly inserted it in my ass. I spread my legs wider as she eased the dildo in…inch by inch. My body swayed between pain and pleasure as wetness oozed down my thigh. Once inside, her thrusts became harder and harder as my thighs slammed against her desk. I climaxed with one last stroke. My heartbeat slowed as she lay on top of me, spent on top of her desk. She stood up, eased the dildo out and spun me around to face her.

"Whenever she sits in that chair, you *will* think of me," I said.

CHAPTER EIGHT

The thought of all my responsibilities rushed back on the plane ride back home. But this time was different. Knowing I had someone beside me made it all doable. We made plans for Mona to finally meet my mother and sister on her next visit. I braced myself before calling Christian to tell him I was back in town.

"Hey Christian, are we meeting halfway, or do you want me to pick Karlos up from school tomorrow?"

"Oh, hey. You're back?"

"Yeah, I just got in."

He chuckled.

"This Mona, she must be special. Karlos said she invited you guys to Alabama."

I paused. "Yeah, she did. We're going to meet her grandmother."

"This must be serious."

"It is."

"How will that work? You can't afford to keep flying to Chicago."

"Why are you always in my pockets? You don't know what I can afford."

"Well, I know you're not working."

"What business of that is yours?"

"Don't get any ideas."

"Ideas? What ideas, Christian?"

"Like trying to move to Chicago. You're not taking my son away from me."

I almost spat the words out. "Taking your son away from you? You act like you're afraid to spend time with him."

"What are you talking about? I spend time with my son! I pay for half his tuition and give you what I can."

"Oh, please! You spend time with him, but you allow Jill to regulate how much time you spend with him. When he gets older, you're going to have to deal with this, Christian. Jill may not always be your wife, but Karlos will always be your son."

"Whatever. If you're thinking about moving to Chicago, you can forget about it!"

My head hurt as I slammed the phone down. I knew it was coming, but I had to admit to myself that I wasn't ready for this fight. Not now. I had too much to lose.

During our quality time alone, I begin to feel Karlos out on Mona being in our lives.

"So, Breezy. Miss Mona is coming to visit next weekend. I wonder what fun things we could do? What do you think?"

"Like the festival we went to?"

"I don't know, something different. You have a soccer tournament that weekend, but we can do something afterwards."

His face lit up. "Can we go drive the go-carts?"

"That would be fun. Is it okay if Miss Mona comes with us?"

"Yeah, she's nice and she said she has nephews that I could play with when we visit Alabama."

I felt relieved as I tried to ease him into my decision.

I was three months shy of graduating. I managed to maintain a 2.7 grade point average, but I was drowning in Corporate Finance II. Anxiety set in as I emailed Professor Will and asked if I could call him.

"Ms. Blue, to what do I owe this honor?"

"Professor Will, I don't know if I can pass Corporate Finance II."

He chuckled. "But you're passing it. Your halfway there!"

"But If I get another C, that will be my second one and I'll be expelled."

"I don't know what your financial situation is, but I tutor students in preparation for Corporate Finance II. I charge one hundred dollars per hour. I meet with students twice a week."

One hundred dollars? My welfare benefits were only $635 per month. There was no way I could afford a tutor. The thought was overwhelming.

"Nikki?"

"Let me look at my finances, because I can't afford *not* to hire you."

The week before Mona came was a blur. I was glad to have another day to prepare when she called to say she wouldn't arrive until Saturday, but she would stay until Tuesday. It was going to be interesting to see how she fit into our everyday life. Karlos had a soccer tournament in Richmond that Saturday afternoon. Luckily, Mona would take the red eye. She didn't seem to mind when I told her we had to drive an hour to Karlos's tournament as soon as we picked her up from the airport.

"That's fine, babe. I have to adjust to his life."

I was later caught off-guard when I called my grandmother to check on her. She sounded excited when I told her I had met someone new.

"She's different than anyone I've ever met, Nana. Unlike those other nuts I chose, she loves me and Karlos. She's coming to visit this weekend. We have to drive to Richmond for his soccer tournament."

"Oh, that's nice. Have you talked to your father?"

"I haven't talked to him in years, Nana."

"Nana's sorry to hear that. I know your father would love to see you and Karlos."

My heart sank when she began to cry.

"Don't cry, Nana. He hasn't been a father to me, and I don't trust him after he snuck and met with Christian behind my back."

"He thought he was being a good father."

"How? By threatening to take my son away from me? By telling Christian I'm a lesbian? Thank God, Christian knows I'm a good mother."

She sniffled. "Family is all you have, and I don't want you or your father to have regrets. Tomorrow isn't promised."

"I know, Nana but…"

"Would you just try for Nana? If I let him know you're going to be in Richmond, would you let him see Karlos?"

I hadn't seen my father in four years. He didn't deserve to see Karlos. My stomach turned at the mere thought of him. And yet, hearing my grandmother cry softened my heart. How could I say no to my Nana?

"You can let him know, Nana. Karlos's game is Saturday morning. Mona, my friend, will be with me."

"I'll call him and let him know. Nana loves you."

I thought about the things we do for those we love. And then I called my sister for support.

"Hey, Ce. What are you doing?"

"Just got in from Ahmad's hockey practice. What's up?"

"Everything. I called Nana to check on her and I told her we're going to be in Richmond for Karlos's tournament on Saturday."

"Okay…"

"She asked if she could let my father know so he could see Karlos."

"Oh no, Nana. Did you tell her what he tried to do with Christian?"

"Of course I did, but she started crying when I said I didn't trust him."

"I know you were like, fuckin' great!"

"Right! And Mona will be with us. She's flying in Saturday morning and we're driving straight to Richmond."

"What are you going to do?"

"I don't know. I wasn't expecting that, but I couldn't say no when she started crying. Maybe we can stop by so you can finally meet her. I have a lot to talk to you about."

"How long will she be here?"

"Until Tuesday."

"Okay. Me, Mommy and Ahmad will drive out on Sunday. But yeah, we need to talk."

I dreaded talking to my father. I prayed that he would be his cowardly self and have my stepmother call me. I packed the car with Karlos's gear and wondered how Mona would fit into our lives. Just thinking of her calmed my nerves. That peacefulness dissipated when my stepmother called that evening.

"Nikki? Hi there. How are you? It's Deena. I hope it's not too late to call."

"Hi, Deena. No, I was studying."

"Your Nana said you were in business school. I don't know how you do it all." There was an awkward silence.

"Your Nana told your father that Karlos has a soccer tournament here on Saturday," she continued. "We would love to see you both."

Thoughts surfaced of my father's threats to take Karlos from me. "Yes, Nana said she would let you know. His tournament is at 11 o'clock at Sodder Field."

"That's only twenty minutes away from the house. Your father and I will be there."

I felt anxious as I thought of seeing my father after being estranged for so many years. Yet, everything felt right as we waited for Mona to land.

"So, Breezy. Guess who's coming to your game?"

"Ahmad?"

"No, Pop Pop and Deena. Remember, they live in Richmond. They want to see you."

"Pop Pop? I thought you were mad at him."

"Well, Pop Pop did something that really hurt Mommy, but I told Nana he could see you. Is that okay?"

Mona's call was the distraction I needed. We laughed on the two-hour drive as Karlos talked about his formidable opponents.

We pulled up to an in-door soccer complex forty-five minutes before Karlos's first game. Karlos grabbed his gear and ran toward his team.

"You sure you're up to being a soccer mom?"

"I don't know if I will be as good you, but I'm going to try. How are you feeling about seeing your father?"

"I won't know until I see him. He had my stepmother call me, but whatever…" I waved at Carol, Karlos's soccer coach, and found a spot on the bleachers. "How was your week?" I asked.

Mona looked over her sunglasses. "I had a couple of meetings with Melissa, and she kept asking me why I was looking at her like that."

"How were you looking at her?"

"All I could think about was you straddling me in the chair she sat in. She leaned over my desk for me to sign checks and I couldn't even look at her."

I winked. "That was the plan."

Soon afterward, the referee blew the whistle and I looked for my father. Karlos's team won their first game and progressed to the next round. Maybe he wouldn't show up after all. I talked myself into thinking I wasn't bothered, either way. We were twelve minutes into the second game when Cody, Carol's son, passed the ball to Karlos on the left side of the field. Karlos was midfield when he shot the ball with his left foot. I heard my father's voice roar over the applause as the ball glided into the net.

"Aye! Breezy! Go Breezy!" I turned toward the sound of his voice. I continued to clap as my throat tightened. Mona gave me a high five as I nodded toward the sideline.

"He's here," I said.

"You okay?" I sat down on the blanket.

"Let's just stay here until half-time." I was sure he had seen us, but he didn't attempt to move, and neither did I. A bit later, I was relieved when Karlos's team didn't make it to the final round. That meant we wouldn't have to stay until the end. I watched my father walk onto the field and hug Karlos. We began to walk toward them as my stepmother did the same. Karlos blushed when my father kissed him on his head.

"Man! Where'd you learn how to kick like that? And you can shoot with both feet? That dude never saw you coming."

"In practice. I'm a righty but I can shoot with my left."

My father hugged him again.

"I'm proud of you, man."

I felt like a little girl as I whispered, "Hi, Dad."

His smile faded when he turned to me. "Yeah, hey Nikki." It felt like we were the only ones in the complex as Mona and Deena stood by. I broke the silence.

"Hi, Deena. This is Mona." They shook hands as my father briefly looked Mona up and down and turned back to Karlos. "This boy should go professional. He's good."

"I don't know about professional, but hopefully he'll play for a Division I school."

My father put his arm around Karlos's shoulder as we walked toward the parking lot.

"How long has he been playing?" he asked.

"Since he was five. I signed him up for a traveling team when he was seven. They play other elite teams in DC, Maryland, and Virginia."

My father continued to stare at Karlos. I wondered what he was thinking. After all those years, I never forgot his words: "You will not turn my grandson gay!" I knew he was surprised that Karlos was a typical little boy who was athletically inclined. Not to say that he couldn't be gay, but he wasn't, as far as I knew. If he were gay, it was my job to love him unconditionally.

We stopped walking and I realized we were parked on opposite sides of the parking lot.

My father tossed a forlorn nod at the rows of cars and asked, "You headed back up the highway?"

"Yeah, Mona just flew in from Chicago this morning. She's tired."

He finally acknowledged her. "So, you're from Chicago?"

"Actually, I'm from Alabama. I've been in Chicago for a while now," she said.

He stepped back. "What took you to Chicago?"

"I was a sales representative for BEAT before starting an arts academy for underserved youth."

"All right, now."

"We gotta get on the road," I interrupted. "Thank you for coming to his game."

My father drew Karlos close before pulling his wallet out. "Pop Pop got something for you," he said. He pulled out a fifty-dollar bill and handed it to Karlos.

"Wow, mom! Fifty dollars! Thank you, Pop Pop."

"Don't spend it all in one place, now. Call your Pop Pop sometimes and keep shooting with that left foot. That's a secret weapon."

I felt awkward as I hugged Deena. Neither my father nor I knew what to do, so we simply said goodbye.

CHAPTER NINE

The ride was quiet on the way back to Maryland. Karlos was asleep in the back seat while Mona and I caught up. In the back of my mind, worry about my Corporate Finance II class persisted. I had to pass, or all my hard work would be in vain. We ordered takeout that night. I went into Karlos's room and kissed him good night after he showered. We never talked about the fact that Mona would sleep in my bedroom. He didn't ask and I didn't bring it up.

I lay down and rested my head between her breasts. We quietly made love and talked about our plans for me and Karlos to move to Chicago. I drifted off to sleep knowing that I was no longer alone.

We spent the next morning laughing and getting ready for Mona to meet my mother and sister.

"Are you ready?" I asked.

"Yes, but I hope they won't hate me for taking you and Karlos to Chicago."

I hesitated. "I haven't had a chance to tell them yet. I'll probably tell my sister before I tell my mother."

"What about Christian?"

"That conversation went left quick. We'll talk about it later."

I was relieved to hear the knock at the door. Mona waited in the kitchen as I ran downstairs. Karlos and Ahmad tackled each other as soon as I opened the door. My sister rolled her eyes as I stepped over them to hug her and my mother. Mona was putting the dishes up as we walked into the kitchen.

"Honey, this is my mother. Everyone calls her Johnnie. This is my sister, Ce."

My mother extended her hand. "I love that hair, girl!" she said to Mona.

"Thank you, but I need to color it again."

My sister chimed in. "It makes me want to cut mine, but I can't with these cheeks."

Our laughter broke the ice as we spent the next hour talking about the boys. I could feel my sister checking Mona out. She hung back when my mother and Ahmad walked to the car.

"She's pretty. Let's just hope she's as pretty on the inside as the out."

I settled into juggling life and love. And yet, my anxiety increased whenever I thought about talking to Christian about moving to Chicago. I was halfway into my Corporate Finance II classes when I realized, yet again, that I was in over my head. I called Professor Will and made an appointment for our first tutoring session. I'd saved enough money from my welfare benefits for three sessions.

We agreed to meet at a small diner where Professor Will met with all his students. The diner occupied a small corner in a hotel two blocks away from campus. I was anxious as I entered and scanned the restaurant. Professor Will waved me over from a corner booth.

"Why are you looking so stressed? Here, sit down." He moved some files to the side.

"I think I should drop this class before I fail it."

He waved the waiter over. "Slow down…slow down," he said. "Failure is *not* an option. At least not on my watch."

We spent the first half-hour eating lunch. He laughed about the first time I brought Karlos to class. He mentioned that I was often the topic of conversation among some of my male classmates. The dirty old man in him surfaced when I told him I didn't play for their team. He slapped the table.

"Hot damn! So, the rumors are true. Shit…I bet you get more ass than me!"

"Probably, but if I didn't need you so much, I would slap you for being so inappropriate. You cost too much damned money. So, concentrate!" That was the day Professor Will and I became friends. After three tutoring sessions, I felt more comfortable with the practice sheets.

Christian called late one evening after one of my tutoring sessions.

"Hey, Nikki."

"Hey, Christian. What's up?"

"Well, I wanted to talk to you about Karlos and Mona."

"What about them?"

"Karlos mentioned that you guys are going to Alabama to meet her family. Don't you think that's kind of fast? I mean, she's only been around for like six months."

"We decided to hold off on the July Fourth visit because of Mona's work schedule. We'll meet her family at some point in time. But what business of that is yours, Christian?"

"I don't even know this woman you're spending so much time with."

"You have a lot of damned nerve. You don't need to know her until I decide you need to know her. Karlos has only been around her a few times. You didn't have a problem letting Jill spend time with Karlos before I even met her ass!"

"Yeah, but she was the only woman I dated. You've dated three different women in his life."

"You're an asshole!"

"I see the writing on the wall. You're spending a lot of time with her. And I'm telling you, you're never taking my son away from me."

I wanted to scream as I spoke through clenched teeth. "How fuckin' dare you! Your insecure-ass wife simply tolerates him, and you allow it. You're going to regret this later, Christian. Mark my words."

"You're not taking my son away from me." He'd become a broken record.

"Karlos will be wherever I am. Period!"

"We'll see about that."

I slammed the phone down and fell apart. I kept that conversation to myself until I could talk about it with the one person who never judged me. I waited until the boys were asleep before calling my sister.

"Hey, Ce."

"Hey, you studying?"

"I just closed my notebook. I'll be glad when this shit is over."

"You'll have earned that damned MBA."

"Right! Well, I wanted to talk to you about something."

"What's wrong?"

"I had an awful fight with Christian."

"Oh no. What happened?"

"I know Mona and I have only been seeing each other for six months, but we've been talking about me and Karlos moving to Chicago once I graduate."

"Cold-ass Chicago? You don't have any family or friends there."

"I know, Ce, but life is too short and this just feels right. It feels so natural. Most importantly, she loves me and Karlos."

"Have you told Mommy?"

"No, so don't mention it until I have a chance to tell her."

"But why can't she move here? Why do you have to be the one who moves?"

"It makes sense for me to move. She's more established with her business there. She's building a performing arts academy. Once I graduate, I can find a job in any industry."

"What did Christian say?"

"He said I'm not taking Karlos away from him."

"I'm sorry, but I can understand both sides. He doesn't want Karlos that far away from him, but Jill doesn't allow them to be as close as they could be. But you deserve to be happy, too. Are you sure about Mona?"

"I've never been more sure."

"Just prepare for a custody battle. You know I'll support you in whatever you decide. I just want you to be happy."

The stress of failing my Corporate Finance II quiz was wearing on me. One day after class, I went to Professor Abrams and told him I was going to drop the course. His response was dismissive.

"Why would you do that? You're too close to midterms. You have time to catch up."

"I'm not getting it and I can't afford to get a C," I said. "I received a C-plus in Corporate Finance I."

Still, he continued to dissuade me from dropping his class. I called my advisor and reiterated my conversation with Professor Abrams. I felt defeated when she, too, encouraged me not to drop the class. Professor Will had made it look easy when he broke down the equations. And yet I couldn't complete them on my own.

Just when I thought my life couldn't get any worse, it did. I put Karlos to bed before sifting through a mountain of bills. My heart stopped when I read the address on one of the envelopes coming from the Maryland Department of Child Services.

Don't tell me they're stopping my welfare benefits.

I couldn't handle another setback. I slowly opened the envelope. I felt sick to my stomach. Christian was taking me to court for custody of Karlos.

I fell to my knees and sobbed.

"How could he do this?" I mumbled to myself. "I'm a good mother. He doesn't know Karlos like I do. What is his favorite color? What does he say when he is afraid? You can't love him the way I do. Your white privilege can never protect your black son. You don't realize that he is a black boy who will become a black man in a society that doesn't value his existence."

I felt crazy, sitting there talking to myself. I wiped my tears and dialed Christian's number.

"Yeah, Nikki." His tone was arrogant.

"I got this bullshit notice in the mail, Christian. You will never have custody of my son."

"Your son? He's my son too and you're not taking him away from me because you have a new girlfriend."

"Is that what this is about? Because I'm dating someone? I deserve to be happy just like you."

"You're not taking my son, Nikki."

I felt like I was about to burst a blood vessel.

"Fuck you, Christian!"

"I'll see you in court," he calmly replied.

I couldn't breathe. I called Mona and broke down as soon as I heard her voice.

"Honey? What's wrong?"

"Christian…"

"What about Christian?"

"He's taking me to court for custody of Karlos." I began to gag.

"Shhh, try to calm down before you make yourself sick," Mona said. "We'll get through this."

"How? I'm running out of money and I don't have a job. I'm going to get kicked out of the program if I don't pass this last class."

She stopped me. "Listen to me. I will do everything in my power to protect you and Karlos. I promise."

I tried to hide my sadness from Karlos as we drove to school the next morning.

"What's wrong, Mom?"

"Mommy's just tired, baby, but I'm okay."

His voice cracked. "No, you're not, Mom."

"I am. How about we get some ice cream after school? But only if you promise Mommy that you'll have a good day."

He hesitated. "Okay."

My heart ached as I kissed him goodbye. How could I convince him that everything would be fine when I didn't believe it myself? I finally got up the nerve to call my mother.

"Why haven't you called me?" she immediately demanded.

"Christian is taking me to court for custody of Karlos."

"What did you say?"

"Christian wants custody of Karlos."

"Is he crazy? What judge is going to give *him* custody? Judges rarely separate children from their mothers unless there are addiction or abuse issues."

"I know, Mom, but…"

"Stop crying. Everything's going to be fine."

"What if he tells the judge I'm gay?"

"He better not! Why do you think he'd do that?"

"I haven't had a chance to tell you, but I want to move to Chicago after graduating. Christian and I had an argument and he said I'm not taking Karlos away from him."

"What about your house? You just bought it."

"It's just a house, Mom. I'll move back home and buy another one if things don't work out with Mona."

She exhaled. "Where will you work?"

"Mom, I'll have an MBA from Johns Hopkins. Coupled with my sales experience, I'll find something. I just don't want to have any regrets."

"What did Mona say when you told her about court?"

"She said she would do everything within her power for me to maintain custody of Karlos."

I waited for my mother's response, and as usual she lifted my spirits with her humor. "I guess I'll be bringing my frying pan to Chicago on the plane." That was her way of letting me know she supported my decision.

CHAPTER TEN

Mona and I often stayed on the phone until the wee hours of the morning. The excitement outweighed the fear I felt as we planned the next phase of our lives together.

"What about this custody battle with Christian, honey? I haven't talked to Karlos about moving yet."

"Well, babe, you have to decide when the right time is to tell him. I think you should tell him before Christian does."

The thought of having that conversation with Karlos made me feel guilty. There we were, moving again. I had to make him understand that the better my life was, the better his life was. Who was I kidding? He was nine years old. He was too young to understand the magnitude of my decisions. I hung up the phone with Mona and prayed that I was making the right decision.

I tried to distract myself from the impending court date. I couldn't afford an attorney, so all I could do was pray.

I made one final attempt to drop the class. Again, both my advisor and Professor Abrams discouraged me from doing so. Hesitantly, I dragged myself to my final tutoring session with Professor Will.

"You ready?"

I closed my notebook and sipped my beer. "All I can do is my best. I just don't know if it's good enough."

"Stop doubting yourself. You'll pass midterms and we'll prepare for the final."

I squeezed his hand. "Thank you for believing in me."

Everything was happening so quickly. Luckily, my custody court date with Christian was postponed due to his orders to be reassigned to Germany. I dreaded having that conversation with Karlos. I made the decision to get past my midterm first.

I felt uncertain as I began my midterm exam. Still, I had enough time to rethink the problems I was unsure of before Professor Abrams's voice echoed through the room.

"Pencils down."

I tried not to second-guess myself as I put Karlos to bed that night.

Please, Father God, let me have passed this exam. It took me twenty-four hours to muster up the courage to access my grade. I clicked on the link for Professor Abrams's email. My eyes welled with tears when I saw the grade: B-.

Thank you, Jesus! Thank you!

I buckled down with newfound confidence and prepared for finals. The decision to sell my house was the distraction I needed. I decided to give the listing to Therez since she sold me my first house and we'd developed a good working relationship. I informed her that I wasn't ready to put the house on the market immediately, though, because I thought it would sell quickly and I needed more time.

My plans for a life with Mona were in motion. And yet, my heart said one thing and my mind said another. This was the first time in my life that I'd met someone who loved me as much as I loved her. I didn't want to miss the opportunity to find true love and happiness. I could have the family I always dreamed of. But…What if she changed her mind and went back to Doug? I anxiously mapped out a plan for the sale of my home to coincide with my graduation.

I decided to take Karlos to his favorite park one day after school. There was calming breeze as I pushed him on the spinning wheel.

"Mom, get on!"

"I don't like this ride, Breezy."

"Please."

I smiled as he sat in the middle of the large ride. I gripped the handle and ran in a circle before jumping on.

"See, this is fun, Mom. We should come here all the time."

I got off and pushed the wheel again. We rode until it came to a stop. I laughed as he got off the wheel and tried to walk.

"You're walking sideways."

"Help me, Mom!" I caught him as we giggled and fell onto the grass.

"How was school today?" I asked.

"It was fun. We ate with the big kids today."

"Cool. Do you still like your school?"

"Yeah, but I wish I could go to school with my soccer friends."

I took a deep breath. "What if you went to a new school?"

"With my soccer friends?"

"Not with your soccer friends here, but with new soccer friends."

He frowned. "I don't want to go to a new school."

"What do you think about making all new soccer friends if we moved someplace new?"

"I don't want to move."

"Moving could be fun. We could have a bigger house. You could make new soccer friends."

"Are we moving, again?"

"We may but, I promise, we'll have a much better life than what we have now."

"How am I going to see Ahmad and Antonio? He's going to forget that I'm his brother."

"Ahmad can always come visit and you can fly on a plane to see your brother and your dad. Trust me, he won't forget you're his brother."

"But I don't want to move from my friends."

"You can visit your old friends and make new friends."

"Where are we moving?"

"To Chicago, so we can be a family with Miss Mona."

"Did she say we could move with her?"

"Yes. She wants us to live with her. Can you at least think about it? Mommy doesn't want you to be sad."

"But I *am* sad."

I was overwhelmed with sadness and guilt as I thought about selling my house. Those emotions were exacerbated by Karlos's sadness. Our home was fairly empty except for his room. I never had the money to furnish it before getting laid off.

Therez assured me the house would sell quickly. We made a plan based on my class schedule for showing times to include a lockbox key when I wasn't available. She told me to give her a call a week before I was ready to start showing the house.

Reality set in: I was selling my second home. Mine was the sole name on the deed. This was the only thing I owned. The thing I had worked so hard for. The sadness deepened. Then I thought about our upcoming trip to Alabama to meet Mona's family. Perhaps getting out of town would lift my spirits.

"Maybe we should wait until after my finals for me to meet your family."

"Honey, you have to meet them sometime. Plus, you need a break."

"Have you told your grandmother about me and Karlos?" I asked.

"Of course. We're very close."

"What'd she say?"

"She asked if I was ready to date someone with a child. I told her that I know what I want and it's you and Karlos. Besides, it will be good for Karlos to meet my nephews, Jacob and Jordan. They're three years older than him. I want you to bring Karlos, but maybe we should wait until after your court date."

"Let me check my schedule. I'll have to bring my books with me." Maybe a trip down South was what I needed after all.

I was nervous about meeting Mona's grandmother. She raised Mona and her brother, Deacon, when their mother passed away. Their father was murdered in a shot-house brawl over corn liquor. I was aware of the preconceived notions that southern women had about northern women. They sometimes called us city girls "fast." I had to make a good impression.

God shone his light down on me a week later when Christian's attorney requested a mediation before the judge. He mentioned that the judge would urge Christian and I to settle our differences for Karlos's sake. My sister joined me that day as we waited outside the courtroom. I wore my best suit, but it paled in comparison to Christian's officer dress uniform. We barely looked at each other as our attorneys negotiated on our behalf. I walked out of court with a commitment to send Karlos back to Maryland once every three months if I were to relocate. I didn't know what brought about Christian's change of heart, but I was grateful.

At the last minute, Christian asked if we could switch weekends, the weekend Karlos and I were supposed to meet Mona in Alabama. I agreed, just to keep from creating any additional conflict so soon after our custody agreement.

I was excited as I packed for the long weekend. As usual, my sister was supportive yet cautious.

"Are you ready to meet her family?"

"As ready as I'm going to be."

"I just don't want you to give more than you receive."

"I know, Ce, but no one has ever made me feel this way."

I soon felt like I was walking on air as I strolled through the Alabama airport. Even the sun was shining differently as I exited the airport.

"I'm here," I said to Mona on my cell. "What are you driving, honey?"

"Look directly in front of you."

I scanned the line of cars for her truck. My smile widened when we made eye contact. She was sitting in a Jaguar coupe. She was stunning as her blonde hair blended perfectly with the champagne exterior. She popped the trunk and I tossed my bag in.

"You look so damned good in this car. Whose car is this?"

She kissed me on the lips. "I hoped you would like it."

"I love it!"

"Happy birthday and early graduation!"

"What?"

"This is for working so hard."

"Babe, stop playing! I haven't graduated yet."

"Well, the truth is that I was tired of driving in that Honda."

"Are you serious? But wait…ain't nothing wrong with my car. You can drive a Honda until the wheels fall off."

She rolled her eyes. "That's what I was afraid of."

We both laughed.

"Babe, are you serious? This is my car?"

"Yup, and I bought a one-way ticket because I'm not flying back to Chicago. We're driving back to Maryland. I'll fly home from there."

I leaned over and mushed her dimple. "This is crazy! What did your grandmother say?"

"She said, 'Oh, so you buying cars now?'"

"Oh, brother. I don't want her to think I asked you to buy me a car."

"She'll be all right. This is my money. She knows you're independent, with your own car and home. I told her it's your birthday present."

I couldn't stop touching the supple interior of the car as we drove to her grandmother's house. I closed my eyes and dreamed about the day I could return the favor and surprise her with beautiful things.

I was nervous as we pulled into the driveway of a rambler with a perfectly manicured lawn.

"We're really in the country. Your grandmother's lawn looks like carpet."

"She doesn't play about her lawn. My nephews started cutting it to make her stop doing it herself." She grabbed my bag out of the trunk.

I took one last glance at my outfit and hoped my skinny jeans and heels weren't too much. I followed her up the steps and walked into a large den with wood paneled walls. The furniture reminded me of my Mema's house. The white couch and reclining chair were covered in plastic. There were black angel figurines placed all around the room. I followed Mona into a living room with an old-fashioned floor television and green cloth furniture. The excitement in Mona's voice was infectious.

"Mama?"

I took a deep breath and sat on the couch. I jumped up when a petite light-skinned woman with wavy hair and keen features walked into the room.

She reminded me of my grandmothers, standing no more than five feet tall. Her gabardine V-neck shirt matched her wide leg pants.

"Well, hello there."

"Hello, Miss Lillian," I said. I nervously extended my hand. Her hands were soft as butter.

"Mama, this is Nikki." Miss Lillian stood back and looked at me.

"Welcome, Nikki. I didn't know when y'all were getting in, but the liver, rice and biscuits are ready. Is this your first time in Birmingham, Nikki?"

"Yes, ma'am," I said. My mouth began to water from nausea as I tried to figure out how I was going to stomach the liver. I hadn't eaten beef or pork in twenty years. I was a city girl, but I knew better than to offend a southern woman by not eating whatever meal she prepared.

"May I use your bathroom, ma'am? I need to wash my hands."

"I'll show you," Mona said. I followed her down a narrow hallway.

I whispered, "It smells good, but I can't stop thinking of that little puppet, Lambchop."

She laughed. "Babe, liver is from a cow, not a lamb."

"Same difference, but I'm going to eat it because she made it." I washed my hands and joined her at the kitchen table while Miss Lillian cleaned up.

"Thank you, Miss Lillian," I said during dinner. "This all looks delicious."

Mona smirked and cut into her liver.

"That's a fancy new car you got. How you like it?"

I almost choked as I tried to stomach my first of piece of liver. "I love it. I was so surprised."

She said, "So was I."

CHAPTER ELEVEN

After dinner, Mona walked me to a small bedroom at the back of the house. "This was my room," she explained. "Deacon had the room across the hall."

I looked around the small room decorated with flowered wallpaper. "Aww…This was your room?"

She sat on the bed. "This will be the first time I'll have slept in the same bed with someone in my mother's house."

I grimaced. "I want you to sleep with me, but I want to be respectful. I don't want Miss Lillian to feel uncomfortable."

"It was her idea," she said. "I think she knows how I feel about you. That's her way of letting me know she supports me."

"Okay. I'm going to jump in the shower and take a nap. I gotta study. I don't want to interrupt your time with your family."

She kissed me on the lips. "You are my family."

It felt as though I had slept for hours when I was awakened by laughter. I brushed my teeth and tapped my face with powder. I walked into a room full of Mona's family. Miss Lillian turned her attention toward me.

"You get enough rest?" she asked.

"Yes, ma'am."

Mona handed me a glass. "Gin and tonic. I thought you would need it."

I sipped my drink as she introduced me to her family.

"This is my brother, Deacon." He was a brawny man who stood at six feet tall. His reddish hair matched his freckles.

"We've heard so much about you."

"I hope it's been good." I nervously prepared myself for the barrage of questions.

"It has been. I thought Karlos was coming with you. The twins stayed with their mother this weekend, so I guess it worked out. They're looking forward to meeting him next time."

"He was excited, too, but his father will be stationed in Germany in a couple of months, so he wanted to spend as much time with him as possible before we move to Chicago."

Miss Lillian abruptly ended her conversation with Mona. "Oh, you're moving to Chicago?"

"Yes, ma'am. Karlos and I are moving to Chicago after I graduate. I'm in business school at Johns Hopkins."

Mona never looked up as she poured herself another drink.

After an hour of conversation, I grabbed the empty plates off the table and began washing them. I felt Miss Lillian watching me, but I dared not turn around.

"Thank you, Nikki, but you don't have to do that," she said. "You're a guest."

"That chicken and broccoli casserole was delicious, Miss Lillian. Washing the dishes is the least I could do, ma'am."

I excused myself to study while Miss Lillian and Mona watched a movie. I was exhilarated from a much-needed nap after studying. I could barely contain myself as we got dressed for a night on the town.

"You know I can't come to Alabama and *not* go to a strip club."

She shook her head. "I know, I'm taking you to the lowest spot in Birmingham."

The Pink Palace looked like a juke joint as cars parked on the grass hill.

"I haven't been here in years, but this should be right up your alley," said Mona.

The doorman eyed us as Mona paid the cover. I felt out of place as we walked toward a small bar near the stage. We were the only women in the club not dancing. I could feel the stares of the men. The dancers looked equally confused as Mona ordered a round of drinks. We moved closer to the stage as she reached in her purse and handed me a stack of bills.

"This is your budget for the night."

I'd already eyed the stripper who would get all my honey's money that night. She was the slimmest dancer on the stage, but there was something about her. She was deep chocolate with thick thighs. She looked to be at least a C cup. Although she didn't have much of an ass, she stood out from the others. The dancer walked toward the edge of the stage, turned around and squatted two inches from our faces. She began to shake her ass so fast that her ass cheeks made a clapping noise.

"That's what the fuck I'm talkin' about!" I yelled.

Mona blushed as I began sticking bills in the stripper's garter. Suddenly, the dancer stood up and began to clap her ass cheeks so loud that you could hear it over the music. Mona grabbed one of my bills and tipped her. At that moment, I noticed a guy standing near Mona. He kept staring at her as I tried to concentrate on the stripper who was spread-eagle in front of me. I felt like I was in a tennis match as I looked from the stripper to the man to Mona. He finally got up the nerve to speak to her.

"Hold up. Aren't you Deacon's sister?"

"Yes."

He smiled broadly. "I used to come over to Miss Lillian's house on Sundays for dinner." He inched closer as I watched the stripper get on her hands and knees. "I always wanted to hug you."

Mona looked from him to me.

"Come on…just one hug," he said.

I couldn't stand another minute. I moved so close to Mona that we could have kissed. "Let him hug you one time because he's getting on my damned nerves."

She rolled her eyes, turned, and opened her arms.

"One hug, and only because you've been to my mother's house for Sunday dinner." He wrapped his arms around her and she promptly pulled away.

"Tell Miss Lillian that Ty said hello."

She turned to me. "Babe, he was just being nice."

"Whatever," I said. "That girl had it busted wide open. His ass made me miss the good part."

I didn't want to leave as we passed a guy selling hot links from a make-shift stand in the parking lot. "I love this damned place," I said.

"You happy now? I love watching you watch them. You turn into a totally different person. It's something I've never seen in a woman before."

"I can't change who I am."

She placed her hand on my thigh. "I don't want you to change."

We woke up to the smell of bacon and coffee the next morning. It smelled like a country diner.

"Come on. I know she went all out."

I followed Mona into the kitchen as she bent down to hug Miss Lillian. "What you in here cooking, lady?"

Miss Lillian playfully pushed her away when Mona snatched a piece of bacon.

"Nikki, I got biscuits, grits, eggs, gravy and bacon."

"It looks like a buffet in here, Miss Lillian," I said. She smiled and placed a cup of coffee in front of me. I looked at Mona as Miss Lillian then placed a container of French vanilla coffee creamer on the table.

"I hope this is the right one."

"Yes, ma'am. That's my favorite. Thank you." Mona smiled as Miss Lillian walked out of the kitchen and sat in her recliner.

"How did she know I like French vanilla?" I wondered.

"She asked me. I heard her leave early this morning. She's never done that for anyone I've brought home. And sleeping in the same bed? Yeah, she likes you."

That weekend flew by. Miss Lillian made us a couple of plates for the ride to Maryland. I could tell she didn't want Mona to leave as they embraced.

"When you coming back?"

Mona kissed her on the cheek. "Maybe in a couple of months. You know we're getting ready for the grand opening of the new building. You may be in Chicago before I can get back home. but I'll try."

I put the last of our things in the trunk and reached out to hug Miss Lillian. I was happy when she embraced me.

"Thank you, Miss Lillian. I probably gained ten pounds this weekend."

"A little extra cushion ain't never hurt nobody. You're always welcome and I can't wait to meet that boy of yours."

We pulled off as Miss Lillian waved from her manicured lawn.

I was the happiest I'd ever been as we started the drive back to Maryland. We were an hour outside of Birmingham when Mona pulled onto the right shoulder.

"What's wrong, honey?" I asked.

"The engine light just came on."

"What does that mean?"

"I don't know, but this is some bullshit! Our family has been buying cars from Emmanuel for years. I should take this shit back right now."

"Do you think we could make it back?"

"I don't know. Let's see if we can make it to the next exit." We drove another ten miles when God smiled down on us. I couldn't believe it. There was a Jaguar dealership as we exited the highway. Mona looked at me in disbelief.

"Do you see that?" she said.

"A Jaguar dealership."

She slapped the wheel. "Thank you, Jesus!"

"This is nothing but God," I said.

Mona pulled into the dealership and called Emmanuel.

"Emmanuel, this is Mona Hatchett. I'm driving back to Maryland and the engine light just came on. It just so happens that there's a Jaguar dealership here. I don't know where the hell I am, but I paid you twenty-five-thousand dollars for this car and obviously it ain't worth a damn."

At that moment, a salesperson came out and greeted us. Mona explained the situation to the salesperson with Emmanuel on speaker. I waited for thirty minutes before she walked back to the car.

"Babe, you're going to have to pick another car off the lot that you like," she said. "We gotta hurry up because I can't miss my flight in the morning. I have a meeting with the bank."

I don't know what she said, but Emmanuel agreed to pick my car up from the dealership. He wired twenty-five-thousand-dollars to the dealership for us to purchase a new car.

"Come on, babe. You see anything you like?"

"But what can I get? Can I get a truck like yours? I'll need a truck for the Chicago winters."

"If that's what you want. You just can't go over twenty-five thousand. There's a truck." She pointed to a small truck and glanced at her watch. I frowned.

"What's wrong?" she asked.

"Why do I have to get the 'baby' truck? I want a big truck."

"You have twenty-five thousand. You can get whatever you like." She and the salesperson followed me as I walked the lot. My eyes widened when I spotted a black Jaguar. It was a sleek, four-door Vanden Plas with a camel-colored leather interior. I opened the door and sat behind the wheel.

"This is it. How much is this one?"

"This is a beauty. It's twenty-three thousand. Let me go get the report." I looked at Mona. "You like it?"

She walked around the car. "It's a beautiful car, but do you like it?"

"I love it! I hope they can work it out."

"Oh, they're going to work it out. We're not leaving here without a car." The salesman returned with the report.

"There are sixty-five thousand miles on it. It's in great condition. Its previous owner was an army general. He only sold it because he couldn't drive anymore due to health issues. We have all the maintenance reports."

He barely finished before Mona spoke. "We'll take it!"

We were an hour outside of Maryland when I called Christian. He agreed to meet us at Karlos's school so I wouldn't have to pick him up in the morning. I was anxious for him to meet Mona for the first time. Christian and Karlos were already there by the time we pulled into the parking lot. I pulled up beside Christian's car. He looked up and did a double take. I waved to Karlos as I got out of the car. He jumped out of the back seat and ran to the front of the car.

"Mom! Whose car is this?"

"It's ours! Do you like it?"

Christian walked to the back as Mona got out of the passenger seat. "This is pretty damned nice," he said. "How'd you afford this?"

"I'm sorry. Mona this is Christian. Christian, Mona."

They shook hands. "I finally get to meet you, Mona," he said.

"Yes, finally." He stood back and looked at the car again.

"Back to this car."

I grabbed Karlos's bag out of Christian's backseat. "It's an early birthday and graduation gift," I said.

Christian looked at Mona. "Must be nice."

"It is," I replied.

I watched him watch us as we drove off. That was the first night Karlos, Mona and I talked about moving to Chicago. I sensed he was becoming comfortable with her being around. We were cleaning up after dinner when he caught us off guard.

"Miss Mona, can you come to my soccer game on Saturday?" Karlos asked.

"I would love to come to your soccer game, but I have to leave early in the morning," she said. "I have a lot of work to do in Chicago."

He lowered his eyes.

"But I will be able to come to all your soccer games, soon," she quickly added. "I know your mom and dad talked to you about you and your mom moving to Chicago. What do you think about that?"

I began to clear the dishes. Unlike my past relationships, it was important that I allow them to develop their own relationship outside of me.

Karlos looked at me for reassurance.

"You can be honest," I said. I wanted him to know that his feelings were important. "What do you think about us moving and being a family with Mona?"

"I think I would like it, but how would I see Antonio and my friends?"

She leaned closer to him. "Your mom and I will make sure you come back to visit your brother and your friends every three months. You can fly on a plane to visit."

His eyes widened. "By myself?"

"Yup. Me and your mom talked about it."

"Okay. I think I can move to Chicago."

Mona and I lay in each other's arms that night.

"Are you ready for all of this?" I dreamily asked her.

"Yes," she said. "I love you. And I can't wait to be with you every night."

CHAPTER TWELVE

I was sad as we dropped Karlos off at school before taking Mona to the airport. He'd fallen asleep in the backseat. My heart fluttered when she opened the back door and he woke up.

"Okay, man. We're at your school. Give me a kiss." He wrapped his arms around her neck as she kissed him on the cheek. "I'll see you soon."

We held hands as I drove her to the airport,

"Okay, lady," she said. "It's time to hit it! You gotta sell the house and graduate. I gotta get Karlos's room ready. We got a lot to do."

I inhaled her scent before finally letting her go.

I continued my tutoring sessions with Professor Will. Deep down inside, I still felt like I couldn't pass my Corporate Finance II final. Again, I expressed my concerns to my advisor.

"During our last conversation, you mentioned moving to Chicago after graduation," she said. "Have you thought about finishing up at Northwestern?"

"Northwestern is a great school, but I just can't start all over again."

"You wouldn't have to start over. We have a partnership with Northwestern. If you drop your class, you can enroll at Northwestern when you move to Chicago. The only caveat is your degree would be conferred from Northwestern and not Johns Hopkins. You've come this far and I'm sure your sessions with Professor Will have helped. Continue to push forward."

I hung up the phone believing I could pass the class.

I was surprised when Therez called late that evening.

"We got an offer! You'll walk away with fifty thousand dollars after my commission. You can sign the contract electronically and we can settle in two weeks."

"Therez...I can't close that soon."

She exhaled.

"Nikki, you told me to pull the trigger. The buyer is a caretaker for her mother, and she needs to close before her mother's released from the rehabilitation center. Besides, this development is at capacity. We may not get a better offer."

"Can you give me a couple of days to think about it?

"I can, but we gotta move on this."

I called my sister.

"How are you going to do that?" she asked.

"I have no idea but I gotta make it work. We don't have much stuff, but my biggest concern is finding a month-to-month lease. I graduate in three months."

"What did Mona say?"

"She said we can find something like corporate housing. Karlos would have to switch schools, but he would go to school with his soccer friends. I thought that would help with his transition. I just want to be happy, Ce. I want this and I want her."

"Well, if anyone can figure this out, it's you."

That next morning, I took a break from studying and placed calls to apartment complexes near Carol and Kenny's house. Frustration set in when the fourth complex stated they didn't offer month-to-month leases. I felt defeated as I made one last call. It was a complex three blocks from Carol and Kenny's house. I was optimistic when the manager stated they didn't

offer month-to-month leasing, but we could work something out if the rent
was paid in advance. I wanted to scream and cry at the same time. That was
the sign I needed that I was making the right decision. We scheduled a date
to walk through the unit. I couldn't wait to call Mona.

"I found a place right near the school Karlos will transfer to," I said.
"It's three blocks from Carol and Kenny's. You could almost walk there."

"That's amazing."

"But there's a catch. The manager said we would have to pay the rent in
advance for a month-to-month lease."

"How much is it monthly?"

"It's $875."

"For a two bedroom? We could do that."

"I have a few bills to pay and then we can put the money from the sale
of the house in a savings account," I said. "I made an appointment to see
the apartment."

"Do you want me to fly in to go with you?"

"You would do that?"

"Of course. I'm asking you to change your whole life. I want to do whatever I need to do to make the transition easy for you and Karlos."

"But you have so much going on at work."

"Work is not going anywhere. And besides, I don't report to anyone. I'm
the boss."

I mentally placed a check mark near each obstacle in my mind. I
couldn't wait to share the news with my two best friends, Toni and Morgan.
I was looking forward to seeing them. Morgan chose a small bistro in DC's
Dupont Circle for us to meet.

She was the first to arrive.

"I knew Toni's ass would be late," I said. Morgan hugged me hard.

"Girl, you know she's always late." We settled into a booth and
scanned the menu.

"So, whose daughter are you having?" She raised an eyebrow.

"I ain't having no one's daughter after that last mistake I made. I know
I'm getting ready to have this cheeseburger."

Twenty minutes later, Toni wandered in like she was on time. "Wassup,
shawties? Y'all know I had to change out of my Metro uniform." She leaned
over to kiss us. We spent the next hour catching up. Nothing had changed.

Morgan was the calm, quiet one whereas Toni was the epitome of a Southeast church girl. And then there was me. I loved God but I cussed a lot.

"So, Blue, how is your house coming along? We haven't even seen it."

"Well…"

"Oh, Lord…" Toni sipped her beer and I decided to just spit it out.

"Me and Karlos are moving to Chicago to be with Mona after I graduate."

Toni looked shocked. "But you just bought your house."

"I have to follow my heart."

Morgan chimed in. "Chicago winters ain't no joke, but let me get my winter clothes ready."

Toni wasn't moved. "Are you sure? What's up with Christian? I thought you guys were going to court for custody."

"He's being stationed in Germany. Thank God we reached an agreement through mediation."

"You love this Mona woman that much?"

"I'm in love with her. I've never had someone love me and Karlos like this. I'm not trying to fit a circle into a square peg anymore. And girl, she's so damned fine. I just want to fuck her all the time and she lets me."

Morgan chuckled. "You ain't nothing be a greasy old man."

Toni's energy shifted. "If you're happy then we're happy. I guess we'll be visiting Chicago."

I decided I wouldn't tell Christian about selling my house until I absolutely had to. I couldn't wait to pick up Mona from the airport and head over to see the apartment.

Her smile widened as she walked toward the car.

"You sure look good in that Jaguar." she said.

"Thank you. My girlfriend bought it for me."

"Where's Karlos?"

"It's Christian's weekend."

We caught up as we drove to the apartment complex.

"Good morning, I'm Nikki Blue. I spoke to Edgar last week about a three-month lease."

"Oh, yes, Nikki. I'm Edgar. It's a pleasure to meet you." He turned toward Mona.

"This is my girlfriend, Mona," I said. They shook hands.

"So, you're interested in a two-bedroom apartment. For three months, correct?"

"Correct."

"And who will be the residents of the unit?"

"Me and my son, Karlos. Mona will travel back and forth, based on her schedule."

We followed him to a second-floor unit with a roommate floor plan. Karlos would have his own bathroom on the opposite side of the apartment. It was small but would do. I walked over and opened the door to the balcony.

"What do you think, honey?"

"It works for what we need."

Edgar clapped his hands. "Wonderful! Let's go down to the office and complete the application. We'll have to do a separate credit check since both of your names will be on the lease."

I exhaled as we reviewed the apartment brochure in the car. Still, I knew my credit was overextended with my school loans and the house.

"Babe, what if my application doesn't go through?"

"I'll just put it in my name. As a matter of fact, while I'm here, let's go into a branch and add your name to my checking account."

I couldn't believe that I found someone so loving and giving. I had to find a way to let her know I loved her just as much.

My hopes were dashed the following morning when Edgar called to say my application was denied. Luckily, Mona's was approved. I wasn't surprised and yet, I was ashamed to let her know.

"My application was denied." I began to cry.

"Why are you crying?"

"Because I don't feel like we're doing this together."

"But we are doing this together. You're in grad school and you bought a house less than a year ago. It makes sense you wouldn't be approved."

"But…"

She interrupted me. "I gotta get ready for this call. Call Edgar to see if I can sign a lease with just my name on it. If so, he can email it. I'll return it with a check for three month's rent. I'll call you tonight. I love you."

I asked myself, *What did I do to deserve her?*

I called Therez two days later to accept the buyer's offer. We would settle in two weeks, which meant I only had a week to move into our new apartment. I braced myself for the conversation I had to have with Karlos. We were having dinner when I revisited the idea of moving.

"So, Breezy, remember we were talking about moving to Chicago when school's over?"

"School's not over, right?"

"No, it's not over but Mommy has to prepare for us to move. There's a lady who wants to buy our house for a lot of money. So, we have to move to a new apartment until you and Mommy finish school."

He looked up. "I have to leave my friends?"

"Yes, but guess what? You're going to the same school as Cody and some of your soccer friends. Our new apartment is right around the corner from Coach Carol and Kenny's house."

His face lit up. "Cody takes the bus to school."

"I know. I thought you would want to take the bus with your friends."

"Can I call him and tell him?"

"Let's surprise him and tell him this when we go over there."

I was relieved yet I felt guilty. I'd worked so hard to keep Karlos in private school. This was the first and hopefully the last time he would attend public school. It wasn't what I wanted, but it was the least I could do to make the move easier for him. Mona alleviated some of my stress by paying for the moving company. I scheduled the move so our belongings would arrive by the time Karlos saw his new home for the first time. He looked out the window as we headed toward the new apartment.

"Where are we going, Mom?"

"To see our new apartment."

"Do I go to school with Cody tomorrow?"

"No, you go to your new school on Monday."

I could barely open the door before he rushed into the apartment. I watched as he slowly walked into his room.

"Mom, it's just like it was before. How'd you do that?"

"Well, almost. The only thing you don't have is the soccer field carpet. Everything else is the same." I stood in his doorway while he made sure everything was in its place.

"Thanks, Mom."

CHAPTER THIRTEEN

I was mentally and emotionally drained when I called Christian to let him know we'd moved into our new apartment. I gave him all the details on Karlos's new school. We agreed to discuss our pick-up schedule once we got settled. I poured a glass a wine before calling Mona.

"Hey, babe. I just got out of a late meeting. I was wondering how everything was going. I'm sorry I couldn't be there to help you."

"You paid the movers and the rent for three months. That's more than enough. I couldn't have done this without you. I'm just exhausted."

"I know you are. How's Karlos doing with the move?"

"I think he's okay. He's excited about taking the bus to school with Cody."

"That makes me feel better. I know it hasn't been easy for you either, but hopefully you're not as stressed."

"I'm not, thanks to you."

I spent the remainder of the week studying and unpacking. Friday couldn't come soon enough. Carol and Kenny invited me and Karlos over for pizza. They wanted to surprise Cody by letting Karlos tell him they would be going to the same school. Their home was always full of laughter. They often had their three children and at least one or two of Carol's soccer players over.

"Are you excited, Breezy?"

His pace quickened as we walked up to their townhouse. "Yes! Cody doesn't know I'm going to his school, right Mom?"

"Nope. Carol wanted to surprise him."

Kenny opened the door and welcomed us. "Hey, Breezy. Man, what took you so long?"

I hugged Kenny and walked into their living room. A few of Karlos's teammates rushed over and tackled him.

"Hey! Hey! Watch the damned beer!" Carol burst into laughter. She was seated at the table holding a deck of cards in her hand.

"Oh, that's all you care about?" I joked. She slapped her cards down on the table.

"Bam! I love you girl but get your ass in here and hand me the bottle opener."

I hadn't known how much I needed their craziness until I was smack dab in the middle of it. Things calmed down as the boys ate pizza in the family room. Carol opened another beer before I could finish the first one.

"Girl, no. I'll be sleeping on your couch tonight!"

She leaned back in the chair, put her feet up on the table and took a swig of the beer. "You're a lightweight. Your ass lives right across the parking lot. This couch is big enough for you and Karlos."

"I gotta study tonight. I have finals in a couple of weeks."

She waved her hand dramatically. "Study, shmudy!...Wait! We haven't told the boys yet. Let's get them. Call them in here, Kenny."

Her mischievous behavior was the exact opposite of Kenny's quiet demeanor. He shook his head and yelled downstairs, "Guys! Come here for a minute."

One by one they ran up the steps, trampling over each other.

Carol sat up. "Well, boys. We have some sad news. When school is over in June, Breezy and Miss Nikki are moving to Chicago." I cringed at the audible gasps.

Cody scowled. "Nooo...Whose team will he play on?"

"Wait, there is a flip side. Cody, you'll have to show our new neighbor how to take the bus to school on Monday. Breezy, tell them who'll be taking the bus with them on Monday?"

Karlos threw his arms up in the air. "Meee!"

Cody looked confused. "What?"

"I'm going to your school on Monday. Me and my mom moved to a new apartment across the parking lot."

Karlos didn't stand a chance as the boys tackled him with Cody leading the way. The sound of their laughter reminded me that life was good.

I was anxious on Karlos's first day at his new school. My heart raced as I watched him run toward a group of kids huddled at the bus stop. I drove back to the apartment with intentions of studying. Instead, I lay across my bed and fell asleep. I woke up staring at the ceiling.

Thank you, God, for your Grace and Mercy. I will have an MBA soon. My son is healthy and I'm in love. What more could I ask for?

Mona came to visit the second week after we moved. I sensed her frustration with work as she constantly answered phone calls.

"I'm sorry. I'm waiting for the bank's decision to refinance my loan for the building. They keep requesting audits."

I ran my hand over her head. "I can only imagine the pressure you're under. A Black woman building a multimillion-dollar facility on the South Side of Chicago? I know those white boys are mad."

She shook her head. "During our first meeting, Melissa and four white men were seated in my conference room. I was running late. Yani told me that we were waiting for one more loan officer. I walked in and sat at the head of the table. They continued to talk about the organization. One of them looked at his watch and said, 'I guess we're waiting for the founder and executive director.' Melissa nodded toward me and said, 'She's here.' They were sick." Mona and I burst into laughter.

We spent quality family time with Karlos by renting movies and games. I loved watching her soothe his feelings when I kept winning.

"Breezy, you can't be a sore loser, dude. Your mom won that game."

I had no mercy for his sulking. "Stop all that whining!" I declared. "Keep trying until you figure out how to win."

I wondered how Mona would develop her own relationship with Karlos outside of me. My curiosity was answered that weekend before she left. She took Karlos with her to pick up a few items from the grocery store while I studied. When they got home, she told me that Karlos had gotten smart with her.

"What? I'm sorry. Tell his ass to get in here!"

She sat on the edge of the bed. "I handled it, babe. We picked up some things that I thought you guys needed. Then I wanted some Wendy's. I pulled up to the drive-through and before I could ask him what he wanted, he said, 'I don't want Wendy's!'"

"No, he didn't!" I replied. "His ass better be glad I wasn't there. What'd you say?"

"I turned all the way around so he could see my face. I said, 'Karlos, I am an adult. I am not one of your little friends.'"

"Did you order his ass anything?"

She began to eat her fries. "Do you see any food other than ours?"

Their interaction reinforced my intent to allow them to develop their own relationship outside of mine. I knew I was on the right track when a week later, Karlos asked if he could call Mona "Mom" once we moved to Chicago. I lovingly told him that he had to ask her, but I was sure that would make her happy.

My Corporate Finance II final still hung over my head like a dark cloud. A call from Toni was the distraction I needed. She invited me and Karlos to a cookout at her new townhouse. I welcomed the break from all the life changes we were experiencing. I was looking forward to seeing my best friends as we drove the familiar Route 301 in Maryland.

"Are we going back to our old house, Mom?"

"No, honey. Toni's new house is close to our old house." I dialed Toni when I entered her development.

"Hey, girl, I think I'm in your section."

"I think I see you, Blue. Drive to the condo at the end and park on the right."

She hung up right before I saw her house. Her guests were standing on her front steps. She didn't tell me there were going to be so many people. Karlos jumped out of the car and ran toward the house. My eyes squinted against the sun. I was so busy trying to make out the faces that I missed the most important one. I walked up the driveway and my mouth dropped.

Mona was sitting between my mother and sister. Everyone laughed as I covered my mouth.

"Congratulations!"

"Honey, what are you doing here?"

Toni hollered over the laughter, "Oh, so she's the only person you see?"

"You said you were having a small cookout," I said, looking around to see Toni's mother, sister Morgan, and a few of their friends.

"I am, but it's your graduation cookout."

"But I don't graduate for another three weeks."

Their collective laughter was what my spirit needed. Suddenly, everyone stopped talking. Mona moved over and made room for me to sit next to her. I tried to read their faces as I turned to sit down. There in front of me, stood Shelly.

He looked angelic as he stood in the sunlight in all white linen with a guitar draped across his chest. His smile was radiant as he glanced at Mona, who began to speak.

"You and Karlos have changed my life," she said. "I'm so proud of the mother you are and the woman you're becoming. Thank you, for finding space in your heart for me. I couldn't put into words how I felt, so Shelly and I wrote this song for you."

She leaned into me as Shelly's voice echoed through the breeze. "Partner for life…would you be my partner for life? If you're searching for forever…I'll be your partner for life. No one could make me feel this free. I want to show you how beautiful love can be."

"I love you and I am so proud of you," Mona said.

"Thank you. I love you, honey." I could hear sniffles behind us. I stood up and turned around. "I can't believe y'all tricked me. I love you all so much for this."

Toni wiped her eyes. "Y'all not gonna have me out here messing up my makeup!" Everyone laughed through their tears.

"The last time you had on makeup was in 1985!" I said.

"Shut up, Blue! Come on here, these crabs are calling us."

While everyone filed inside, Mona, Shelly and I sat on the steps.

"Wow Shelly, I forgot how amazing your voice is," I said. "What a beautiful gift. Thank you."

He beamed. "Your other half helped me write the song. It belongs to you and her. It's titled *Partners*."

I turned to Mona. "You feel that way about me?"

She caressed my face. "For life…"

We spent the rest of the day with those that I loved the most. But anxiety crept into the back of my mind.

I had to graduate. I couldn't let them down.

I trudged through the last days of studying in preparation for my finals. Christian helped with Karlos while I pulled all-night study sessions. I was overwhelmed and overstimulated. I tried to ignore Dean's call, but something made me pick up.

"Hey, Dean."

"Wassup with your educated ass?"

"I'm sick of this shit. I just want to run away."

"Your woman told me about your surprise cookout, but I had a gig in L.A."

And just like that, a thought crossed my mind. I needed to do something that made me happy. I deserved it.

"When will you be back home?"

"I got back a couple of days ago. I'm at my mom's. What's up?"

"Mona has been so good to me and Karlos. I want to show her how much I love and appreciate her."

She sucked her teeth. "Y'all bitches are sickening."

"That's why your ass is single. Anyway, she's good to me and she deserves to have someone be good to her for a change. All them other low-budget hoes before me took but never gave."

"I knew I would love you two together. Just call me a day before to make sure I'm not working."

I woke up that morning with a new attitude. I had one final tutoring session with Professor Will. I felt confident when I got most of the equations right. He winked at me as we clinked our beer bottles.

"You're ready!"

"What if you're wrong?"

"I, young lady, am rarely wrong."

I opened my eyes the morning of my final exam and asked God to give me the strength and guidance I needed to endure. I reveled in having the apartment to myself and I took my time getting dressed. I was too nervous to eat. The air was stifling as the class began to fill up. We had an hour to complete the exam. Some of the equations looked familiar but I ran into a few snags toward the end. I felt lighter when I called Dean.

"What are you doing tomorrow? I just finished my final exam. I graduate in a couple of weeks, but I'm going home to Chicago next weekend."

"Oh, it's home now? Those bitches who been chasing her are gonna be sick!"

I laughed. "That's why I'm calling. I want you to go with me to this jewelry store in Tysons Corner. I want to buy her a ring."

"Oh, you ain't playing!"

"Not at all!"

We made plans for me to pick her up the next day.

I called Dean when I pulled into her mother's driveway. She jogged down the steps, stopped dramatically in front of the car and clapped her hands. I couldn't help but laugh as she mouthed the word "Biiiiiiitchhh."

"Get in here! I gotta be home by the time Christian drops Karlos off."

She opened the door and felt the butterscotch leather seats. "I know you did some prostitute shit to get this."

We laughed and caught up on the drive to Tysons Corner. I had a couple of hours to find the right ring. Dean and I gawked over several designs and cuts of diamonds. The salesperson was courteous but didn't engage us. Her eyes widened when I told her I was looking for a two-carat ring. She whispered to another saleswoman and pulled out a tray of rings.

"Two carats?"

I ignored Dean as I scanned the tray until a bright stone caught my eye.

The salesperson described it in detail. "This is a cushion cut. The clarity or shine is brilliant. It's totally colorless."

"That's it," I said. She turned the price tag over and Dean nudged me as the saleswoman shined the ring. Cost, fifteen thousand dollars.

"Are you really going to pay that much for a ring?" Dean asked.

"I sold my house but that's all I can afford right now."

"Right now?"

I pushed past her and tried on the ring. It was breathtaking.

"I know for a fact that no one has ever bought Mona anything like that," Dean said. "She did all the giving."

"Good, it's her turn to receive." I turned toward the salesperson. "I'll take it."

"You've made a wonderful selection," she said. "Let me go and shine it one more time before wrapping it." Ten minutes later, the salesperson returned with an older white man. She had a troubled look on her face.

"Ma'am, there's been a mistake on our part. Unfortunately, your selection was mismarked. This isn't white gold, it's a platinum setting."

My heart sank. I couldn't afford a platinum setting. "What does that mean?"

"It means that we must sell you the ring at the price that's listed," he said.

"What's the difference in cost?"

"Fifteen hundred dollars. By law, I had to inform you of what you're purchasing. Gia will ring you up before wrapping it. Please think of us for your future purchases." He placed his card on the counter before returning to the back office.

Dean nudged me again. "Oh, her ass is fired. You got that shit set in platinum!"

"Thank God, because I couldn't spend another dime."

My joy was temporarily cut short when Gia ran my debit card for the ring.

"Miss Blue, I'm sorry but your purchase was declined."

"Declined? There's over forty thousand dollars in that account."

"It wasn't declined for insufficient funds, but the code is requiring the account holder to contact the bank."

My cellphone rang. Mona.

"Babe, I just got a message on my phone from the bank. What are you buying for fifteen thousand dollars?"

I had to think fast. "I wanted to buy myself a graduation present. I haven't been able to do something nice for myself in a long time."

"What costs fifteen thousand dollars?"

"A fabulous watch I've always wanted."

"Let me call the bank and let them know I'm making an out-of-state purchase. I can't wait to see this watch. Call me later. Love you."

I was relieved when she believed me. I would never spend that kind of money on anything for myself.

CHAPTER FOURTEEN

The week flew by as I prepared to fly to Chicago. I couldn't believe I was finally finished with my courses. I promised Karlos that this was the last time I would be in school. I just wanted to be a mom.

This would be the longest visit since Mona and I decided to be together. I finished packing my suitcase and realized I would have to check my bag. How was I going to travel with a fifteen-thousand-dollar ring?

Mona and I were going to our house in Michigan after she picked me up from the airport. I sat on the side of the bed. *Think, Nikki! Think!* I didn't want to just give her the ring. I wanted to give it to her in an unforgettable way. One that she would never forget. I looked around the room and wondered what to do. My eyes settled on my jewelry box. A smile danced across my face as I rifled through it. I picked up a sterling silver chain. I removed the cross and placed the chain around my waist. I removed her ring from the box and looped it through the chain. That was the only way I felt comfortable carrying the ring on board.

I tossed and turned that night. I finally fell asleep only to wake up in a cold sweat. I sat up in the middle of the bed. I dreamt that I received a C+ in my Corporate Finance II class. I tried to shake the thought from my mind. Please God, let this be a nightmare and not reality. I lay in the dark, staring at the ceiling, until I fell back asleep.

I tried not to think about it on the cab ride to the airport. I felt as though I was floating as I walked through the airport. I approached the scanner and whispered to the TSA agent as I gently raised my shirt. "I have a necklace with a diamond ring around my waist. It's a surprise and I didn't want to pack it in my bag."

She nodded and guided me through the scanner. I fell asleep upon take-off. I was exhausted from not sleeping the night before.

I felt refreshed when I called Mona as soon as we touched down. "I'm here."

I was nervous as I waited for her to pick me up from the airport terminal. Our relationship was still so new and exciting. I couldn't stop smiling as I got into the car and kissed her on her cheek.

"I've missed you. How was your flight?"

"There was a little turbulence. You know I hate flying. Where's Misty?"

"She's at the doggy hotel for the weekend. She's been up there with me before, but not with you."

"I don't know how you stay up there by yourself. It is pitch dark at night. Honey, we need to get an alarm system for both houses. I know you're a country girl, but I'm from the city and we don't play that."

"You're such a scaredy-cat. Being up there alone allows me to get away from all my responsibilities in Chicago."

"Whatever…but wait until you see the surprise I have for you."

"Wait until you see the surprise I have for *you!*" Mona replied.

I rolled down my window and enjoyed the fresh Michigan air. The perennials in the front yard were in full bloom.

"I forgot how beautiful it is up here. You can actually hear the birds chirping instead of police sirens."

"There's so much I want to do to the house, but wait until you see what I've done already," she said.

We walked onto the screened-in porch. Mona unlocked the heavy metal door and pushed it open. She screamed before I could get in the door.

"Babe!"

I stumbled as she backed into me. "What?"

"Look! It's a mouse." She backed onto the porch.

"Where?"

She pointed toward the couch. "Right there."

I focused my eyes.

"Honey, it's dead."

"How are you going to get it up?" she said.

"Ugh...I don't know."

"I can't do it! I can't!"

I laughed. "I don't want to do it either, but one of us has to. And what if there's another one somewhere?"

"Don't say that."

I spent the next twenty minutes coaxing Mona into holding a plastic bag while I scooped up the mouse with a dustpan. We opened all the windows in the house and peered into each room for other mice.

When I carried her bag into the bedroom, I stopped and squealed. "You got it!"

Sitting in our bedroom was the dresser I wanted from an antique shop in town. It was a white dresser with a black-and-white harlequin design.

"Thank you, I love it," I added. I leaned into her before quickly pulling away, not wanting her to feel the chain around my waist. We unpacked and placed our clothes in the dresser before driving into the quaint beach town for groceries.

"I love it here. It feels like we're a thousand miles away from Chicago."

Later, she opened a bottle of wine while I put the groceries away. We sat side by side on the couch as she poured the wine. I listened as she vented about work but saved the best for last.

"My construction loan was approved. Now I just have to transition the after-school arts program into a full-fledged performing arts school."

"What? How are you just going to say that so calmly?" She smiled when I started dancing. "Congratulations! You're the real head bitch in charge! When do you start construction?"

"In sixty days. I have so much to do."

"The hard part is over. You did it!"

She sipped her wine. "You make me feel like I can do anything."

"You can, but I also want you to know I'm here for you. There'll never be a time when I'm not. I want to take care of you the way you take care of me." I took her glass out of her hand. She leaned back as I straddled her and kissed her lips. "I have a surprise for you."

"What is it?" She placed her hands on my hips as I leaned into her.

"I am so in love with you. You're everything I've dreamed of. I deserve you and you deserve me." I sat up and removed my shirt. I slowly unbuttoned my jeans and pulled them down over my hips. Her eyes traveled from my breasts to my navel. I smiled at the confusion on her face when she saw the chain. I reached down and felt for the ring.

"This…is for you." I slid the ring around until it rested above my pubic hair.

"Babe…"

"I wanted to show you how much I love you."

"But we can't afford this and your watch."

"There is no watch. They almost spoiled my surprise, so I had to make something up before you figured it out."

She turned the ring over. "So, this is what you were buying?"

"Yes, do you like it?"

"I love it, but what did you do for yourself?"

"This is what I did for myself. I'm happy when you're happy. Try it on."

I leaned back as she unclasped the chain. I took the ring off and gently placed it on her finger.

"It's a little loose but we can get a ring guard."

She moved her hand as the diamond glistened. "No one has ever given me something like this."

"I don't know how those hoes let me jump to the front of the line, but I'm here to stay," I proclaimed.

I was in heaven as we drove back to Chicago. Those feelings were interrupted during our dinner at a restaurant in Hyde Park. That was the first time I realized how visible she was in the community. We were barely seated when a woman walked up to our table.

"Aren't you the Chicago Academy of Performing Arts lady? It's the CAPA school, right?"

"Yes, how are you?" Mona said.

The woman moved closer. "My daughter started in your program when she was thirteen," she began. They indulged in a long-winded conversation as I sat there feeling like an intruder. That was the first time I felt invisible in Mona's presence. She sensed my discomfort and tried to lighten the moment once the woman left.

"I don't think anyone knows my name anymore. They just call me 'the CAPA lady.'"

"I wish we could just be ourselves," I said, noticing her smile fading.

I didn't waste any time searching for a job when we returned to Chicago. Mona was well connected, but I wanted to create my own identity outside of hers. I fell back on what I knew. I could sell anything or any product that I believed in. I searched online for the top advertising agencies in Chicago. I started with the low-hanging fruit and submitted my résumé to a few agencies I had worked with during my NSBA days. I was encouraged when I landed three interviews. I spent the next couple of days researching each agency and their clients. I was excited when Mona asked what I was going to wear for my interviews.

"I don't know. I've always wanted a Brooks Brothers pantsuit."

"Then let's go find the perfect suit for your new job."

I was nervous the morning of my first interview. The office was located on Wacker Drive. I nervously smoothed out the jacket of my slate-grey pantsuit. I located the office on the elevator board and took the elevator to the sixteenth floor. The office was decorated with bold colors and modern furniture. The corporate logo took up an entire wall. A young Latina looked up after ending a call.

"Good morning. I'm Nikki Blue. I have an interview with Rebecca Walsh."

"Yes, Miss Blue. Rebecca is expecting you. Have a seat and I'll let her know you're here." I sat down and watched the clock.

"Miss Blue, Rebecca will see you now," the receptionist said after a few minutes.

I was surprised when I stepped into the office and a young Black woman was seated behind a large, oakwood desk.

"Nikki, good morning. I'm Rebecca Walsh. Thank you for coming in today."

I extended my hand. "Thank you. Hollister is legendary in the advertising industry."

"Yes, we are, but we are looking to add new talent and voices to our corporate initiatives. Please, have a seat." I sat in the chair directly across from her. I scanned her office for any clues on where she went to school as she shuffled papers on her desk.

"Your résumé as well as your experience is quite impressive," she said.

I couldn't believe a Black woman named Rebecca Walsh was the vice president of sales at one of the top advertising agencies in Chicago. Most of my interactions with advertising agencies had been with young white men and women. I wondered if her sleek chignon hid the character of a real sister. I quickly regained my train of thought.

"Thank you," I said. "Most of my experience has been in print but on the client side. The agency side would be a welcomed challenge."

We spent the next hour with me fielding questions on why I chose Hollister versus another agency. I was confident I was a fit as she explained the daily routine and expected goals of an account executive. The interview ended with her commitment to contact me for a second interview if she also thought I was a fit for the agency.

I went through back-to-back interviews with two other advertising agencies that week. I had my heart set on Hollister. And yet, I became discouraged when I didn't hear back from any of the agencies. What if none of them was interested?

CHAPTER FIFTEEN

I received a call for a second interview at Hollister that Friday. I was ecstatic. I decided not to tell Mona about the second interview. I didn't want to jinx it. I took a risk in wearing a chartreuse sleeveless dress with a matching duster. I paired it with a single strand of pearls and ecru slingbacks. I was calm enough to read the receptionist's energy.

"Good morning. I have a second interview with Rebecca."

"Yes, good morning, Miss Blue, she's expecting you. Follow me."

I tried not to look surprised when I walked into a room with four people seated at the table. Rebecca motioned me to an empty chair.

"Good morning and welcome back, Nikki."

"Good morning and thank you."

"We're excited to welcome you back for a second interview. The team was equally impressed with your background. So, before we get started, let me introduce you to the Midwest sales team." I tried to relax as I glanced around the table. There were two young white women, one older white man and an older Black woman.

Rebecca began with a barrage of questions. Jeff, a director, was terse in his questioning. The older Black woman, Grace, nodded when I elaborated on why I believed my military experience had laid the foundation for my discipline and determination. I left the interview knowing I gave it my best shot.

Mona and I were having dinner at home when my phone rang that evening. "I don't recognize this number." I put my finger to my lips and answered the call. She watched my facial expression change as I listened to Rebecca offer me the position.

"Thank you," I said. "I'm excited to join the Hollister team. I look forward to hearing from your assistant for next steps."

Mona leaned in as I giggled. "You're looking at the new Midwest account executive for Hollister!"

She stood up and embraced me. "Congratulations! Maybe I should have hired you after all."

I began clearing the dishes. "You can't afford me."

I had one week before starting at Hollister. I was relieved that some of our financial pressures would be alleviated. It was important that I begin to contribute to the household. We were trying not to deplete our savings from the sale of my house. I added another responsibility to my plate by looking for a private school for Karlos. He would be entering the eighth grade, given that he'd skipped a grade in elementary school. I was adamant about enrolling him in a private school, but I put that on hold until I completed my training at Hollister.

Mona surprised me with a celebratory dinner.

"I'm so proud of you. I don't know if I could work, raise a child, and go to school."

"You didn't have to. You built a successful business without a degree."

"Yeah, but I've always regretted not finishing school."

"What's going on with the grand opening? You've been tossing and turning in your sleep. You are so bad! A Black woman, building a multimillion-dollar performing arts academy on the South Side of Chicago? That's crazy. What are you planning for the grand opening?"

Her eyes lit up.

"I want do to something that has never been done on the South Side."

"Shit, you're already doing that! But how are you going to top the building?"

"That's why I love you. You're my biggest cheerleader, outside of my grandmother," she said. "Check this out: I'm thinking about asking Char to fly in from L.A. to host the event. We'll market it to VIP clients for corporate sponsorships. But I wanted to know if you're okay with me asking her."

Charlene Wells was an A-list actress in Hollywood. She and Mona had dated off and on for years. She was known in the industry as Char. I was intimidated when Mona told me of their affair. I became more comfortable as I gained more insight into their relationship. I'd never been an insecure person unless someone gave me reason to be.

"That's your friend and if she can help you have a successful grand opening, then I support you."

"Thank you, babe. I appreciate that."

I spent the rest of the weekend preparing for my first week of training at Hollister. I decided on a black pantsuit paired with a pinstriped shirt and black pumps. Per Poppy's email, I parked in a garage three blocks away from the office. I made a mental note to wear flats and carry my heels.

"Good morning, Poppy." She smiled this time.

"Good morning, and congratulations, Nikki. Let me show you to your cubicle. You're in training this week but I think you'll be shadowing Savanna." I followed her to a tiny cubicle in the middle of the office. I was surprised to find a bouquet of flowers with a card and a basket of chocolate kisses on top of a binder.

"Savanna sits right next to you. She should be in shortly. Training starts in the main conference room at ten. Why don't you get settled and I'll come and introduce you to the team."

I looked out the small window overlooking a building. It wasn't much of a view, but it was mine. I sat down and opened the card. It simply read, *Welcome to the team! Savanna.*

I had begun reviewing the binder when I heard movement in the cubicle beside me. A young Black woman's head appeared over the partition.

"You must be Nikki. Happy First Day! I'm Savanna." She extended her hand.

"Thank you so much for the flowers and chocolates," I said.

She gripped my hand and gave me the universal sister-girl look. "You gonna need that chocolate."

She pulled up a chair and we delved into the binder until Poppy interrupted us. Poppy walked me up and down both sides of the office introducing me to the team. There were three new hires already seated in the conference room. At ten o'clock on the dot, a slim white guy walked in. He had on a European-cut suit with a blue shirt that matched his blue eyes.

"Good morning and welcome to Hollister. I'm Patrick Barbeau, manager of the Midwest team. We will spend the first week immersed in training. Your second week will consist of role-playing and pitching to our executive team."

I was glassy eyed after listening to Patrick talk nonstop for two hours. We broke for lunch and returned to where we left off. I was drained by the time I walked to my cubicle to pack up for the day. Savanna stood over our partition.

"Was it what you expected?"

"Yes and no. I was an advertising manager for a nonprofit for several years. Being on the agency side is a little different."

"That's more than what I had when I started. I have a graphic design background. I had the messaging down but not the sales part. Hopefully, we will be on the same team. Get some rest. You have four more days with Patrick."

I realized I hadn't had time to call Mona. "Hi, honey," I said.

"Hey working lady. How was your first day? I was surprised when I didn't hear from you."

"I know. I was in training all day and then I grabbed a sandwich while looking over my binder. I'll be in training for two weeks, but I think I'm going to like it."

I researched private schools in Hyde Park for Karlos while on my lunch breaks. The Sadona School was the only private middle school in the neighborhood. I knew the thirteen-thousand-dollar-per-year tuition would be a bone of contention. I subtly brought it up after dinner one night. I sat on the bed while Mona changed her clothes.

"How was your day?" I asked.

"It was good. I secured a grant for staffing for the upcoming year. How was your and Karlos's day? I want to sit down and talk to him to see how he's adjusting being away from his friends. I don't want him to think I'm too busy."

"I think he's doing okay but I wanted to talk to you about the Sadona School."

She began to remove her makeup. "What about it?"

"I looked at other schools, but I really like Sadona."

"Babe, are you really thinking about him going to a school that costs fifteen thousand dollars?"

"It's thirteen thousand."

"Fifteen, thirteen…same thing. Why would we pay that kind of money for one year of middle school? And you're talking about Dematha or St. Augustine for high school because of their soccer program?"

I held my ground. "He's always been in private school and it's important he stays in private school. It will increase his chances of getting into a good college."

"I know for a fact that tuition for both those high schools is ten thousand per year. That's forty thousand dollars for high school."

"But we still have our savings from the sale of my house. Coupled with my commissions at Hollister, we could manage it."

"Thirteen thousand for one year of middle school?"

"His education is important to me."

"Oh, and it's not important to me?"

"I have half the tuition in my savings. I'll figure out the rest."

"So now it's 'I' instead of 'we'?"

I didn't respond as she walked out of the room. I thought about the times I had to fight Christian to keep Karlos in private school. Why must his education be an ongoing battle? Enrollment in a private middle school would help him get into a select high school. He could eventually secure a soccer scholarship into a Division I college. If not, he could focus on his academics. I was determined to give him opportunities I never had. I had to focus on making myself stand out at Hollister. Surely, she couldn't say no to Sadona once I began earning commission.

I was thrilled when I was placed on Savanna's team at the end of my training. We would report to Patrick. My excitement was heightened when I reviewed the new organizational chart. Grace Hazelton was the head of our department. She was a southern belle who happened to be an AKA. She reminded me of the ushers at church who could speak volumes with a look.

She was a woman of few words. Her dark brown skin stood in beautiful contrast to her vibrant St. John suits. It helped that Savanna was also an AKA. I leaned on her for guidance as I practiced my first pitch with Grace.

"She's scary," I said.

"I know. She's harder on us because we're only two of four Black account executives and the only women. She'll push us to be better. We represent her and she'll never let you forget it."

I had one week to prepare for my first presentation to Grace. Mona and I were running on empty. She worked late trying to complete punch lists for construction of her state-of-the art building while running the existing programs. Something had to give. The only thing that alleviated our combined stress levels was our salacious sex life. I always wanted her and no matter how tired she was, she never said no.

I woke up one morning and found her staring at the ceiling.

"What's wrong, honey?"

She wiped a tear from her eye. "I don't know if I can do this."

I sat up and pulled her closer. "What's going on?"

She shook her head. "I have so many people depending on me. My staff have families. My kids…these are the children who were never excited about school, let alone college."

"But you're giving them hope. They see what's possible. Look at what you've accomplished."

She covered her face and cried as I held her.

"It's going to be okay," I said softly. "I'll do whatever I can to help you. I'm adjusting to this new position, but I can help you secure corporate sponsorships for your opening. I should be able to help you in two weeks. Just let me graduate first."

I kissed Mona and got up to get ready for work. I was surprised when she didn't join me for our morning bath. I went to check on her and saw that she had pulled the covers over her head.

"Honey, it's almost eight!"

"I'm not going into the office today," Mona declared.

I'd never seen her not go into the office unscheduled. I sat on the side of the bed. "What if I make you some breakfast?"

She didn't respond.

"It's going to be okay. Get some rest. I'll let Misty out and feed her before I leave. Call me if you need me, okay? I love you."

Worry set in as I rushed to feed Misty before heading to work. What could I do to alleviate some of Mona's stress?

I was drained after role- playing with Savanna all morning. I thought about Mona on my way to lunch. Her voice was almost a whisper when she answered the phone on the third ring.

"Hello."

"Hi, honey. I'm on my lunch break. How are you feeling?"

"Fine."

"You're not, and you don't have to pretend to be. Have you eaten?"

"I'm not hungry."

"You have to eat something. I'll check on you before I get off."

I'd never seen her so despondent. I glanced at my watch and made a spur-of-the-moment decision. It was going to be tight, but I could do it. I grabbed my purse and changed into my flats. I took the back elevator down-stairs and swiped out. Luckily, there wasn't a line at the deli. I ordered two entrees, paid for our lunch, and ran to the garage. I drove at least seventy miles per hour on Lakeshore Drive. I parked in front of the house and ran up the steps. Misty met me as I deactivated the alarm. I raced up the stairs to the kitchen and yelled out to Mona.

"It's me." I grabbed a bottle of water out of the refrigerator before heading upstairs. She was sitting on her side of the bed when I walked in. Her eyes were puffy from crying.

"What are you doing home?" she said in a scraggly voice.

I held up the bag.

"Room service!"

She ran her fingers through her hair and looked around the room. "What time is it?"

"A little after one. I gotta get back to work but I was worried about you." I walked to her side of the bed and laid her lunch out before kissing her. "I gotta get back to work. Please, eat. I love you."

I had twenty minutes before I had to swipe back in. I opened my container in the car and scarfed down a couple of bites before racing back to the office. I exhaled when I stepped out of the elevator and swiped in ten minutes after two. I caught my breath as I walked to my cubicle and changed into my heels. I couldn't help but smile when I took my phone out of my purse to place it on silent. Mona's text read *I love you.*

CHAPTER SIXTEEN

I was hopeful I would find her in a different space when I got home that evening. My hopes were dashed when I walked into a quiet house. I kicked off my heels and headed down the hallway to our bedroom. I opened the curtains.

"Hi, honey." Her half-eaten lunch was on my side of the bed. She pulled the cover further over her head. "Can I get you something?"

"No, thank you."

I felt hopeless as I gathered her leftover lunch and placed it in the refrigerator. I sat on the couch and ate the rest of my lunch before feeding Misty and setting the alarm. I changed my clothes, took a bath, and slid into bed beside her. Without saying a word, Mona turned over and wrapped her arms around me. It was seven o'clock in the evening, but I held her until she fell asleep.

The sun shone bright through our floor to ceiling windows the next morning. We went through the same routine as the previous morning. This was the second day that she wasn't going to work. I thought of how her voice messages and emails were piling up. Yani was a competent assistant, so I knew she'd reschedule Mona's meetings.

Suddenly, a light went off in my mind. I would be taking a risk, but I had no other choice. I kissed Mona goodbye before getting dressed and heading to work. I pulled out of the garage and grabbed my cellphone. I swallowed hard before dialing the number.

"Miss Lillian. It's Nikki."

She paused. "Hello, there. How are things?"

I exhaled. "Not too good, ma'am. I'm sorry to call so early, but I didn't know what else to do."

"Nah…don't worry about it."

"She's going to be angry with me for calling you but…I can't get Mona out of bed. She's so stressed over this building. She's been in bed for two days. I can barely get her to eat."

"Mm, hmm. I see."

I began to ramble. "I know how close you are, and I was hoping maybe you could call her. Please, don't tell her I called you."

"No, I won't tell her and thank you for calling."

I tried to focus at work as I prepared for my first pitch with Savanna and Grace. I'd just changed into my heels when Savanna appeared at my cubicle.

"You ready?"

I rolled my eyes. "I need a drink."

"You and me both."

We gathered our files and headed toward Grace's office. I followed Savanna's lead as she stopped at the threshold of Grace's office and knocked on the open door.

Grace looked over her glasses and motioned us in. We sat in the two chairs directly in front of her huge desk. The large bay window offered a landscape view of Wacker Drive. Her undergraduate degree from Tuskegee was mounted beside her AKA plaque. She hung up the phone and adjusted her glasses.

"Welcome to the Midwest team, Nikki."

"Thank you, Grace. I'm excited to be a part of the team."

"Good. I take it that Savanna has brought you up to speed.

"Yes, she's been very helpful."

"I fought hard to have you both on my team. I know you're working together will help us secure the number one position in the department. Your sales background coupled with Savanna's media background we will be a force to be reckoned with."

The house was quiet when I got home that evening, as it had been for the past two days. I changed into some sweats before heading to our bedroom. I was surprised when I rounded the corner and saw Mona sitting in the middle of our bed with her phone.

"Hi, honey," I said.

"You called my grandma?"

"What?"

"She called me this morning."

"What did she say?"

She had a twinkle in her eyes as she glared at me. "She said she's going to call tomorrow morning and if I'm not in my office, she'll be on her way up here."

"Miss Lillian is gangsta." I lay down beside her.

"Thank you," she said.

"For what?"

"For always knowing what to do. My mama is the strongest woman I know. She reminded me of who I am. So, I have some ideas. Char will be in town for an event next month. She said she wanted to meet you. We're also going to start planning for the grand opening."

"Okay."

"I know you have a lot going on with your new job, but I need your help." She began to scroll through her phone. "I wrote down some ideas for selling corporate sponsorships for the opening. I came up with the idea for a magazine. The corporate sponsorships will include a monetary donation and an ad in the CAPA Magazine. The ads will highlight their programs and initiatives."

"That's two additional revenue streams."

"Yeah, but I don't have anyone on my team who can sell. I don't have time to hire anyone."

"You need someone who can hit the ground running."

"Can you help me?"

I paused. "Of course, I can, but I ain't cheap. You're going to have to pay me in trips, shoes, and ass."

I arrived at the office early to calm myself before my pitch to Grace. She sat stone-faced as I presented. I ended with a strong pitch on why the client should hire Hollister. She leaned back in her chair.

"I recommend more emphasis be placed on their target market. Other than that, well done."

Savanna nudged me as we walked back to our cubicle.

"We got this."

Our hopes were crushed when we weren't awarded the contract the following week.

Meanwhile, I tried not to look for my final grade from Johns Hopkins each day in the mail. I threw myself into securing corporate sponsorships for CAPA. I couldn't contain my excitement when Mona came home and handed me a computer bag.

"Miguel said this is the computer most compatible with his. He loaded all the programs you'll need. He also created a CAPA email account for you. You're now connected to our intranet."

"Thank you. This is everything I need to get started."

"Good. I'll introduce you to Miguel via email. Thank you, babe. I appreciate you helping me."

"Anything for you."

That next week was a whirlwind as I solicited Hollister clients during the day and CAPA clients at night. I was in my element when Savanna and I secured two new clients. I was finally winning, personally and professionally.

I remember the day as if it were yesterday. I stood in the foyer, sifting through the mail. I was surprised to find two envelopes from Johns Hopkins. My throat tightened as I read the first letter…*We regret to inform you*…The words became blurry as my tears stained the ink. I had received a C+ in my Corporate Finance II class.

I failed. Five years of my life, wasted!

I fell to my knees and sobbed. I had failed myself and everyone who believed in me.

I dragged myself upstairs, got into bed, and cried myself to sleep. I woke up praying it was a dream. I pulled the cover over my head when I heard the security sensor chime.

"Babe?" My chest heaved as Mona walked down the hallway. "What's wrong?"

"I failed. He gave me a fuckin' C-plus."

"But can you take the class over?"

"I can't."

"There has to be something you can do. Can you call your professor?"

"No. His class was the one I tried to drop but he, Professor Will, and my advisor all told me not to."

"There's gotta be something you can do. You tried to drop it, but everyone encouraged you not to."

"You can only receive one C in business school. You're expelled if you receive two. This was my second C."

Not even Mona's arms could console me that night. I woke up to her caressing the back of my head.

"You were crying in your sleep."

I exhaled. "What is God trying to tell me?"

I pulled myself together as she ran our bathwater. I didn't recognize myself in the mirror as my bloodshot eyes stared back at me. I wanted to run and hide, but then remembered my military experience.

I didn't know how I was going to do it, but I had to drive on.

I was relieved that Mona wasn't home when I arrived. I changed my clothes and got into bed. I was falling asleep when the alarm sensor chimed. Mona called me from downstairs.

"I ordered some food, babe."

"I'm not hungry," I replied. She came upstairs and sat on the bed.

"Babe, you have an envelope from Johns Hopkins."

"It doesn't matter."

"You're not going to open it? It could be something about your grade. Do you want me to open it?"

"It doesn't matter."

It seemed like forever before she spoke. "It says you've been selected to speak at the scholarship luncheon for graduates."

"They must have sent it before final grades were submitted."

"I think you should go, to say thank you for the scholarship you received," she said.

"Great! How would that look? Thanking them for a scholarship and not graduating."

Mona lay down beside me. "You never know what can come of it. The letter says you have seven days to accept or decline. We'll get your ticket. Maybe seeing Karlos will make you feel better. Promise me you'll think about it."

I had no intention of going, but I could never say no to her. And yet, I waited until the very last minute to respond.

The next couple of days flew by as I tried to distract myself with work. I called Carol to speak to Karlos before his bedtime. Just the sound of his voice lifted my spirits.

"Mom! We beat Bethesda yesterday."

"What? What was the score?"

"Four to three. I was midfield and crossed it with my left foot to Cody and he scored with a header."

"I know Carol went crazy."

"Everyone did. They dogpiled me and Cody."

"That's crazy."

"When are you coming to my game?"

"I'm not sure. Your dad wants you to spend the summer with him before he goes to Germany."

"But you said you were just going to be a soccer mom after you graduate."

"Mommy will try to make one of your games soon."

"Remember the little college mouse I made for you at school? Do you have to wear a hat and coat like that?"

I wiped my tears. "Yes, honey. It's called a cap and gown." Why did he remember that little mouse at that moment? Was that a sign?

CHAPTER SEVENTEEN

It never occurred to me to inform my advisor that I wouldn't be graduating. I assumed she knew. Mona was right. It was the right thing to do to thank the corporate sponsor. I braced myself before reading the first letter in its entirety. The bold print jumped off the page: "You have seven business days to appeal the decision." I looked at the date. I had less than a week left to respond. Under what pretense could I appeal? I failed. I had nothing to stand on. I thought of Karlos's little graduation mouse. My mind told me the idea was absurd, but God whispered... *Trust Me.*

Melancholy set in as the plane hovered over D.C. I was overwhelmed with anxiety, but I knew I'd made the right decision to go to the luncheon. I signed in at the reception desk as a scholarship recipient. The large ballroom was half-full by the time I arrived.

"Nikki!" I turned to find Minnie smiling at me. "I'm so happy you decided to join us."

"Minnie, it's so good to see you. I don't know where I'm supposed to sit."

She placed her hand on my shoulder. "You'll be sitting with the other scholarship recipients up front." She guided me to the recipient's table. I was the only Black scholarship recipient. I began to review the program when an older white gentleman sat beside me.

"Good morning. Which scholarship recipient are you?" He was a distinguished-looking man with a salt-and-pepper buzz haircut. His wired-rimmed glasses covered warm brown eyes. I extended my hand.

"Good morning, sir. I'm Nikki Blue, the BG&A scholarship recipient."

"BG&A is one of our long-term partners," he said. "Which specific scholarship were you awarded?"

I shifted in my seat. "I was awarded the scholarship for single parents. I enrolled in the program after earning a master's in human services from Lincoln University."

He leaned in. "What were you doing prior to Lincoln?"

"I worked in various sales positions after returning from Desert Storm. I was a medic in the army."

His eyes lit up. "Thank you for your service. I served in Vietnam."

I squared my shoulders. "Thank you for your service, sir."

Our conversation ended when Dr. Coleman walked to the podium and began the program. I made the decision to speak from my heart and not prepare a speech. What difference would it make? I wasn't graduating.

I was the last recipient to speak. It felt like I walked a mile to the podium when Dr. Coleman announced my name. The room seemed larger as I looked beyond the podium. I smoothed out my list of BG&A executives and thanked them for selecting me. I took a deep breath before explaining how the two-thousand-dollar scholarship came just in time. I had no way of paying for my final semester. I described the shame I felt being laid off and having to rely on public assistance. I painted a picture of how my desk was an old dresser drawer. Many nights I had to use the back side of used paper to print my case studies because I couldn't afford to buy paper. I thanked the BG&A executives for being the light at the end of the tunnel. I managed to finish my speech without crying. I tried not to notice attendees wiping their eyes as I walked backed to my seat. I had barely sat down when Minnie approached me.

"Nikki, Dr. Jensen and I were just talking about what an amazing testimony that was to your will to succeed. You're the student this program was designed for. Oh, dear, forgive me. Dr. Jensen is the program chair. Pardon me, Dr. Coleman is signaling for me."

Dr. Jensen leaned in closer. "You have an amazing story. We'll have to invite you back post-graduation to speak to future recipients."

My shoulders slumped. "That won't be possible, Dr. Jensen. Unfortunately, I won't be graduating."

He looked over his glasses. "Why on earth not?"

"I received a C+ in my final class, Corporate Finance II. That was my second C."

"Was your professor aware of your academic status?"

"Yes, sir. I had several conversations with him and Minnie regarding dropping the class and retaking it in the Fall. They both encouraged me not to drop it. I sacrificed one hundred dollars per week for six weeks of tutoring with Professor Will."

"What was Professor Will's recommendation?"

"He also encouraged me not to drop the class." I lowered my head.

"As a practice and in deference to the professor, I rarely intervene when a professor makes a decision relative to grades."

"I understand, sir."

He placed his hand over mine. "It was indeed a pleasure meeting you. You're a special young lady. Why don't you send me a letter reiterating your situation? Graduation is three weeks away. I'm not making any promises, but let me look into it." He reached into his jacket and pulled out his business card. "Send me a letter as soon as possible. Again, thank you for your service."

"Thank you, sir."

The air was sucked out of the room as I read his card. It read, Robert A. Jensen, Ph.D., Program Chair. I didn't know why, but I felt lighter on the cab ride to my sister's house. I could barely breathe when I finally told her the truth.

"Just think, you weren't going to go. You were supposed to be there. That was nothing but God. What are you going to do?"

"You know who your sister is. He said to write him a letter as soon as possible. I started writing the letter on my phone in the cab."

"I know that's right! We're going to pray."

I allowed myself to just be a mother that weekend. I didn't tell Karlos I would be in town that weekend. His face lit up when I waved from the sidelines during halftime. Nothing else mattered when he shot from midfield earning a hat trick. His teammates went wild as he ran up the sideline and pointed at me.

"That's for you, Mom!"

The next week flew by as I played catch-up with my client calls at Hollister. One evening as I got home from work, I kicked my heels off in the foyer and went through the mail as usual. I was surprised to see a priority envelope from Johns Hopkins. I sat on the bench and prayed before opening the envelope. I glared at the first sentence:…"After careful consideration, I have reversed your final grade of C+ to B- for Corporate Finance II."

I was numb as I read the sentence over and over. I lay on the bench and closed my eyes. This time, my tears were tears of joy. *Thank you, Father God, for your Grace and Mercy*. I was too wound up to cook dinner that night. I ordered Mona's favorite takeout and set the table. I ran into the den when I heard her keys jingle in the door. I held the letter up in my hand and began to dance. Her dimples deepened as she laughed.

"Hey, babe."

"Dr. Jensen changed my grade!"

"He did? What does that mean?"

I fell into her arms. "It means I'll have an MBA in three weeks."

She hugged me more tightly. "Oh, babe. I'm so happy for you."

I couldn't stop talking as we made plans to travel to D.C. for my graduation. She kept looking at me and smiling.

"You did it, but I knew you would. Just think if you hadn't gone to thank the sponsor!"

"I know. I'm so glad you convinced me to go. Thank you for always believing in me."

"I'll always believe in you. Even when you don't believe in yourself."

She surprised me after a Saturday lunch date. "Let's go shopping. I need to buy you a graduation outfit. You gotta look like all that money you borrowed to get this MBA."

I felt like a princess as we shopped on Michigan Avenue. I settled on a black pleated miniskirt with a matching cable knit shirt. The outfit couldn't hold a candle to my shoes. I knew they were the ones when I spotted them. I held up a pair of two-toned black and camel-colored Mary Janes. The four-inch block heel was in stark contrast to the white leather across the instep.

"These are the ones."

"How much are they?"

"If I tell you, I'll have to kill you!" I said.

My cheeks hurt from smiling on the plane ride to D.C. Mona reserved a hotel room at the Baltimore Harbor so we would be close to the campus. I was finally proud of myself when we woke up and ordered room service.

"You ready?"

I laid my clothes on the bed. "Yes, God! Thank you so much for loving me through all this."

I got dressed and left her in the hotel room. All graduates had to arrive on campus an hour early to pick up our caps and gowns. My sister was bringing Ahmad, Karlos, and my mother. The next time I saw my family, I would be walking across the stage to receive my MBA.

I got emotional when I heard the music boom through the speakers. Mona sent me a text with a heart to say that she was sitting with my family in the fourth row of the bleachers. The stage seemed so far away as we were led to our seats. I felt ten feet tall walking onto the field to thunderous applause. There were five departments announced before the business school. My palms became sweaty as Dr. Jensen announced our names alphabetically. When a department representative motioned us to stand, we got to our feet, marched down the middle of the field and waited for our individual names to be announced. My heart raced when Dr. Jensen called my name. He shook my hand firmly, handed me my degree, and said, "Hoorah!" I walked off the stage clutching my degree tightly, as if they were going to take it back.

I was midway to my seat when I heard his voice. "Nikki!"

I turned in the direction of the voice and saw my father. Time stood still as he smiled and gave me a thumbs-up. I cried as I returned his gesture. He was here. How did he know?

We left the field as we entered it, one department at a time. I maneuvered through the throng of graduates. I spotted my mother's smiling face and made my way to the bleachers. Slowly but surely, I found my sister and my brother. My mother was the first one to hug me.

"I'm so proud of you."

"Thank you, Mom…" Before I could say another word, my father appeared.

"Look at you, girl!" The years of hurt and betrayal vanished as I fell into his open arms. I finally had his approval.

"How did you get here?"

"We drove. Let me introduce you to my old lady, Julie." I was caught off-guard when a white woman stepped around him and handed me a gift bag.

"Congratulations, Nikki."

"Thank you. I'm happy you and Dad could make it." I couldn't believe how much she looked like my stepmother, Deena. My aunt Ros had mentioned that they were having marital problems, but I was surprised to learn they'd divorced after twenty years of marriage.

My thoughts were interrupted when I recognized a familiar face in the crowd. My eyes squinted against the sun as he waved. Standing there, looking just as surprised, was Tim, the best friend of my ex, Valencia.

"Nikki! Congratulations! I didn't know you were at Hopkins."

"Hey, Tim. Thank you. What are you doing here?"

"A friend of mine graduated. He's in the psychology department."

Someone touched my waist and I turned to see Mona. She handed me a bouquet of red roses. "Congratulations, babe."

"Thank you, honey."

I felt Tim's glare. "Tim, this is my girlfriend, Mona." I smiled as they shook hands.

I wanted to laugh as he watched her hug Karlos. The drag queen in me emerged as I thought of Martin Lawrence's hilarious catchphrase:…"Now run tell dat!"

CHAPTER EIGHTEEN

As Mona and I headed back to Chicago, I realized I was becoming the woman I'd always dreamed of becoming. I had my MBA. I had true love. I had transitioned to Chicago with an exciting new job. Karlos would spend the rest of the summer with Christian before he left for Germany before he joined us.

As I settled into my new life in Chicago, I began to realize how visible Mona and her work was. I felt like I was married to a celebrity. We couldn't go anywhere on the South Side without someone recognizing her. I was happy for her, and yet my feelings of invisibility resurfaced. She rarely introduced me as I stood there feeling uncomfortable. Whenever I entered the house, I entered through the back door. I wondered if her staff saw me coming and going to our private residence. Though I began to correspond with her graphic designer via email, I'd never met him or any of her staff.

I'd been back in Chicago for a week when Mona told me Char was in town. I wore a form-fitting suit to work that day. After all, she was one of Mona's exes. Mona had taken a half day from work and ordered Char's favorite Jamaican food. I heard their laughter from the kitchen as I entered the back door. I dropped my purse on the table in the den and took a deep breath before walking into the kitchen.

"Hi, honey." I walked over and kissed Mona.

"Hey babe, this is Char. Char, this is my honey, Nikki."

Char's presence was more magnificent in person than it was on the big screen. I leaned over and hugged her.

"Lord......you're more beautiful in person."

She laughed the hearty laugh she was known for.

"Bless you. That's expensive makeup, suga. So, you're the woman who got her off the market." She smirked as she looked me up and down.

"Yes, ma'am! I caught these bitches slipping!"

She burst into laughter and gave me a high five. "I know that's right!"

I excused myself for the rest of the evening. I wanted to give them time to catch up, but most importantly, I wanted Char to know that I was secure. Afterward, Mona and I spent the rest of the evening discussing her plans for Char hosting the grand opening.

With so much on my plate, I began eating my lunch in the conference room at Hollister. I also made calls and solicited CAPA sponsorships using my cellphone. My strategy was to wake up an hour early and leave voice messages regarding sponsorships opportunities. Potential sponsors would often respond by lunchtime. I loved the rush of pitching CAPA's grand opening and switching gears to Hollister clients.

I kept a low profile at Hollister as I navigated the learning curve. I interacted with other team members only when necessary. I noticed a shift in my white counterparts when Savanna and I started reaching our revenue goals. They began to make snide comments during team meetings.

Heather was an androgynous-looking rep who had the longest tenure at Hollister. "I guess the rest of us better take notes from Savanna and Nikki," she noted at one meeting.

I couldn't help but smirk as I leaned closer to Savanna and said, "What's her problem?"

"She wants to be a director so bad," Savanna whispered. "She was pissed when Grace hired Patrick over her, and he had less experience."

Slowly but surely, some of my colleagues began to probe into my personal life. I never offered much other than I had a son, I was a veteran, and I'd graduated from Johns Hopkins.

During my first month at Hollister, we welcomed a new team member. Barry Moore was dressed impeccably when Patrick introduced him to the team. He reminded me of the gay men from my high school days. As time went on, he began to comment on my attire.

"Yes, Miss Nikki. You betta let the kids have it!"

"I'm just trying to keep up with you," I said. I wanted him to know I was "family," but I was always wary of who knew Mona. I finally had the life I always dreamed. However, I began to struggle with being out in my personal life and closeted in my professional life.

The temperament of the administrative staff began to change. Whenever I walked into the break room, the Black admins would stop talking. I struggled to engage in their office gossip about their heterosexual conquests and office affairs. They were aware of the fact that I'd never mentioned a man in my life. There was one assistant, Gail, who always ignored me. She was the ringleader. She held court as the other assistants laughed at her mean-girl gossip. I tried to ignore them as I ate my lunch. I made a mental note to ask Barry what the issue was. He knew everyone's business. I didn't have to wait long to find out. My question was answered one day after a departmental meeting.

Our colleagues applauded me and Savanna when we shared the fact that we'd been "hazed" by Grace. It felt good to be recognized for exceeding our team goals. I was refilling my coffee when Barry approached me.

"Miss girl ain't feeling you."

"Who?"

He nodded toward Gail.

"Why do you say that?" I asked.

"When you were reporting out the numbers, she held up two fingers and said, 'She need some dick in her life.'"

"What? Who was she talking to?"

"The admin team."

I was incensed. Why did I have to keep coming out? My sexuality had nothing to do with my performance. I'd almost forgotten Barry was standing there.

"Bitch, please," I said. "I know she didn't with that tired drag queen weave. I'm going to work this like the white girls."

"What are you gonna do?"

"Where's Rebecca?" He looked around the room and nodded toward Rebecca, who was talking to Grace. I squared my shoulders and walked over to them.

"Excuse me Grace, may I steal Rebecca for a moment?"

Rebecca looked surprised as Grace walked away.

"I know I'm new to the team, but I come to work every day and do my job without question," I said. "I'm pissed."

She placed her hand on my shoulder and guided me out the door. "What's wrong?"

"Barry told me that while I was presenting, Gail put up two fingers and said in front of the admin team that I needed some dick in my life."

Her eyes widened. "What brought that about?"

"I don't care what brought it about. It's unprofessional. Did she think she was outing me? Well, good luck with that. I came out to the world at the age of thirteen. What does my sexuality have to do with my performance?"

"I'm so sorry, Nikki. I didn't know."

"How would you know? No one else announces their sexuality."

She nodded. "How do you want me to handle this?"

"I would like her written up, unless she wants me to file a discrimination case with HR."

"You have every right to feel that way. I'll speak with her before the end of the day."

I left the meeting knowing that wasn't the end of it. At least not for me.

I vented to Mona that evening as she tried to calm me down.

"So, everyone knows?"

"I couldn't care less."

She hesitated. "I used to date Lewis James, the director of diversity at Chicago State. He's Grace's best friend."

"I didn't know that."

I couldn't sleep that night as I had flashbacks of being bullied in high school by mean girls like Gail. I woke up that morning with memories of the gay men of my youth and their advice. *….Never let them see you sweat.* I pulled out a spandex orange, floral-printed skirt and matching ribbed tank top. I couldn't stop thinking of her as I ironed a white high-collared shirt. I put the shirt on and tied it in the front. I paired the outfit with a pair of squared-toe, orange sling-backs.

I swiped in an hour early. I changed into my heels and tapped my face with powder before walking to Gail's cubicle. The office was quiet except for the whirring of the air-conditioning. She was startled when I leaned against her cubicle.

"I heard you had something to say to me."

She turned and adjusted her thick glasses. "What?"

"I heard you had something you wanted to say to me."

"I don't know what you're talking about."

"I thought you would say that, but let me let you in on a little secret. If I could give you all the dick that gets thrown at me that I don't want, perhaps you wouldn't be so miserable."

She chuckled.

"And if you ever have something to say to me, my cubicle is right over there and we can do this."

I walked away feeling vindicated. I was sure everyone in the office knew what had transpired but no one ever mentioned it.

The calendar was winding down to the date of the CAPA grand opening. I was ten thousand dollars from reaching Mona's goal for the magazine. While I worked on it, I managed to stay out of her staff's way. The only staff member who knew I was Mona's partner was Yani. I suspected Mona was relieved when she didn't have to explain who I was to more people. I could imagine the challenges she faced, being a Black woman building a multimillion-dollar facility in a white, male-dominated industry. The fact that she was bisexual was an additional threat to her business. Knowing this, I buried my feelings.

I began to miss my family and friends. Mona must have sensed what I was feeling because she offered to fly my mother in for the grand opening. I missed Karlos more than ever, but I knew Christian wasn't going to send him to Chicago until the end of the summer. I didn't know why, but my intuition told me I would need my mother.

Mona assigned me a cubicle space with access to all CAPA technology. To minimize the awkwardness, I limited my time using the office space to after hours. I would call Mona to ensure that Melissa had left for the day. I had no interest in meeting her. Mona couldn't hide her distain.

"Yeah, that nut is gone for the day."

"What's wrong?"

"She wants to use this security company to wire the new building, but he's way over budget. He must be one of her friends. I'm running out of time and the other vendors didn't have good reviews. I may have to go with the guy she chose."

I made a point of not talking about CAPA unless she brought it up. I wanted our home to be our sanctuary. I was thrilled when I secured the final sponsor for the magazine two weeks out from the grand opening.

"I'm sorry I couldn't do more."

"You did more than enough. You reached the goal I needed so I didn't have to pull it from another line item."

"I know, but I was only a couple of hundred over. Next time, if I have more time, I can raise more."

She raised her wine glass. "So, when are we going to Miami?"

CHAPTER NINETEEN

Mona purchased my mother's airline ticket the week before the opening. She decided that she would have a private reception for the band members at our home. She insisted on soul food to complement a catered menu. I couldn't think of a better cook than my mother and she was more than happy to oblige.

Mona was excited as we sat in the den after dinner and reviewed the marketing materials. "Close your eyes," she said, "Now, open them."

"Oh, my God! How did you get Avis Banks?"

She sipped her wine. "Char connected me to her manager, and guess what?"

"What?"

"She agreed to perform at half her fee because we're a nonprofit."

"That's crazy."

"I know, right? That leaves me with enough money to book another artist." She gave me a mischievous look and pulled out another draft. "I'm waiting on a call from another artist, just in case." She just got off tour with Avis. She's willing to do it. She's checking to make sure she doesn't have another gig. I had Miguel create two markups just in case she falls through."

Avis Banks was a legendary R&B singer who made a successful transition to acting. Most Black people grew up singing her songs. And Isabelle White was a jazz artist who had a major neo-soul following.

"People are going to go crazy with this lineup."

"You think so?"

"I know so."

That Wednesday before the grand opening, I was surprised when I opened the garage door and saw Mona's truck. I walked into the house and smelled a delicious aroma. There were candles and gardenias on the table.

"What are you doing here?" I asked.

She laughed. "I live here."

"But why aren't you at work?" I sat at the counter as she pulled a dish out of the oven.

"I needed to clear my head. My construction punch list is done, so I thought I would make dinner for you for a change."

I got up and pulled the cover off the dish. "An apple pie? Where did you get this from?"

Mona looked amused. "I made it."

I squinted my eyes. "You made it? How? It has the little crisscross strips that you see on commercials."

"I just felt like making a pie."

"I can't believe you made this. You've been holding out. You can draw, paint, sculpt, put up drywall, build buildings, and now you're baking pies with the little strips."

"They're called lattices, babe. Let's eat. I got something else I want to show you."

I helped her clean the kitchen before feeding Misty and heading upstairs. I was floored when we reached the top landing. There was a trail of red roses leading to our bedroom. She guided me to the chairs in front of the bay windows. She lit some candles before sitting down and holding my hand.

"I know I don't tell you this enough, but hopefully I show you how much I love and appreciate you. I never thought I would find you. You love me for who I am. I know it's not easy being with me and all that comes with that..." She lowered her head.

"I love all of you..." I said.

Before I could finish, she reached under her chair and pulled out a small box. I exhaled as she opened it. Tears streamed down my face as I stared at a brilliant Tiffany cut diamond.

"It's beautiful."

She gently placed it on my finger. I leaned over and kissed her. "How did you keep this from me?" I asked.

"I almost slipped up and left the box on the bed. I showed it to Yani and she was like, 'Dang, Nikki must be special.' I said, 'She is.'"

"I hope you always feel that way."

I smiled all the way to work that morning. We were five minutes into our morning meeting when Savanna stopped mid-sentence.

"Wait a damned minute!" She looked at my hand. "When did that happen?"

"Last night."

She picked up my hand and held it closer.

"I'm trying to be like you when I grow up."

The fact that she never inquired about who gave it to me let me know that my conversation with Gail was office chatter. They were either nervous or respected me too much to speak on my personal life. I preferred to think it was the latter.

I was looking forward to having my mother and Miss Lillian with us to celebrate Mona's accomplishments. I couldn't help but beam with pride as we shopped for our outfits.

And yet, I sensed her anxiety when she said, "I just pray everything goes well."

"It will. We're just going to claim it."

I took Thursday and Friday off to do the things I knew she wouldn't have time to do. I went grocery shopping and scheduled the housekeeper in preparation for my mother and Miss Lillian's arrival. This would be the first time they met. I felt as though I was still earning Miss Lillian's approval and I was grateful that my mother was arriving before Miss Lillian and Deacon. I felt like a kid as I waited for them outside the airport terminal. Mom started dancing as I waved from the car. I jumped out and kissed her.

"Your mother's here!" she announced.

"I know and I'm so happy. We have so much to do."

She hopped into the front seat. "I need to go to the grocery store. How many people am I cooking for?"

"About twenty. Is that okay?"

"That's fine, but we just need to go to the store early in the morning so I can prep everything. Where's Mona?"

"At the site, making sure her staff is ready."

"She needs to get some rest before Saturday."

"I know. Miss Lillian and Deacon will be here in the morning. She's the only one who can make her rest."

I put my mother to work soon after we got to the house. Her eyes widened when she walked through the door.

"This is wonderful. Is this iron?" She ran her hand along the banister for the spiral staircase.

"Yup. Mona had it shipped from Mexico when she was there. Another one's upstairs."

"How many floors?"

"Four. Come see the rest of the house and the room you'll be in. Miss Lillian will sleep in the room upstairs. You'll stay in the room down here. You have your own bathroom." We headed to the bedroom on the first floor.

"I'm going to be down here by myself? Y'all are all the way upstairs if someone tried to get me."

"Ain't nobody going to get you, Mom. Misty would have been your security, but she's at the doggy hotel. Don't worry, we have a security system. You know I wouldn't be in this big house without one."

I gave my mother a tour of the house and couldn't help but feel proud as she studied each piece of art.

"Did Mona paint all these?"

"No, only some. She hasn't had time to paint or sculpt because she's been so busy with the new building."

My mother and I talked and laughed as she cooked one of Mona's favorite dishes.

"I'm sorry I got you slinging pots already, Mom. Mona loves liver and I don't know how to make it, so she'll be happy you're here."

"That ain't nothing. It won't take me no time."

I didn't realize how much I'd missed my mother. She had dinner ready and the kitchen cleaned by the time Mona drove up. I rewarded her with a couple of glasses of wine as I set the table for dinner. I still got excited when

I heard the garage door shut followed by the sound of Mona's footsteps. I got up and opened the door.

"Hi, honey." She kissed me on the lips and smiled when she saw my mother sitting on the couch. "You're here!" She walked over and kissed my mother.

"Your dinner's ready. I made liver, rice, and onions."

Mona kicked off her heels. "Is that what's smelling so good?"

My mother had fixed Mona's plate by the time she changed into her sweats. We sat at the table while my mother sat at the counter.

"I gave you two pieces, but there's more when you're ready," my mother said.

Mona looked at me. "Babe, do you know how to make liver?"

"No, ma'am. Mommy will have to teach me how to make it. I must really love you because I can't imagine touching it."

She shook her head and rolled her eyes. "I haven't had liver and rice since the last time I was home." My mother beamed.

"Great, Mom," I said. "Now she's going to expect me to make it like you."

"Well, you better learn."

I made sure my mother was comfortable before setting the alarm and heading upstairs. I ran the bathwater as Mona lay across the bed in the guestroom. I sat on the bed and began to rub her feet.

"How's everything at the building?"

She exhaled. "So far so good. I spent the last two hours going over the guest list and seating chart with Yani and the staff. We'll do a walk-through tomorrow night when Char gets in. She's staying at the Drake, downtown. She will be here at the house for the reception with the band. She hasn't seen my grandmother in years so that'll be nice. How are you?"

"I'm fine. I'm just worried about you. You gotta rest before Saturday. Is there anything else you need me to do?"

"Not really. Thank you for handling the sponsorships and the ads for the magazine. I couldn't have done this without you."

"I can't wait to see it."

It was nice having my mother there when I went to make Mona's breakfast.

"Good morning, Mom. You sleep okay?"

"Yeah, but this house is too damned big. I kept hearing people walk by outside. Scared the shit out of me."

"You better stop watching all those killer shows."

"Ask Mona how she wants her eggs cooked and I'll make them," she replied, ignoring my advice.

I yelled upstairs to get Mona's order. My mother had a full breakfast ready by the time she walked into the kitchen.

"Well, you look nice," said Mom.

"Thank you, but I won't be able to fit any of my clothes by the time you leave."

My mother looked like a proud chef as Mona wolfed down her breakfast, looked at her watch, and gulped down her orange juice.

"What's your day like, honey?"

"Mommy and I have to go to the grocery store to get the food she's cooking for the band. You need me to do something?"

"No, I'll try to be home by noon. My grandmother and Deacon should be here by then. I'll call you to see where you are if I'm running late."

It soon felt like old times as my mother and I strolled down each aisle checking items off her list.

"I'll season the chicken early in the morning. You know I can't have nobody in the kitchen while I'm cooking. I don't want nobody stealing my secrets."

"I know, Mom." I was just happy to have her with me. I watched the clock as we finished shopping. I prayed Mona got home before Miss Lillian arrived. I was still nervous around her. I wondered if she thought I was like all the other women in Mona's life.

CHAPTER TWENTY

I was happy to see Mona's truck as I drove past the house and parked in the garage. My mother and I carried an armful of bags into the house. Mona was on the phone when we walked in. She moved the phone so I could kiss her on the lips. There was a knock at the door less than thirty minutes later.

"I think Miss Lillian is here," I whispered.

Mona ended her call and rushed downstairs. I heard Miss Lillian's southern drawl.

"How you?"

"Come on in here, lady."

"What are you doing home in the middle of the day?"

"I wanted to be here when y'all got here."

"I was doing seventy all the way here," Deacon chimed in. "Let me get Mama's bag."

I made my way downstairs. "Hi. Miss Lillian." I walked over and kissed her on the cheek.

"How you doing?"

My mother stood up and hugged her. "Hi, Lillian. I'm Johnnie."

"I can't wait to have some of your famous fried chicken I heard about," said Miss Lillian.

"I'm going to get up early in the morning so it'll be fresh."

"Can I get you some water, Miss Lillian?" I asked.

"Y'all got that fancy water or regular?"

"We have both, ma'am."

"I'll have the regular one."

"Are you hungry, ma'am?"

"Nah, we ate on the road."

Mona and Deacon came upstairs with Miss Lillian's bags.

"Hey Nikki, and you must be Johnnie." Deacon embraced my mother and sat at the counter. He turned to Mona. "What do you need me to do before I head over to my friend's house?"

"I need you to follow me over to the building and make sure the guys bring the chairs over and set them up downstairs," Mona said. "We're expecting about twenty band members and VIPs."

Miss Lillian interrupted them.

"When am I going to see this multimillion-dollar building you say you built?"

Mona grabbed her keys off the counter. "Since you don't believe I do any work, come on."

I was surprised when she leaned over and kissed me on the lips in front of our mothers.

It was almost seven o'clock in the evening when Mona and Miss Lillian walked in the back door. I was surprised to hear Char's voice. They walked in with several bags of takeout food. My mother was starstruck when Char leaned in to hug her.

"Hey, Momma Johnnie. We bought jerk chicken, but I heard it ain't as good as your fried chicken."

My mother laughed. "Probably not."

We ate and communed as Black women do in the kitchen. My mother and I cleaned up when Miss Lillian went to bed.

"Babe, I'm going to drop Char back off at her hotel," Mona said. "I won't be too late. I gotta be at the building by seven in the morning to set up for the band."

Char hugged me and my mother. "Okay, Momma Johnnie. I'll see you and your fried chicken tomorrow."

The morning of the grand opening was a whirlwind. I got up and ran our bath while Mona slept. She wasn't a morning person, so I quietly joined her in the tub.

"Babe, would you please lay out my clothes for me? I probably won't get back here until four. The doors open at seven."

"Sure, honey. Call me if you think of anything else."

My mother and Miss Lillian were already in the kitchen by the time we got downstairs.

Mom said, "I didn't know what you wanted, so I made the same as yesterday."

Mona kissed my mother and Miss Lillian. "Can we get you to stay?"

My mother chuckled. "It's too cold here for me."

"Miss Lillian, I bought Carnation milk for your coffee," I said.

"Well, thank you for remembering. I'll have some coffee with you."

I made our coffee as Mona finished her breakfast and rushed off to the new building. I was grateful my mother was there to help me entertain Miss Lillian. She helped my mother prepare for the band's reception. I took the time to lay out clothes for myself and Mona. I took her dress out of the garment bag. I'd forgotten how beautiful it was. She chose a sheer black, bell-shaped gown with a camisole slip. I hung it from the railing of the canopy bed. I pulled out three pairs of heels for her to choose from. My outfit was just as stunning, with a white, high-collared blouse and elaborate side tie. Black taffeta would hug my hips before fanning out into a train. I paired it with a pair of black satin ballerina slippers since they wouldn't be visible under my dress.

I took a nap before getting ready for my hair appointment. It was nice to have a moment to myself as I drove to the salon. I called and checked on Karlos as I waited for my hairstylist. I was disappointed when Christian didn't pick up. It was Saturday and they were probably at a game. I felt revitalized after getting my hair done. Miss Lillian was taking a nap and my mother was talking on the phone when I walked in.

"That girl really knows how to cut your hair."

"Thank you, Mom. I'm going to lay down for a minute."

I went upstairs, tied my hair up and lay across the bed in the guest room. At that moment, anxiety set in. The CAPA grand opening would be my first public event where I would meet Mona's staff. Who was I fooling? I wasn't looking forward to being in the same room as Melissa. I tried not to think about it as I drifted off to sleep.

Mona had been at the building for eight full hours. When she got back to the house, she looked tired as she kicked her shoes off.

"What time is it?" She wearily looked at her watch and lay down beside me.

"A little after four."

"Do you have time to take a quick nap?"

"If I take a nap I won't get up," Mona said. "Can you make some coffee?"

"Oh, yeah, you're tired. You never drink coffee."

"I know, but you make it look so good."

"What time do we need to be ready?"

"I need to leave at 5:30, but Deacon will pick you all up at 6:30."

Miss Lillian was sitting at the kitchen table talking to my mother when I got downstairs.

"Did you get some rest, Miss Lillian?"

"I sure did. I like what you all have done to Karlos's room. He has a lot of trophies."

My mother chimed in. "He's been playing soccer since he was four."

I made Mona's coffee and rushed upstairs. "Thank you, babe, and thank you for laying my clothes out."

"You're welcome."

She smiled sleepily. We got undressed and got into the tub.

"I hope Char can get the VIPs to make donations. She's going to ask a few times throughout the evening. We also have donation cards at each table."

"I'm sure you'll raise a lot of money tonight," I said. "Do you realize what you've accomplished?"

"I haven't had the time to think about it."

I touched her face. "You're doing amazing work by helping little Black girls and boys realize their dreams."

I began to apply my makeup in the bathroom while she got dressed in the guest room. I soon finished and walked into the guest room. The sheer black gown on her was perfection.

"You look like a fuckin' million dollars! I want to eat you!" I yelled as I jumped on the bed. Mona blushed and shook her head.

"You just love me."

"I do love you, but you're going to be the most beautiful woman in that building tonight," I told her before she left the room. As I began to get dressed, I could hear Miss Lillian tease her.

"Well, don't you clean up nice."

"Thank you, lady," Mona said. "I try to do a little bit."

"Oh, I love that," my mother added. "That looks real rich."

I leaned over the balcony as Mona left. "I'll be ready in twenty minutes, Mom. Are you ready?"

"Me and Lillian been ready."

I grabbed my purse and shoes then gathered the train as I swished down the steps. "Mom, could you please close the clasp on my skirt?"

"Now, that really shows off your shape."

"Thank you, Mom."

Miss Lillian had a slight smile on her face. "Y'all really know how to do it up."

Like clockwork, my phone rang and Deacon said he was outside. I grabbed my keys and followed Miss Lillian as my mother held my train.

"No, Miss Lillian, please, you sit in the front." I got into the back seat as my mother gathered my train and shut the door.

"Thank you for picking us up."

"You're welcome," he said. "You ladies look wonderful. Mama with her lace, Johnnie with that black tuxedo, and you with the train. I love it!"

The city allowed Mona to cordon off one of the streets to accommodate valet parking. There were strobe lights and a red carpet as we pulled up to the front door. The handsome valet attendant opened the door and Deacon jumped out to assist our mothers before helping me. He looped his arm through Miss Lillian's as we walked into the building. Rounded wooden walls opened to a large vestibule. Art and photographic images of black dancers and actors hung on the walls. I was in awe as we walked into the atrium. There were at least fifty tables draped in ecru table linens with black ribbons around the base. The stars shone through the retractable glass ceiling. The stage was front and center. I looped my arm through Miss Lillian's.

"What do you think, ma'am?"

She had tears in her eyes. "It's absolutely beautiful."

Just then, Mona made her way through the throng of guests filing in. Without saying a word, she embraced Miss Lillian.

"This is all for you."

Miss Lillian held Mona's face in her hands. "I knew you could do it." She beamed with pride as Mona gave us a tour of the building. The atrium was full of guests by the time we returned. I held my mother's hand as we followed Mona and Miss Lillian to our table in front of the stage.

My heart was full of joy, seeing the pride in both our mother's faces. Waiters came to take our drink orders just as the music began. The crowd applauded wildly as Char walked onto the stage in a feathered orange dress that swirled around her thighs with each step. The color paled in comparison to her blond pixie haircut. Her presence was grand.

"Y'all look fabulous! I'm glad I dressed for the occasion," she joked. "I'm Char Winters. Welcome to the grand opening of the Chicago Academy of Performing Arts, also known as CAPA!"

When the house lights went down and Char introduced Mona, I remember thinking *This is a moment to remember*. The audience gave her a standing ovation. She bowed and motioned for the audience to take their seats. Char raised her arms and the audience stood longer and applauded even more loudly. I watched as Mona tried to compose herself. Receiving recognition was difficult for her. Most people didn't know how shy and introverted she was. She was the opposite of her business persona. She wiped her tears and again motioned for the audience to be seated. She went on to thank the corporate sponsors and VIPs. She paused before stating that she wouldn't be the woman she was without the love and support of her grandmother. Miss Lillian blushed as Mona pointed to her.

The audience roared before she waved her staff onstage. One by one, she thanked each staff member by introducing them by their titles and the roles they played in building CAPA. But when she thanked Melissa, who linked hands with Mona before taking a bow, I felt nauseated. I never expected Mona to introduce me as her partner, but didn't I deserve recognition? She could have thanked me when she thanked the corporate sponsors. That would have been the perfect time. They would be able to put a face to my name. I was in a daze for the rest of the program. It was all I could do to hold myself together.

My mother sensed my sadness. "You look like the first lady."

"I don't feel like the first lady, Ma."

I excused myself and rushed out of the building as the program ended. I walked down the street and called my sister. I broke down as soon as I heard her voice.

"What's wrong?"

I could barely speak. "Mona didn't even…she thanked everyone but me."

She was silent.

"She thanked everyone but me…" I repeated.

"I'm sorry. You worked so hard to help her. I guess she's not comfortable acknowledging you."

"She could have thanked me as a volunteer. She thanked Melissa for being her right hand." I turned my back as guests walked by.

"Where are you? You can't let anyone see you crying."

"I walked outside, but we're having a reception at the house. Now I have to go and pretend in my own home." I gathered my skirt and dabbed my eyes with the hem.

"Try to calm down, because you have to go back in there."

"I know. I just needed some air."

"Are you in an area with light?"

"Yeah, I walked across the street. It's well lit."

"It's going to be okay. Call me in the morning."

I leaned against a light post and tried to compose myself. I took my compact out of my clutch and tapped my face before heading back into the building.

I managed a faint smile as I walked through the crowd and found my mother.

"You ready, Mom? I have to find Deacon and Miss Lillian."

"What's wrong?"

"Nothing, Mom." Mona appeared as we turned to leave.

"Where have you been, babe?"

"I needed some air."

She knew something was wrong but now wasn't the time to address it.

"Yani is going to drop you all at the house. Deacon left early in case the band got there before we did. He has my keys."

"Okay." She recognized the sadness in my eyes, and I saw the same in hers.

There were a few guests at the house by the time we arrived. I asked Yani to make sure our mothers were comfortable until I changed clothes. I would have to reach deep into my trick bag to pull that evening off. I rummaged through our closet and pulled out a pair of white-washed, bell bottom jeans. Silver studs ran along the slits from my ankles to my knees. I paired them with a red V-neck CAPA T-shirt. My ensemble was complete with a pair of silver strappy sandals. I retouched my makeup and dabbed perfume behind my ears and wrists before heading to the reception.

CHAPTER TWENTY-ONE

O ur den was packed by the time I got downstairs. I headed over to my mother and Miss Lillian. "Mom, Miss Lillian, are you okay?"

Miss Lillian raised her plate. "Yani made our plates. I haven't had fried chicken like this since my mother's."

"Let me know if you want more," I said, adding, "Okay, Mom. I'm going to thank some of the VIPs and sponsors." I made eye contact with Char as she walked toward me.

"The show was amazing!" I told her. "I'm sure you helped Mona raise a lot of money. The audience was starstruck. Oh, and that damned dress was crazy!"

Char wrapped her arm around my waist as her eyes traveled the length of my body. "Chile, not as crazy as these jeans. No wonder I ain't heard from Miss Mona."

"I got tricks," I said.

She sipped her cocktail. "So I've heard."

I was exhausted by the time the last guest left. Surprisingly, both our mothers were still alert as they chatted about the event. Mona finally joined us on the couch.

"You ladies better get some rest. We want to take you to see the house in Michigan in the morning."

We went upstairs and washed our faces. We were too tired to take a bath before getting into bed.

"What's wrong, babe?"

"I'm just tired. Congratulations, that was an amazing grand opening."
She moved closer.

"I know you. What's wrong?"

"Let's talk about it tomorrow."

The next morning, our mothers made breakfast. We continued to recap the
evening's events while on the road to the Michigan house.

"What made you buy a house all the way out here?" I heard something
in Miss Lillian's voice, but I couldn't put my finger on it. It was the same tone
I heard when Mona bought my car.

"Sometimes Mama, I just need to get away from Chicago," Mona
explained.

My mother chimed in. "It looks like a little dollhouse."

"I know, right, Mom?" I said. "We wanted something small since the
house in Chicago is so big. We have three acres. Misty loves running around
like a little pony."

They looked surprised when Mona opened the door and they walked
into a modern-day farmhouse. We had two leather couches that we purchased from an import furniture store in town. The walls were decorated
with some of Mona's art as well as a few up-and-coming Black artists. My
mother and Miss Lillian walked from the front to the back of the house.

The sun began to shine as we walked the property. Deacon's voice
startled us.

"I almost couldn't find this place. This is nice." He walked over and kissed
us on the cheek, one by one. Then I overheard his muffled words to Mona.

"This is nice, but don't you think it's a little too soon?"

Mona shot him a look that made him join our mothers as they walked
toward the house. The silence between us was awkward.

"So…my grandmother doesn't think you're happy for me."

"Why would she think that?" I asked.

"She said you didn't look happy at the grand opening."

"You thanked everyone but me."

"What did you want me to do? I couldn't thank you as my partner."

My voice became a whisper. "You didn't thank me – at all. Not as your partner, but for helping you like everyone else on your team. Do you know how that made me feel?"

Mona didn't respond as she walked back to the house ahead of me. After our brief visit, we secured the property and headed back to Chicago. Our mothers sat in discomfort as we rode back in relative silence.

The next morning couldn't come fast enough. Deacon and Miss Lillian prepared to get on the road while my mother sat her bags by the back door in preparation for her flight.

"It was nice having you here, Miss Lillian," I said. Her hug didn't feel the same.

"Yes, it was good seeing you and Johnnie. Call me if you need me." She turned to hug Mona. "I'm proud of you, girl. Don't make me come up here." Mona giggled like a little girl as Miss Lillian pinched her cheek. We waved goodbye as we watched their car turn onto Lakeshore Drive. I tried to lighten the somber mood.

"Do you have everything, Mom?"

"Yup. If I forgot anything, just mail it to me."

Sadness enveloped me as the three of us arrived at the airport. I didn't want Mom to go. I often felt alone in Chicago.

Mona grabbed my mother's bag out of the trunk and hugged her. "Thank you for coming."

"Any time." She turned to me and I hugged her tightly.

"I love you, Mom. Thank you for being here."

"Just call me whenever you need me to come. Love you."

The silence was unbearable as Mona and I drove home. I didn't have it in me to pull my hand away when she reached for it.

"I can't handle knowing that I hurt your feelings."

"I love you, and I'm in love with you, but I never expected to feel invisible," I replied. "I know you can't always acknowledge me as your partner. But is it because you work with kids? Or are you not comfortable with acknowledging me...period?"

She hesitated. "I don't know."

"But you have to know."

"I'm a private person and I don't feel the need to broadcast my personal life."

"I don't broadcast my personal life. I just don't hide it."

"This makes me so sad. What can I do to fix it?"

"I don't know."

For the next few days, we walked around each other on eggshells as uncertainty permeated our space. The fact that we were in love was all I had to hold onto. She surprised me early one morning when I opened my eyes, and she was staring at me.

"Good morning," I said. "How long have you been up?"

"I couldn't sleep."

"You thinking about work?"

"About us. I never want you to question if you matter. I promise to do a better job of showing you what you mean to me."

She turned over, grabbed two envelopes off her nightstand, and handed them to me. I pulled out a roundtrip ticket to Miami. She laughed as I screamed and threw my arms around her neck.

"I've always wanted to go to Miami."

"Miami is one of my favorite places. This is for helping me with the magazine and the corporate sponsors."

"Thank you. We've been so busy that I almost forgot our birthdays are coming up. I thought we were just going to hang out in Michigan."

"We need to get away and besides, with that tuition at Sadona, we won't be able to go anywhere for a while."

"Wait – Karlos can go to Sadona?"

"Yes, babe. He can go to Sadona. That's the best private middle school nearby until we choose a high school."

"That makes me so happy! I guess I'll keep you."

That weekend, I made up an excuse for why my hair appointment took two hours instead of one. I rushed from the salon to Neiman Marcus. The way I felt about shoes was the way Mona felt about watches. I circled the jewelry case until I found the perfect diamond watch. I used the personal account I had never closed before opening our joint account. The watch cost half my emergency fund, but she deserved it. I hid the watch in a sock before stuffing it in the bottom of our suitcase as we packed.

"I had Yani push my meetings back. I'm not going to do any work while we're in Miami. I can't wait to take you to my favorite spots. What do you want as a birthday present?"

"This trip is my present."

"No, you earned the trip for being a selling machine."

"Okay, then what's my limit?"

"One thousand, lady."

"And I can have anything or go anywhere I want in Miami?"

"Yes."

"Because you know I cannot go to Miami without going to the Queen of Hearts."

She shook her head. "And that's what you want for your birthday?"

"That's not all I want but let me think about it."

I could barely contain my excitement as we landed in Miami. "Are we taking a cab or a shuttle?"

She nodded toward a black town car. "This is us right here."

"Oh, you are showing out!"

I rolled down the window and people watched as our driver drove down Collins Avenue. I felt special when we walked into the dreamiest hotel I'd ever seen. Our room was a stark white oceanfront suite. "This is insane."

Mona opened the door and we stepped onto the seventeenth-floor balcony. She pulled me in front of her and wrapped her arms around me. "Happy birthday, babe."

"Thank you, honey. This is beautiful."

We changed our clothes and ordered room service while taking in the view. I felt special as we showered and got dressed for dinner. She was stunning in white linen pants with a matching shirt tied in the front. I felt sexy in a white miniskirt paired with a white V-neck T-shirt. My pewter four-inch sandals completed my outfit.

I'd never felt so much in love. Being with Mona made me realize why the relationships I'd had before her didn't work out. I had to go through them to get to her. We made love well into the early morning. We ate breakfast watching the waves roll in. I left Mona on the balcony to start the shower. I caught my breath when I returned to find a Gucci box sitting on the bed.

"Honey!"

"Yes, babe?"

"What is this?"

She walked in from the balcony and sat on the bed. "One of your birthday presents. It's what I wanted for you, but you still have to tell me what you want."

I crawled onto the bed and opened my arms. "But all this is my birthday present."

"You have one thousand dollars to do whatever you want."

"You're so good to me."

"I hope you like it."

I carefully unwrapped the bow. "It's so pretty. I want to take my time."

I opened the box and lifted the tissue paper. I picked up a four-inch, snakeskin heel.

"These are hot! I love them!"

"They looked like you."

I jumped off the bed and tried them on. "How do they look?"

"Sexy, like you."

I stopped and stood over our suitcase. "I love that you know me. You never have to ask what I want."

"I feel the same way."

"I wanted to spoil you, too," I said. "Close your eyes." I reached into the suitcase and took the box out of the sock. I opened her hands and placed the box in them.

"Open your eyes."

She opened her eyes and looked down. "What's this?"

"One of your birthday presents."

"But it's your birthday."

"I know, but our birthdays are only ten days apart. We might as well celebrate them together. Besides, I share you with so much of the world that I want these moments to be special. Open it."

She playfully peeked into the box. "Babe! This is the watch I wanted. How'd you know?"

"I saw you looking at it when we were shopping for our outfits for your opening."

"But I tried on other watches."

"I know, but you couldn't stop looking at this one."

"I love how you love me."

I leaned over and mushed her dimple. "You deserve me."

CHAPTER TWENTY-TWO

We spent the rest of the day on the balcony watching drunken tourists dance at the pool party. We slept our cocktails off before ordering room service.

"What are we doing tonight?"

"Queen of Hearts! Baby, baby!"

She shook her head. "Thank God I'm a secure woman. Why do you like strippers so much?

"It's the mind-fuck of it all. It's fascinating. Especially when they do all those tricks. They have to practice that shit. That's hot! So, yes, that's what I want to do tonight."

We showered and got dressed for a night in Miami. The Queen of Hearts was twenty minutes outside of South Beach. There was a long line when we pulled up to the roped-off entrance. The line was longer by the time we walked into the largest strip club I'd ever seen. Half-naked bottle girls sauntered in and out of VIP sections with sparkling topped bottles. I reached behind me and grabbed Mona's hand.

"Let's sit at the bar before it gets too crowded."

We grabbed two empty seats and turned our chairs toward the main stage. Just then, a pretty brown-skinned bartender placed menus in front of us. "I'm not just saying it because I work here but our food is off the chain," she said. "I'm Nessa. What can I get you?"

"We'll have a gin and tonic and a Corona. Maybe we'll order something later."

Mona whispered into my ear, "You're going to eat something from here?"

"Honey, this is one of the most popular strip clubs in the country. All the ballers come here. The food has to be good." I turned my chair back toward the stage. The club was packed. I sat back and sipped my beer as a stripper brushed up against us.

"Look at her ass," I said. "That's real!"

"How can you tell?"

"Look at how it jiggles."

I tipped a few dancers as we ordered another round. They had amazing bodies, but no one caught my attention. Mona looked bored until I convinced her to order some barbecue wings. The alcohol was setting in as we ordered a third round. I tipped a few strippers until I couldn't take it anymore. Nessa looked at me as she set a plate of wings in front of us.

"Everything all right?"

I leaned over the bar.

"Where are the sistahs?"

She looked at the main stage. "They're all sistahs."

"No, where are the chocolate sistahs? What's up with all these redbones?"

"Oh, you want a chocolate sistah? Hold on. I'll be right back."

She washed and dried her hands before leaving the bar.

"That's crazy. All these dancers and no chocolate sistahs? Shit...they're the baddest ones."

Mona nodded. "I know one thing..."

"What?"

"These damned wings are good."

We hadn't realized Nessa had returned to the bar. "I got something for you," she said. "Chocolate's set starts in fifteen minutes. I told her to look for the pretty ladies at the bar." She smirked like she had a secret.

We were almost finished with the wings when Nessa nodded at us. We turned around and saw a gorgeous dark-skinned stripper. I stopped eating and wiped my hands. Chocolate didn't utter a word as she slowly danced between us.

"That's what the fuck I'm talkin' about," I said. I reached in my bra and pulled out a wad of ones. She smiled and turned her back to us, her ass bouncing against my legs.

"Where have you been all night?" Her voice had an East Coast twang.

"Nessa said y'all walked in right after my first set." She leaned back and caressed her breasts.

I gently pulled her against me and whispered in her ear, "Give my baby some."

She peeled herself off me and slid over to Mona. "This my shit!" she said, bending over in front of Mona and bouncing each ass cheek to "The Motto" by Drake... *Tell Uncle Luke I'm out in Miami too. Clubbin' hard, fuckin' women, there ain't much to do.*

"Tip her, honey."

Mona raised both hands. "I got barbecue sauce on my hands."

"She don't care if you get barbecue sauce on her ass," I said.

Mona struggled to tip Chocolate as she rotated her thighs. A pretty stripper with thick thighs and hazel eyes began dancing against Chocolate. I took half the bills from Mona and we tipped them at the same time when they began to kiss. The hazel-eyed stripper grabbed Chocolate's ass briefly then walked away. Chocolate tossed her hair and leaned back onto Mona.

I couldn't help myself. "How much would something like that cost me?" I asked. She continued to dance against Mona.

"You a mess!"

"Is your girl down?"

Chocolate threw her head back and laughed. "Passion is down for whatever I want."

"How much would that cost?" She placed her hand on my thigh while the other remained on Mona's as she bounced her ass against us.

"A band, but I don't get off until two."

"Let me talk to my wife. I'll leave my number with Nessa." She ran her hand up Mona's thigh. Mona shook her head as Chocolate sauntered off.

"Damn! I just got these pants out the cleaners."

"You act like she got booty-juice on you."

"She may have. But...really babe? I know it's your birthday but..."

"You said...I could have whatever I want."

"I know, but a thousand dollars? What if they set us up or want us to join them?"

"I ain't sharing my wife with nobody. Come on, babe. Life's too short. Let's live."

"Why can't I ever say no to you?"

I kissed her as she reached in her purse and handed me her debit card and five hundred dollars. I went to the ATM and withdrew the balance. I walked back to the bar, grabbed a napkin, and wrote my number down before wrapping one hundred dollars inside. I folded it up and motioned to Nessa. I handed her a twenty-dollar bill before handing her the napkin.

"Tell Chocolate to call me when she's on her way."

Mona kept staring at me on the cab ride back to the hotel.

"I don't want no stranger in the bed we're sleeping in."

"I ain't crazy. I'll book another room for the night."

"What if she keeps the hundred dollars and not show up?"

"She's not going to leave nine hundred dollars on the table. I've dated a lot of strippers. They're trying to pay bills like everyone else." I called the concierge at the hotel and booked a room a few doors down from ours.

"I can't believe you got me doing this," Mona said.

"Oh, please, babe. You're just as excited as I am."

She changed into a pair of drawstring sweats and a tank top. I wore a burgundy silk short set. We walked a few doors down and was surprised to see that the concierge had included chocolate covered strawberries with my champagne. Chocolate called just as Mona popped the champagne.

"They're on their way," I reported.

"I'm going to sit over here," Mona said.

I opened the curtains as she lay back on the chaise that faced the bed. I scrolled through the playlist on my phone and selected Norah Jones's "I've Got To See You Again." I turned it down low enough so we could hear what they sounded like when it was getting good. The words struck a chord as I hit repeat. I crawled onto the chaise and kissed her deeply.

"Thank you for loving me unconditionally," I said. The knock at the door interrupted us. I was surprised to see Chocolate and Passion with minimal makeup. Their hair was pulled into ponytails.

"Hey …" Passion followed Chocolate into the room. I could tell she was impressed. "This shit is dope! I've always wanted to stay here."

I sat on the edge of the chaise as Passion checked the view. The two dancers were more beautiful in street clothes. Chocolate had on a V-neck T-shirt with stretch denim jeans and thigh high boots. Passion was more subdued in overalls and a crop top that barely contained her ample breasts. She dropped her backpack as they sat on the king-sized bed.

"What're your real names?" I asked. Chocolate leaned back on the bed, untied her ponytail, and shook it out.

"Ebony."

I leaned back on Mona's thigh and looked at Passion.

"Tatiana, but everyone calls me Tati."

"I'm Nikki. This is my wife Mona. It's my birthday and she said I could have whatever I want."

Ebony tossed her ponytail. "And what do you want? Y'all gonna dip in?"

I chuckled. "I don't share my wife. We just want to watch." I got up and dimmed the lights before joining Mona on the chaise.

"Help yourselves to whatever you like in the bar," I added.

We watched Tati pour their drinks. "I saw y'all when you walked in the club," she said. "I was like, damn, they fine. I don't know why I can't say no to Ebony."

"Because I love men, but I want you." Ebony took Tati's drink out of her hand and placed it on the nightstand. Tati's body relaxed as Ebony nuzzled her neck. Ebony lay beside Tati and began to undress her. I heard Mona's breath rate increase as Ebony sat on top of Tati and removed her tank top. She reached down and cupped her breasts. Her ass cheeks spread each time she moved against Tati. Ebony threw her head back as Tati gripped her ass.

"I've missed you." Tati's voice was deep with desire.

"Then show me …"

I began to flow as Ebony opened Tati's legs with hers. I could hear their wetness as their bodies moved together. Sweat dripped down the arch of Ebony's back. Her ass bounced as she thrust one last time before rearing back and climaxing. She thrust into Tati and collapsed on top of her.

"You got the best pussy in the world." Tati began to masturbate. Ebony pulled her hair back and reached into the backpack. We watched as she pulled a dildo out and strapped up. Her long nails glistened in the dark as she positioned the strap around her waist. She pulled out a condom and slipped it on with ease. Tati moved to the center of the bed as Ebony joined her. I wanted to scream when she knelt between Tati's legs before rubbing her face in her hair. Tati spread her legs wider. I leaned into Mona as she placed her hand between my legs. It was as if Ebony was torturing us as she stretched out and opened Tati's legs before eating her. Mona's hand felt warm inside my shorts. She moaned when she felt my wetness.

"You're so nasty."

"Me? You're the one who has your fingers inside of me." We watched as Ebony sat up and slapped Tati's ass. She pulled Tati onto her knees and slowly entered her. She stroked in and out before removing the dildo and entering Tati's ass. Tati's moans became louder as she reached between her legs and began to masturbate. Mona leaned into me.

"Is it in her ass?"

"Yes, she's masturbating with her other hand."

Ebony shoved the dildo into Tati one last time as Tati climaxed and fell onto the bed. Ebony turned Tati over and they kissed passionately. I was startled when Mona stood up and pulled me to my feet.

"Let's go," she said.

"Thank you, ladies," I said to the dancers. "The money is on the bar. The room is paid for. Enjoy yourselves."

Mona and I walked to our room in silence. We could barely get into the room before she pinned me against the door. I surrendered as she fucked me like a prostitute.

CHAPTER TWENTY-THREE

That salacious morning was cut short when Mona's phone rang at six a.m. I gently nudged her.

"Babe, your phone is ringing."

She jumped up and reached for it. "Hello...What? Have you been drinking?" She sat straight up in the bed.

I heard Melissa's voice through the phone. She was crying. "You never acknowledged me as your partner, the co-founder of CAPA," Melissa said. "I helped build this motherfucker! You want everyone to think you did it by yourself. Fuck you, Mona! Fuck you!" Melissa's voice became a muffled cry.

Mona tapped the mute button. "She said she's going to kill herself," she told me. She unmuted the phone and started to respond.

"What are you talking about? CAPA was my idea. Yes, you helped me with the startup, but the idea and the model was mine. You were my girlfriend and I hired you."

No wonder she was so pissed. Melissa felt like she was the cofounder and was never given credit. I became irritated as their conversation became more emotional.

"Hang up the phone," I said.

Mona placed her hand over the phone. "Babe, please..."

"Please, what? I'm sick of this shit."

She looked at the phone and realized Melissa had hung up.

"Please, don't make this worse."

I was incensed. "Oh, I'm making it worse? She wants a reaction and you're giving it to her."

I got out of bed and walked onto the balcony and watched the sunrise. I felt like the walls were closing in on me. Mona startled me when she stepped onto the balcony and sat in the chair beside me.

"I'm sorry, babe, but we have to leave on the first flight back home."

My voice cracked. "I made plans for your birthday today."

"My birthday isn't until next week. We can celebrate at home."

"It won't be the same."

She moved closer and wiped my tears. "I have to get her out of my life, personally and professionally."

"You've been saying that for almost a year."

"I think I have a way to get her out of my life, but I need to talk to Frank as soon as possible. I don't feel comfortable having such a personal conversation over the phone." Frank Morton was Mona's attorney. They were close friends and he knew about her relationship with Melissa. He'd been her attorney since she founded CAPA.

We were on edge as we packed and headed to the airport a couple of hours later. She looked dejected as she listened to me cancel her VIP golf package at the Stoneridge Resort.

"I'm sorry," she said.

"So am I."

The silence was unbearable on the flight back to Chicago. We barely put our bags down before she called Frank. I headed upstairs, wondering how I would manage this kind of hurt.

A week after she made that phone call to Frank, she joined me as I sat in the bay window of our bedroom.

"It's done."

"What's done?"

"Melissa. I'm done with her, personally and professionally."

I didn't respond.

"Frank handled it. I had to pay a lot of money, but…"

"How much?"

She exhaled.

"Fifty thousand dollars and a nondisclosure agreement."

"That's a lot of money."

"It's worth every dime. Thank you."

"For what?"

"For loving me while I figured this out."

I placed my hand on top of hers. "I will always love you. I just need you to meet me halfway. Don't ever leave me out there by myself."

We were finally a family of three when Karlos arrived later that month. I would never forget the look on his face as he ran through the house.

"Mom, this is one whole house?"

"Yup, this is our whole house. Come see your room." It warmed my heart when Mona stopped outside his bedroom door.

"Close your eyes." She opened the door and pulled his suitcase inside. "Now, open them."

He opened his eyes and squealed as he jumped on his queen-sized bed. "This is my room?"

Mona had decorated his room with a sports motif using all his soccer trophies. She meticulously took the time to hang his Team USA jerseys on the wall.

"Wow, Mom! You found all my trophies."

I sat at the foot of his bed. "Of course, I did. Thank Miss Mona, too. She decorated your room."

"Thank you, Miss Mona. This is so cool."

"You're welcome. We gotta add your new jerseys once we find a high school. Sadona doesn't have a soccer team. Let's go see the rest of the house." Misty trotted along, escorting him through each room of the house.

We spent that first night chatting about a new school and making new friends. I cleaned the kitchen while Mona helped Karlos unpack. I was worried about his bedroom being on the first floor and ours being on the fourth. I felt better when Misty marked her spot in his room as Mona and I kissed him goodnight.

"Okay, Breezy, Misty may come in and out of your room. She's just getting used to you being here."

Mona rubbed his head. "You can shut the door so she won't come in but, that's just her way of protecting you."

"It's okay. She can come in."

We began to spend more time at the house in Michigan on the weekends. It soon became apparent that Karlos had no desire to join us. He wasn't remotely interested in mowing the grass on three acres of land – The typical lazy pre-teen. Watching him sulk as Mona fussed ruined the sanctity of being away from the city.

We were ecstatic when he became friends with Alejandro, a neighbor's son. Ale's family was from the Dominican Republic. Like Karlos, he had also played youth soccer. I naturally gravitated toward his mother when we were both checking the mail in Chicago.

"Ale! *A it gon. Fok mal travay*." She clapped her hands.

"Hi. I'm Nikki, Karlos's mom. I love your language. What did you just say?"

She laughed sheepishly. "I just said, 'Come on boy. I have to go to work' in Creole. We're from the Dominican Republic. Most people from the Dominican Republic speak Spanish but there's a large population of Haitians. I'm Babette." From that day forward, Karlos chose to stay with Ale whenever we went to Michigan.

During the summer of 2005, we narrowed down Karlos's high school choices to two, Dematha and Holy Cross. I had my heart set on Dematha. It was closest to our house and most importantly, it was an all-boys school. I thought Karlos would be distracted at a coed school. I wanted to keep him as busy as possible to keep him out of trouble. I came up with another idea to keep him busy: I began researching modeling agencies. The Siobhan Daniels-Kent Talent Group (SDK) was the top children's agency in Chicago. I had an eye for a product that I could sell, and I could sell anything I believed in. Karlos had a face that could make money. I coyly brought up the idea to Mona one night.

"So, honey, I was thinking of ways Karlos could work his way through high school and even college."

"Like an after-school job?"

"Oh, he's definitely going to find an after-school job. I think kids should start working as soon as possible. It keeps them out of trouble and teaches them life skills," I said. "I mean something making more money."

"Like what?" Mona asked.

"I think I can get him signed to a modeling agency."

"He's definitely handsome enough. My only concern would be if he can handle the adulation that comes with that industry."

"I know, but it would be my job as his manager to ensure he remains humble."

"Well, if anyone can get him signed, it's you."

I searched the SDK website for submission guidelines that evening. They requested natural, nonprofessional photos. I selected a few photos of Karlos where his features were prominent. I said a prayer, pressed submit, and closed my laptop.

Karlos graduated from Sadona the summer of 2006. I couldn't contain my excitement when we went shopping for his graduation suit. We were going to make sure he stood out when he walked across the stage. The fact that Mona had dated men in her past gave Karlos a perspective that I, myself, did not have. She was much more familiar with the essentials of how a man should present himself. Karlos was equally excited as we walked the aisles of a men's fashion store. We hadn't been in the store more than ten minutes when I noticed the face of the salesperson light up.

"Aren't you the CAPA lady?"

Mona smiled graciously, but I recognized her discomfort. "Yes. I am. How are you?" She continued to sort through the suits as Karlos's energy shifted.

The salesperson persisted. "My niece graduated from CAPA and she just applied to Morris College Prep. My sister couldn't get her to leave CAPA whenever she picked her up from your after-school program."

Mona motioned to Karlos. "My son is graduating from middle school, and we need to find a suit, shirt, and tie."

The salesperson was more than pleased to assist us. We settled on a khaki, European-cut suit with a salmon-colored shirt. He beamed as Mona held a yellow and khaki paisley tie against the shirt. "This is perfect," she said. I sensed their relief when we left the store. Karlos leaned between our seats.

"Gosh, Mom. People don't even know your real name."

Mona chuckled. "Sometimes I prefer it that way."

I was aware of our collective anxiety as Karlos's graduation approached. Mona began to find herself in public settings where she felt obliged to introduce Karlos as her son. I'm sure most people in the community wondered where he came from. We would often have pillow talk regarding questions about her personal life. She heard rumors about people wanting to know if she dated men or women. I never asked how that made her feel, but I knew it had to be as difficult for her as it was for me.

Karlos began to sense a sadness that neither of us could explain. He knew I struggled with being out yet partnered with someone who was not. I recall his concern as I laid out his suit the morning of his graduation.

"Your mom picked out some socks to go with your shoes."

"Mom, do you ever get sad when people get excited over Mom and act like you're not even there? Like, she can say I'm her son, but she can't say you're her partner."

For Christ's sake! Why is he making me think about this right now?

I knew he and Mona noticed that I became quiet whenever we were out in public as a family. And yet I tried to put on a happy face.

"Why would you ask me that?"

He lowered his head. "You just seem sad."

I busied myself by smoothing his shirt out. "Well, I'm not sad today. I'm very happy. You're going to high school. Can you believe you're going to be a ninth grader?" I playfully punched him in the chest.

"I know. I wish Dad was here."

CHAPTER TWENTY-FOUR

The sun shone brightly as we drove to Sadona's graduation ceremony.

"You ready, dude?" Mona adjusted the rearview mirror.

"Yup. I can't wait to sleep late this summer," Karlos replied.

I was on cloud nine until people began to stop Mona to talk business. Neither Karlos nor I could hide our annoyance. This was his day and I'm sure he just wanted to be with both his mothers to celebrate. Nevertheless, I smiled.

"Breezy, there's Ale and Babette. We're going to sit with Babette. Hurry, go find your class."

Mona and I made eye contact as a councilmember chatted her up. She nodded as I motioned to our seats. I sat next to Babette and we chatted about where the boys would attend high school. We agreed the boys should go to the same high school.

"Sorry, honey. You know she couldn't wait to tell me that her husband was Karlos's math teacher."

I mustered a faint response as the councilmember watched us. "I'm sure."

I was determined to put on a happy face for Karlos. Each student chose a song to walk to as their names were announced. We applauded his classmates and turned toward the door when Karlos's name was announced. The audience went crazy when he walked out to Yung Joc's "It's Goin' Down"...*This a Nitti beat, here we go again, Bad Boy, South Ghettoville, USA*. He simulated driving a motorcycle with his arms and danced toward the stage.

He smiled when he made eye contact with me and Mona. I thought, *Yeah… that's a moneymaking face.*

Karlos was over the moon at the idea of staying home and playing video games all summer. Mona alleviated the stress of her CAPA responsibilities by converting our basement into an art studio. She spent hours painting late into the evening. I would dutifully bring her food, wine, and water whenever she forgot to eat.

"You've been down here for hours. I made you something to eat."

She leaned back on her stool and tilted her head. "What do you think?"

I walked behind her and looked at the painting.

"I forget you're an artist."

She laughed. "I forget, too. What do you see?"

I looked at an old painting that she had painted over.

"Her facial expression is different. In the original painting, there was a sense of loss, unrequited love. Maybe she was in love with someone who wasn't in love with her. In this painting, she looks like love has been returned because she's holding the flowers upright versus upside down."

She looked at me. "I painted this piece when I was seeing Doug and Melissa. This reflects where I am now." She pulled me onto her lap.

"Sometimes, I get sad because I don't know what my passion is," I said.

"Oh, babe. Don't be sad. You're an amazing salesperson. That's a skill many people don't have."

"I know, but it's not my passion and I don't know what is. What did God give me that touches people's lives?"

She kissed me on my cheek. "You'll find it, in time."

Her words echoed in my head as I thought about preparing Karlos's submission to the SDK Talent Group. Maybe becoming his manager would become my passion. Still, something was missing.

My schedule at Hollister became hectic when our department went through a reorganization. Savanna and I were taken aback when we were summoned into Grace's office.

"As you ladies know, we are going through a reorganization. Both you ladies have been instrumental in achieving our departmental goals, but let me cut to the chase. Patrick will be promoted to director of sales. Nikki, you'll be promoted to sales manager and Savanna, you'll continue to serve as an account executive. We'll announce the changes at our next meeting."

Savanna playfully nudged me as we walked back to our cubicles.

"Congratulations, mama!"

"Thanks, but are you okay with the changes?"

"Girl, that makes sense. You just got your MBA in marketing. That, coupled with your sales background, is a no-brainer. I'm going to miss you, but do the damned thing!"

I was thankful that she was happy for me. As the only two Black account executives on Grace's team, we made a pact to always support one another.

I couldn't wait to share the news with Mona and Karlos. The timing was perfect, as my promotion would be effective before Karlos started high school. St. Augustine was ten thousand dollars per year. That was a huge sacrifice for our family, but I knew it would pay off in the long run.

I was surprised to see the truck in the garage that evening. Misty met me at the door. Mona was sitting in the den when I opened the back door.

"What are you doing home?"

"I know we planned to go back to Miami for the Fourth of July, but I need to go home."

I sat down beside her. "Is everything okay?"

"Deacon called me. Mama fell. She's okay but she's forgetting things more often. I asked him if I needed to come home and go with her to her doctor's appointment, but he said it was just a follow-up."

"You should go, honey."

"Can you take off?"

"It shouldn't be a problem since I've been hitting all my numbers. By the way, you are looking at the new sales manager for the Midwest territory."

"Look at you! I told you that you'd find your passion."

"I don't know if sales is my passion, but it's what I'm good at. I'll put in a request for the time off. I just need to make sure my team secures their ad placements before I leave. Where's Karlos?"

"He's in the basement playing games with Ale. Babette asked if he could stay for dinner while she worked overtime."

"Okay. Let me change and I'll start dinner."

Karlos and Ale sounded like a herd of horses as they ran up the steps.

"Hey, Mom. It smells good. What are you cooking?" He and Ale sat at the counter.

"Spaghetti. Guess what? I got a promotion at work today."

"Are you the boss, like Mom?"

"I wish, but I'll be making more money. Speaking of more money, would you be interested in modeling or acting? I think I can get you signed with a talent agency." They looked confused as they munched on potato chips.

"What's a talent agency, Miss Nikki?" Ale asked.

"It's a company that gets you modeling and acting jobs with ads in magazines or television commercials."

"Do you have to pay them money to find me a job?" Karlos asked.

"No, a company will pay you to advertise their products. Like, if the company paid you to convince people to use their toothpaste. The talent agency takes 20 percent of whatever you make."

Ale's eyes widened. "Like, Breezy would make a thousand dollars?"

"It depends. As his manager, he would have to pay me 15 percent."

"Mom! You would charge me?"

I laughed. "You think I'm going to be working for free? I do have a full-time job. It's going to take time and money to run you around to auditions. You have to really think about it because your attitude and confidence is more important than your face. You're too short to be a runway model but you can do print."

"I think I want to try. Modeling will help me get a lot of girls, girls that look like Kiya Spalding."

"And that, sir, is why you're going to an all-boys high school! Who's Kiya Spalding?"

They snickered as they ran back downstairs. I made a mental note to find out who Kiya was.

I was overwhelmed as I prepared to take Karlos to 's back-to-school night. There were at least two hundred students and family members in the auditorium. Something in me was triggered as I watched priests greet the male students. I scanned the auditorium and was dismayed at the lack of female and Black teachers. That feeling was amplified when Father O'Toole approached me and Karlos. Father O'Toole was an older white man with a salt-and-pepper jarhead haircut.

"Welcome to St. Augustine, young man." He extended his hand to Karlos and then me.

"Welcome, Mrs. Calabrese," Father O'Toole called me by Karlos's last name.

"Hello, Father. I'm Ms. Blue."

He gave Karlos a brief orientation on his class schedule. I flashed back to the way my uncle used to glare at me. I shook my head to escape the feelings I often suppressed.

I was elated when I received a response from the SDK Talent Group two weeks later. Karlos and I were anxious as we headed to our interview. Mona wished us luck and kissed us goodbye before we headed up north.

"Your haircut is crazy, Breezy. You ready?"

"My stomach hurts."

"It's natural to be nervous, but I have a feeling they're going to want to sign you. And if not, at least we tried."

We pulled up to a high-rise on Halsted Avenue. The lobby was designed with steel columns and twenty-foot ceilings. A young assistant graciously welcomed us. She made a call and asked us to be seated. Fifteen minutes later, a tall well-dressed white guy walked through the glass doors.

"Good morning, I'm Jonathan. Thank you for accepting our interview." We shook hands before he turned to my son. "Karlos, welcome to the SDK Talent Group."

We followed Jonathan to a large cubicle with a view of Halsted. He motioned for us to be seated. "Can I offer your something to drink?"

"No, thank you." Karlos's voice was firm.

"Again, I'm Jonathan Harlow. I'm one of the agents for our youth division. That includes print and film." He opened a binder on his desk and laid out Karlos's photos.

"After reviewing Karlos's photos, we'd like to invite Karlos to join the SDK Talent Group. Based on his images, we believe Karlos could secure bookings in print and film."

I turned and winked at Karlos, who immediately asked, "What does that mean?"

Jonathan laughed. "That means we want you to represent the SDK Group as one of our talents. I'm going to give your mom some information as well as a contract to review. She'll decide if you guys are interested in representing SDK. We want you on our team, Karlos."

I contained my excitement until we got into the car. I turned to face Karlos while "The Next Episode" by Dr. Dre and Snoop Dog blared through the speakers...*La-da-da-da-da...*

"You're going to be a model!"

He recited the lyrics as he pretended to Crip Walk.

"Oh, my God! You gotta call your mom." I dialed Mona's number and placed it on speaker before handing him the phone.

"It's me, Mom."

"Hey, dude. How'd your interview go?"

"They gave Mom some information to think about if I want to model."

"Whoa...they want to sign you?"

"I think so."

I chimed in from the front seat. "Yup, they want to sign him."

CHAPTER TWENTY-FIVE

We spent the last week of summer preparing for Karlos's first day of high school. We decided I would drop him off at school. Although we lived near a metro station, we didn't think it was safe for him to take public transportation to school.

Mona and I continued to get dressed for work. Still, I was the parent who always made a big production for every occurrence. "Come up here and show us your uniform," I called down the stairs.

"Mom, it's just a uniform."

"Boy! You better get up here! This is your first day of high school."

His steps shook the spiral staircase as he bounced upstairs. I couldn't believe this moment had come. He was becoming a young man right before my eyes. He looked handsome in his brown oxford shirt tucked into his khakis.

"Who is this, honey? Turn around, shawty."

He blushed as Mona straightened his collar. "Mom's so funny."

"You know your mom. We're so proud of you. You had to have good grades to attend and you did it."

"And you better continue to get good grades," I added, "as much as we're paying for tuition. No good grades, no soccer."

"I know, Mom."

I tried not to cry as we gave him a laundry list of things to remember.

I became emotional once more as we pulled up to a long line of cars dropping students off. The young men of St. Augustine looked studious as they lugged their bookbags over their shoulders. I watched as a priest ushered the boys into the entrance. My voice cracked as I talked myself out of crying.

"Okay, Breezy ..."

"What's wrong, Mom?"

"I'm just so proud of you. Give me a kiss." He leaned between the seats and obliged me.

"Love you."

I drove off, pulled the car into the main parking lot, and fell apart. I cried like I did the first day I dropped him off at daycare. I had prayed and sacrificed so much for this day. He was becoming everything I asked God for. He was everything society said I couldn't have.

Five o'clock couldn't come soon enough. I opened the sunroof of my Vanden Plas and glided down Lake Shore Drive to the school. I anxiously looked for Karlos as I pulled into the drive aisle. I tried not to wave when he saw me.

"Hi, Mom."

"Hey, Breezy. How was your first day?"

"Oh my God, Mom! I'm really in high school. My bookbag is so heavy."

"It looks heavy. Do you have a lot of homework?"

"Yup, and I have a lot of notes I have to review. Me and Ale met the soccer coach. I have to show you and Mom the permission slip."

"They're recruiting on the first day?"

"Yeah, Mom. Tryouts are in a week."

He repeated the same story as Mona listened over dinner. Everything was falling into place...or so I thought.

Karlos began to manage his new responsibilities of being in high school with little help from us. He settled into a daily routine of completing his homework before anything else. We checked in on how he was feeling.

"How are you, Breezy?" asked Mona. "I know you have soccer tryouts next week. You think you can handle your schoolwork and soccer?" I heard the concern in her voice.

He gave Mona his undivided attention. "Oh boy, Mom. I know I can because I did it before, but I have a lot more homework now."

I remained silent. I wanted him to know she cared about him and his feelings just as much as I did. He kissed us and went to his room to finish his homework.

"So, honey," Mona said to me, "I know how much you want him to play soccer, but what about the modeling stuff? Don't we have to make a decision by the end of this week?"

"Yeah, we need to talk about that. I know he can handle his schoolwork and soccer, but do you have any concerns about him modeling?"

She raised her eyebrow. "That's a lot. Do you think you're putting too much on his plate as well as yours?"

"No. It's not like he'll have auditions every day. Plus, I think school, soccer, and modeling will keep him busy. He won't have time to get into too much trouble. If we see that he's struggling, then modeling will have to go. Can we look at the contract tonight and make a decision?"

"That's fine," she said.

I was pleasantly surprised when we reviewed the SDK contract that night in bed. I focused on the language regarding parent and talent responsibilities while Mona focused on the financial aspects.

"What do you think?"

"I think it could be a great opportunity for him. Can you commit to what it's going to take? Because your work schedule is definitely going to be impacted."

"As long as I hit my numbers at work, Grace is pretty flexible."

"We have to keep him grounded. I have a lot of friends in the entertainment industry who struggle with balancing their personal and professional lives. Karlos is a handsome kid and I don't want that to consume him."

"I think we've done a good job so far." I waited for her response.

"You should sign the contract. It looks fine to me."

I signed the contract when I got to work that morning and emailed it to Jonathan.

Karlos's first week of high school flew by. I couldn't help but smile when I walked into his room to grab a jacket out of his extra closet and saw that he had tacked his school calendar up on his wall. His homework and soccer tryout dates were circled with a red marker.

Our lives seemed to be safely on autopilot as I prepared for my first presentation to a major client as sales manager. Although I had four account executives under me, I was assigned specific accounts. I spent the whole day preparing for my presentation.

Just as I shut my computer down, an email popped up on my phone from Jonathan. I read his confirmation of our signed contract, welcoming Karlos to the SDK Group. I quickly typed a response confirming Karlos's photoshoot with their photographer, Gianni.

Over dinner that night, Mona and Karlos listened intently as I told them about Jonathan's message.

"Gianni? He probably has a dramatic Italian accent. I can hear him now, Mom. *Si*, Karlos!" We all laughed.

"I know, right?" I laughed, adding. "We gotta get your haircut. Oh, and don't you need new cleats for tryouts?"

"I know. I tried on my old cleats and my toes are crunched up."

"Boy, don't wait until the last minute to tell us you need something. I can't remember everything."

"Gosh, Mom. I really feel like a high schooler."

"You ain't seen nothing yet."

That second week of high school was a whirlwind. I took Karlos to get a haircut before purchasing new cleats for tryouts. Selecting a time slot for Karlos's photoshoot with Gianni that Thursday threw a monkey wrench into my schedule. My presentation was scheduled for that Friday, but I had to put the finishing touches on my presentation and submit it to Grace. I confirmed Karlos's photoshoot time and looked at my schedule for the rest of the week. Everything depended on Grace approving my presentation. I would have to make revisions before leaving early on Thursday. Thank God, I worked well under pressure.

I pumped Karlos up as we drove to school that morning.

"You better go out there and show your ass today!"

He laughed. "I know, right Mom?"

"Are you nervous?"

"A little. This is high school soccer and it's more competitive."

"You got this!" I assured him.

I stopped to get coffee on the way into the office. I was relieved to find a sticky note on my desk from Grace. She had written minor edits on my presentation. Other than that, she wrote that it was a go. I felt like a boulder had been lifted off my shoulder. I transferred all calls to my voicemail and made the final edits to my presentation. I took my time driving to St. Augustine. Karlos's tryouts weren't over until six o'clock. I parked and closed my eyes for a short nap. I was awakened by deep voices as players walked to their parents' cars. I couldn't read Karlos's face as he got in.

"Hi, Mom."

"How were tryouts?"

He lowered his head.

"Did you make the team?" I persisted.

"There are only eleven starting positions. I didn't make the varsity team."

"What does that mean?"

He startled me when he squealed. "It means your son got one of the starting positions on the junior varsity team. I made it, Mom!" He started laughing.

"You scared me. I'm so proud of you."

"And guess what?"

"What?"

"Ale made the team too."

"That's so cool. Guess what's even cooler?"

"What?"

"You have your first photoshoot with Gianni on Thursday. I chose the latest slot so you wouldn't need an early release."

"Whew. I thought you were going to say Friday. That's our first soccer practice."

"Nope, but sometimes you'll have to miss practice if you have an audition. But don't worry. We'll work it out."

I exhaled that night as I gave my presentation one final review before submitting it to Grace. I reviewed the list of clothing Gianni requested for Karlos's shoot. I skipped my lunch break in order to leave the office early. I raced toward St. Augustine, ran in and signed Karlos out. He quickly changed clothes in the back seat. We had forty-five minutes to get uptown.

Gianni's studio was in a residential building. I rang the bell and waited to be buzzed in. We walked to an apartment on the first floor. A handsome young man stood in the doorway.

"You must be Karlos and Nikki. I'm Jeremy, Gianni's assistant. Gianni will be here shortly." I was awestruck as we walked into a studio with large lamps and cameras.

"Karlos can change into the first outfit Gianni requested," said Jeremy. "Let me know when you're ready."

I sat on a couch outside the room while Karlos changed. I heard what I assumed was Gianni's voice. He had a thick Italian accent as he directed Jeremy in adjusting the lights. I let Jeremy know that Karlos was ready. He instructed Karlos to sit on a stool before pulling out a makeup palette. Karlos flinched as he moved closer.

"I'm just going to even out your skin tone."

I tried not to laugh as Karlos side-eyed me. Gianni stepped from behind a large screen as Jeremy applied pomade to Karlos's hair.

"Karlos Calabrese! My fellow Italian. Ah...I see why Siobhan signed you. Mom, we're going to get started."

For the next ninety minutes, I watched as Gianni directed Karlos.

"Chin up! Eyes to the right. Shoulders back." The rapid click of Gianni's camera made it real. Karlos began to tire just as Gianni finished his last roll of film. He placed his hand on Karlos's shoulder.

"Wonderful, young man. Mom, would you like to see some of the shots?" I got up and motioned for Karlos to follow me.

"Siobhan will select the final headshots she will use for his auditions and go-sees. I think we've got some strong shots." He knelt and showed us several images.

"Jonathan will be contacting you once Siobhan selects the final images. He has something special."

CHAPTER TWENTY-SIX

I stayed up late that night practicing in the mirror for my presentation. I tried on my suit to get the full effect. The next morning, I felt confident as I applied my makeup. I was surprised when Mona walked into the room and plopped on the bed.

"What are you doing up this early?" I asked.

"I couldn't sleep. I didn't tell you last night because you were getting ready for your presentation." She closed her eyes.

"What's wrong?" I sat on the bed.

"I have to go home. Mama's test results came back. She has stage four cancer of the brain." She laid her head on my lap.

"Oh, honey. I'm so sorry. I'll reschedule my presentation so we can go with you."

"I don't want you to do that just yet. I'll fly out today and call you when I think y'all need to come."

"I'll purchase open tickets and if you don't need us to come, we'll save it for when you do," I said.

I held her in my arms as she sobbed.

"I don't know what I'm going to do without her."

I tried to be present as Karlos chatted on the way to school. I decided not to tell him about Miss Lillian until Mona gave me an update. I was relieved that no one was in the office when I arrived. I sat at my desk and reviewed my presentation one last time. I sat back in my chair and prayed for God to give Mona the strength she was going to need.

Grace and I soon jumped in a cab and headed to our meeting. I tried to focus as she gave me last-minute pointers. We were whisked into a conference room full of white male executives. I introduced myself and began my presentation. I couldn't read their faces. but I read the most important one in the room: Grace. She looked at me and offered a slight nod. She didn't speak to me until we stepped onto the elevator.

"You knocked it out the park. Now, we wait for their decision. I hope I'm not overstepping boundaries, but Lewis mentioned that Mona's grandmother isn't well. I want you to know I'm praying for your family."

I thanked her for her kindness and stopped to get a cup of coffee as she returned to the office. I looked at my watch and called Mona.

"Hi, honey. Are you there yet?"

"I just landed. Deacon is picking me up. I don't know if I can do this."

I reassured her as best I could before we hung up. I didn't mention my presentation.

I left the office early to spend some quality time with Karlos. I called my mother as I waited for his soccer practice to end.

"Hey, Mom." She heard the sadness in my voice.

"What's wrong?"

"Mona left for Alabama this morning. Miss Lillian is in the hospital."

"What happened?" she asked.

"She has stage four brain cancer. I think she's been sick for a while but didn't want Mona and Deacon to worry. It doesn't look good, Mom."

"I'll put her name on the prayer list. When are you going to be with Mona?"

"She said she'll call me when I need to come. I have to purchase open tickets for me and Karlos."

"Poor Lillian. Call me and let me know how she's doing."

I reapplied my makeup when I saw Karlos walking off the field.

"Hi, Mom."

"Hey, honey. How was practice?" My voice cracked.

"What's wrong, Mom?"

"Your mom had to fly to Alabama this morning. Your Mema is in the hospital."

"Why? What's wrong with Mema?"

"She has brain cancer."

He began to cry. "Is she going to be okay?"

I couldn't bring myself to tell him the truth.

"I don't know. Your mom will let me know when we need to fly down."

"Why didn't you tell me?"

"Your mom just told me. She didn't know how sick she was."

"Do Jordan and Jacob know?" He was thoughtful enough to remember Deacon's sons.

"I don't know, but don't tell then until your mom calls me. Come, sit up front with me." He got out of the back seat and fell into my arms.

"I don't want Mema to die. Mom is going to be so sad."

I rubbed his head. "I know, honey. We'll have to be strong for her, but it's okay to be sad." We sat in the parking lot until he stopped crying.

At home, I could barely get him to eat after he got out of the shower. When he climbed into bed, I pulled the covers over him and kissed him on the forehead. Misty must have sensed his sadness because she stayed at the foot of his bed that night.

I set the alarm and lay across our bed. Mona called late that evening to tell me that Miss Lillian chose not to have the recommended chemotherapy. I fell back asleep knowing that it was just a matter of time. I tried to put on a brave face for Karlos, but I was losing the battle. It was all I could do to function at work. I watched the clock constantly as I waited for Mona to call. It was obvious that I wasn't doing a good job of holding myself together.

It was rare for Grace to stop by my cubicle. "Congratulations, Nikki. We landed the account." I turned my chair around and pumped my fist in the air.

"Well done," she said. "You should take a few days off. You've earned it."

"Thank you, Grace, but I'll need to take some time off whenever it's time for me to go to Alabama."

"Please, let me know if I can do anything."

"Thank you, I will."

I trudged through the day as the clock ticked. Karlos called to ask if he could spend the night over at Ale's.

"It's a school night, Breezy."

"I know, Mom, but Miss Babette said she'll wash my uniform."

"Okay. Just make sure you finish all your homework."

In all honesty, I was happy to have the house to myself. It was the first time I could openly grieve. My mother-in-law was dying and there was nothing I could do about it. I fed Misty and went to bed. I thought I was dreaming when I heard myself whimpering in my sleep. I slept on Mona's side of the bed that night. Smelling her scent on her pillow made me feel closer to her.

The next day, I distracted myself in our staff meeting while Grace announced that I closed a new account. I managed a faint smile as the team applauded. That moment of joy was interrupted when my phone vibrated. I excused myself and stepped into the hallway.

It was Mona. "Hi, honey," I greeted her.

"You need to come."

"We'll be on the first flight in the morning."

I rushed to my cubicle, gathered my belongings, and walked to Grace's office.

"Grace, I need to go."

She removed her glasses. "Take as long as you need. Just keep me posted."

I cried all the way home. Misty followed me to Karlos's room as I began to pack his things. I sobbed as I pulled a black suit and shoes out of his closet. I wiped my face when I heard Karlos deactivate the alarm.

"Hey Misty, girl." He walked into his room and jumped when he saw me with his suitcase. He dropped his bookbag and collapsed into my arms.

"Mom, no..."

"She's still with us, but we need to leave for Alabama first thing in the morning."

"Is she in pain?"

"The doctors are giving her a lot of medication, so she won't be in pain, but we don't want her to suffer. She told your mom that she wants to be in her own home. They'll bring her home from the hospital and make her comfortable."

The next morning, we rode in silence as we dropped Misty off at the doggy hotel and circled back to park the car. This was the first time that

Karlos would experience the loss of an immediate loved one. I wanted to wrap him in my arms and absorb his pain. He must have felt my longing to hold him because he lifted the arm rest between our seats on the airplane and laid his head on my lap. Neither Mona nor Deacon wanted to leave Miss Lillian's side, so we took a cab to the house. Deacon was smoking in the driveway when we arrived. He reached for Karlos and hugged him.

"Hey, man."

"Where's Mom?"

"She's with Mama."

"How's she doing?" I asked.

Deacon wiped a tear from his eye. "Not good."

"Are the boys here?"

"Yeah, they're in the house." My legs felt weak as we followed him inside. Walking to Miss Lillian's room was one of the hardest things I'd ever done. Mona looked up when I walked into the room. I caught my breath as Karlos draped his body across Miss Lillian's feet.

"Mema…" I walked around her bed and embraced Mona.

"Can she hear us?"

"Yes, but she goes in and out."

"Breezy, why don't you go find your cousins." He peeled himself away from Miss Lillian and looked at Mona.

"Can I kiss her, Mom?"

"Of course, babe. She can hear and feel you."

He bent over and gently kissed Miss Lillian on her cheek.

"I love you, Mema."

"Did you see that, Breezy?" Mona said. "Her breathing increased when you said, 'I love you.'"

I leaned over Miss Lillian and held her hand in mine before kissing it. "Miss Lillian, it's Nikki. I love you, too." I pulled a chair closer to her bed. Suddenly, she started sniffing.

"What's wrong, honey?" I asked.

Mona gently caressed Miss Lillian's arm. "I think it's your perfume."

"I'm sorry. Let me go and wash it off." I rushed to the bathroom and washed my perfume off. I went back into the room and stood at the foot of her bed. I felt connected to Mona in a way that would bind us together forever. I watched as the woman I loved watched the most important woman in her life make her transition. My presence felt invasive as I witnessed something so profoundly intimate. I wanted to be respectful of their final moments together.

"I'm going to lay down, honey."

She simply nodded. I tossed and turned all night as I listened to Mona's sobs.

I showered and got dressed before sunrise. I walked into the living room and saw that the boys were asleep on the couch. Deacon motioned to me from the kitchen.

"The boys are going to be hungry. Come ride with me to get some breakfast for everybody."

I grabbed my purse and joined him in the car. "How have you been holding up?" I asked.

He shrugged his shoulders. "It hasn't set in yet."

"I'm so sorry."

He wiped his eyes as we pulled up to Sonic. I handed him my credit card when the cashier gave him the total. His phone rang as we were pulling out of the drive-through. He paused before leaning back in his seat. His voice trembled.

"Mama's gone."

He floored the accelerator as he sped through the back roads and came to a screeching halt before running into the house.

I heard their sobs as soon I walked into the house. Jordan, Jacob, and Karlos were stretched over Miss Lillian's body. Mona was holding her hand. I went into the bathroom and ran cold water over a washcloth and handed it to Deacon.

Mona was inconsolable as she caressed Miss Lillian's face. "I need to call hospice."

Deacon covered his face with the washcloth and walked out of the room. I pulled a chair to the side of the bed and held Miss Lillian's hand. Jacob stood up and ran out of the room sobbing. I reached over and pulled Jordan and Karlos closer to me.

Deacon returned to the room and whispered in my ear, "The coroner will be here soon. Take the boys out back so they won't see them take Mama out."

I touched Karlos's arm. "Get your cousins. Let's go out back and get some air."

He reached over and pulled Jordan away from Miss Lillian. I joined the boys on the back porch as they sat around the pool. "Your Mema is no longer suffering" I explained.

When I went back in the house to check on Mona, I saw that Deacon was trying to pull her away from Miss Lillian.

"Come on, Mona," he begged.

I couldn't bear to watch him separate them. I quietly left the room. It seemed like an eternity before the coroner arrived. I went into Mona's childhood room and sat on the bed. I will never forget the sound of her weeping. It was the most heart-wrenching sound I'd ever heard.

CHAPTER TWENTY-SEVEN

The house was quiet when I slid the bedroom door open. Miss Lillian's bedroom door was closed and I assumed Mona was asleep in her bed. Deacon was in the guest room making calls to family. I walked into the living room and all three of the boys had resumed their positions on the couch. I went back into the room and closed the door. I reached in Mona's purse and found her cellphone. I punched in her code and began the somber act of calling her closest friends. I swallowed hard before calling Char.

"Hey, Char. It's Nikki. I'm sorry to call you so early but I wanted to let you know that Miss Lillian passed. I know Mona would want you to know."

There was a moment of silence.

"Thank you for calling me. I'm so sorry to hear that. When I heard your voice and not Mona's, I knew she'd passed. You're a special woman to call me. How is she?"

"Not good."

"Oh, sweetie. I'm so sorry. I'm in L.A. on set, but please give her my love. I'll reach out to her some time tomorrow. Thank you for letting me know."

I forwarded an email to Grace informing her of Miss Lillian's passing. I requested bereavement days off until the following week. Mona walked into the room and I stood up and held her in my arms. Her voice was a whisper.

"How do I live without her?"

"She'll always be with you. She gave you everything you need to move through this world without her."

She pulled away and lay on the bed. I lay down beside her, pulled the covers over us and watched her sleep. The next couple of days were a blur as Deacon and Mona planned Miss Lillian's funeral. The morning of Miss Lillian's service, I couldn't get her out of bed. I'd gotten up early to shower and lay her clothes out. Deacon made sure the boys were dressed. But Mona was curled up in a fetal position.

I realized that her brother was the only one who could get her out of bed. The boys were eating when I walked into the living room and motioned to Deacon.

"I can't get Mona out of bed," I whispered.

He gently brushed by me and slowly walked toward Miss Lillian's room.

"Now, you know Mama would make you get out of this bed," he told her. "She's in a better place. Come on baby, let's get you up."

She began to cry so hard that she gagged. I ran to the kitchen and got a glass of water. I handed it to Deacon, and he tried to sit her up. His voice was firmer this time.

"Mona, Mama would not want this. We got to send her off right and that includes you."

She sat up and took a sip of water before falling back onto the bed. He pulled her up and gathered her in his arms.

"Do this for Mama," he said. I watched as he guided her into the bathroom.

It took two hours to get her ready. The boys were standing beside the limousine. Deacon and I stood on either side of Mona and guided her down the steps. Her black Chanel sunglasses hid her puffy eyes. I looked up and Miss Lillian's neighbors stood at the end of their driveways. I tried to hold myself together. I'd never seen something so beautiful yet so sad.

We remained silent as cars stopped and allowed the limousine to pass as the limo wove through the country roads. There were cars lined up as far as the eye could see when we arrived at the church. It was packed by the time we entered. We steadied Mona on both sides as we guided her to Miss Lillian's casket. I pulled Karlos between us as Mona leaned over Miss Lillian and wept. Deacon guided her back to her seat. I placed my hand around Karlos's shoulder as he leaned into me and sobbed. I guided him back to the pew then sat beside Mona and motioned Karlos to sit on the other side of me. I needed to be able to console either one of them. I managed to hold myself together until I read the program. My name was listed as Miss Lillian's daughter-in-law. Karlos was listed along with Jacob and Jordan as her grandsons. Selfishly, I found solace in being recognized by the most important person in Mona's life. I wouldn't have been acknowledged if Miss Lillian hadn't given us her blessing.

It was my turn to cry.

The hardest part of the service was watching Miss Lillian's casket being lowered into the ground. Deacon and one of their male cousins had to hold Mona up before guiding her back to the limousine. There were cars lined up around the street by the time we returned to the house. The house was full of extended family and friends. Deacon led Mona to her room where she climbed into bed and pulled the covers over her head. We were shocked when she walked into the living room two hours later. Her cousins surrounded her as she sat on the couch. I took the opportunity to make her a plate. She shook her head when I handed it to her.

"Please, honey. You have to eat something." She reluctantly took the plate while her cousins continued to tell childhood stories. I was thankful they could make her laugh even if temporarily. It seemed like a dream until everyone left.

Sadness hung in the air as we made plans to return to Chicago. I was surprised when Mona said she wanted to drive back to Chicago.

"Are you sure, honey?"

"I don't want to see or talk to anyone. I just want to drive."

"I'll reserve a car."

The remaining time in the house was bittersweet as I watched Karlos tussle with Jacob and Jordan. I was thankful he had his cousins to help him through their shared loss.

Karlos and I followed Mona's lead as we drove back to Chicago. We listened to music and talked only when she initiated a conversation.

"Breezy. I heard you, Jacob, and Jordan talking about getting tattoos."

"Tattoos?" I yelled. "You're too young for a tattoo. I'm sorry, honey. You were talking to him."

"It's okay. But what were you guys talking about?"

"We were talking about all of us getting the same tattoo for Mema. They would get the tattoo and send a picture to me so I can get the same one."

"What would the tattoo be?" Mona asked.

"Mema's name."

She looked at me. "How do you feel about that, babe?"

"I think he's too young for a tattoo, but this is an exception. I'm okay with it if it's not visible."

"So...I can get one?"

"Let's see what your grades look like after your freshman year. If they're good, then you can get it. How does that sound?"

I heard the disappointment in his voice. "Okay."

We got home, switched cars, and picked Misty up from the doggy hotel before it closed. I waited in the car while Karlos and Mona went in to get her. It warmed my heart to see them laughing as Misty pulled Mona to our truck. She licked Karlos as he put her in the back seat with him.

"How did they say she was?"

Mona handed me Misty's report card. It read, "Misty was a good girl but wasn't her usual playful self." I was amazed at how pets were in tune to the emotions of their owners.

"Aww Misty...you were sad?" I asked.

Karlos rolled the window down as she stuck her head out. "She's happy we're home, Mom."

We ate dinner in relative silence that night. I began clearing the dishes.

"Dinner was good, babe," Mona said. "I'm going to lay down."

Karlos waited for Mona to walk up the steps before speaking. "Mom is so sad."

"I know, honey. She'll be sad for a long time. Sometimes she may not want to talk, but please don't think it's anything you've done. I think you should take a couple of days off from school. You have to give yourself time to grieve."

He lowered his head. "Do you think mom would be mad if I went back to school? I think my friends and soccer would help me not be sad."

"She wouldn't be mad. She would want you to do whatever doesn't make you sad. Are you sure you're ready to go back?"

"I don't know."

"Just think about it and let me know in the morning."

I was exhausted that next morning when the alarm went off.

"Are you going to work?" Mona asked.

"No, I'm going to see if Karlos wants to stay home or go to school. I talked to him last night and he's torn. He thinks seeing his friends would make him feel better, but he doesn't want you to be mad at him for going back to school."

She rolled over. "I know it's a lot for him to process."

"I told him that. I'm going to see what he wants to do."

I let Misty out and stood in the doorway of Karlos's room.

"Breezy? How are you feeling? Do you want to stay home or go to school?"

He burst into tears. "I want to stay home with Mom."

"It's okay to be sad. You can stay home, but your mom may not feel well enough to get out of bed today."

"I want to stay in case she gets up."

"Okay." I kissed him on the forehead and pulled the covers over him and headed back to bed.

"Is he going to school?"

"No, he said he wants to stay home in case you get out of bed." She lay her head on my chest and got up just as I was starting to drift off.

"Where are you going, honey?"

"To talk to Karlos."

The aroma of bacon soon drifted through the vents. I heard laughter as I came down the steps. They were sitting on the couch in the den eating breakfast.

"Mom! We're watching *Major Payne*. Mom has never seen it."

"I asked him what he wanted to do today, and he said make pancakes and watch *Major Payne*. Did we wake you up laughing too loud?"

"No, I was dreaming that something was burning."

"We made pancakes, eggs and sausage."

"I'll eat later. I'll let you guys finish your movie."

"Come watch it with us, mom."

We tried to spend as much time with him as a family as possible. I was grateful when Mona convinced him to return to school two days later. I was even more surprised when she said she was going to work.

"Don't you think it's too soon, honey?"

"She would expect me to."

CHAPTER TWENTY-EIGHT

We ate breakfast as a family that morning before returning to school and work. I was greeted by multiple coworkers when I walked into the office. My eyes welled with tears when I reached my cubicle. There was a large floral arrangement on my desk. I was overwhelmed when I read the card signed by our entire team: "Our condolences for the loss of your mother-in-law."

In the midst of our family trauma, I had forgotten about the SDK Talent Group. I opened an email from Jonathan and read the message and the attachment. I was speechless when I opened two headshots of Karlos. I couldn't believe how striking his images were. His eyes were captivating. His Robert DeNiro mole stood out on his handsome face. Jonathan confirmed that the attached headshots were the images Siobhan had chosen for Karlos's auditions. I hoped that this was sign of better things to come.

Our house in Michigan became our refuge. Being a city girl, I preferred to clean the inside of the house. We would often go to the farmer's market to find the freshest produce. Mona reveled in the country traditions of her childhood. She would wake up early and mow the lawn. I would make our lunch and we would sit on the screened-in porch, talking about how we wished we could stay there forever. Misty ran around the three acres like a racehorse. I wasn't raised with pets, so I hadn't realized that they were like children who needed just as much love and attention. As Mona continued to grieve over Miss Lillian's passing, we came up with an idea as a tribute. We planted a weeping willow in the backyard. The weeping willow represents the ability to withstand the greatest challenges while bending but never breaking.

We were beyond excited when I received a call from Jonathan regarding Karlos's first go-see. It was for a local school furniture company. I was excited until Jonathan stated the go-see could take two to three hours. He reiterated that we needed to be on-site at one o'clock sharp. He reminded me to carry at least ten copies of Karlos's headshots. I hung up knowing that Mona wasn't going to be happy with Karlos missing a half day of school. I cringed at having to tell him he would miss soccer practice. I would have to sign him out of school by noon to get up north by one o'clock.

I decided to cook one of their favorite meals for dinner that evening. We made a habit of sharing something good that happened to us each day. I chose to share first that evening.

"Okay...so, I had a telephone call today and..." I paused for a dramatic effect.

"Come on, Mom. What happened?"

"You, Karlos Calabrese, landed your first go-see for SDK Talent Group!"

"Seriously, Mom?"

Mona offered her usual response. "Whoa..."

"Yup, but we have to follow some very specific instructions. And there are a few drawbacks. You'll have to leave school early that day. The go-see is up north so I'll have to sign you out at noon. You would also have to miss soccer practice that day."

"He'll be missing more than half a school day," Mona said.

"I can't miss practice so soon in the season," Karlos added. "I'll have to do extra sprints for missing practice."

"Well, we have to make a decision as a family. I told you that I could get you signed, and I did. Not all of your go-sees will require you to miss school or practice."

"But, Mom ..."

"We don't have to go but it won't look good declining your first go-see."

"How much would he make before the agency takes their twenty percent?"

"It depends on how much the client is paying. Regardless, it's better than nothing."

"Let's see how it works out this time," Mona said. "That's if he gets the job."

I made sure my numbers were at eighty percent before requesting the day off. I was nervous as we sped up north that day. The process was like Gianni's photo shoot, except this time I couldn't be there to guide Karlos. I tried to read his face when the corporate representative stated Jonathan would hear from them within forty-eight hours. I waited until we got outside to ask a million questions.

"What was it like?"

"Man, Mom. It was crazy! I was nervous, but then I felt comfortable. I think I'm going to like modeling."

My intuition was confirmed when Jonathan called two days later to tell us Karlos had booked his first job. We received a copy of the ad and Karlos's fee was deposited into my account three days later. We went out to dinner to celebrate.

"Your money is in my Navy Federal Credit Union account that I opened years ago," I announced. Karlos beamed with pride when Mona said she was proud of him.

Mona and I then talked until the wee hours of the morning. I knew she was healing when she talked about getting in shape for her fall fundraiser. She suggested hiring a personal trainer.

Our lives continued to flourish when Jonathan called to inform me that Siobhan wanted Karlos to audition for a role in a short film. We were floored as we discussed the possibility of this opportunity leading to larger jobs versus the prospect of Karlos becoming overextended. We all agreed that school came first. Still, Karlos showed us that he could juggle his responsibilities when he finished the first semester of high school with a 2.9 grade point average.

There were at least ten young men waiting by the time Karlos and I arrived at an off-site location. We were directed to a room with a single chair in the center of the circle. The parents were directed to sit in the chairs lined up against the wall while the young men were directed to take a seat within the circle. I sat up when the door to the studio opened and in walked Siobhan Daniels-Kent. Her heels clicked on the smooth concrete floor. She looked like the boss, with her crisp, white, high-collared shirt paired with tailored black pants and red heels. Her red matte lipstick was flawless. Her long black hair bounced as she walked to the chair in the center of the circle.

"Good morning. I'm Siobhan Daniels-Kent. I've handpicked you all to audition for a client who's producing a short film. If selected, you'll be required to commit to a six-week production schedule. Today, I'll assign characters to each of you. I want you to improvise according to the character you're given. Let's get started!"

Siobhan handed out character descriptions to each young man. It was nerve-wracking as she called out each character name. Some of the boys thrived while others struggled under the pressure. I held my breath when she called out Karlos's character. I watched him morph into his character right before my eyes. I waited with bated breath while Siobhan made notes after the final improv. She was hard to read as she ran her hand through her thick mane.

"You guys are making my job hard. Please join your parents and when I call your name, return to your seats." The young men looked nervous as they joined us. There were only five positions available and there were ten young men.

"That was crazy, Mom. I felt like I had to boo-boo when she called my character's name."

I tried not to laugh out loud. "I'm not saying this because I'm your mother, but you're a natural. You were so believable."

"I hope Siobhan thinks so."

"It's Miss Siobhan," I corrected.

We sat on pins and needles for twenty minutes before Siobhan made her decisions.

Karlos was the last name Siobhan called. She thanked the participants who weren't selected and asked the remaining five to tighten up the circle. She briefed them on the production schedules they were instructed to share with their parents. Karlos was all smiles.

"You're going to be in a movie, but guess what?"

"What?"

"We cannot add another damned thing to your schedule!"

We couldn't wait to share the news with Mona over dinner that evening. So many good things were happening and yet, I still wondered when I would find *my* passion.

I remember the day that changed my life forever. And yet, I didn't connect that event to my declining health until much later. Mona was working from home. I got home early after a client presentation. I opened the back door and walked into a thick fog of dust. I began to gag as I called out to Mona. I stepped back onto the porch and fumbled for my cellphone when she didn't respond.

"Honey, where are you?"

"Upstairs."

"There's dust all over the den."

"What? I'm coming," she said. I could barely see her as she stood over the balcony.

"Goddamn it!" I covered my mouth and walked toward the kitchen. It too, was covered in dust.

"It's everywhere, honey! I can't breathe."

"I told him he needed to put plastic on that brick wall."

"Who?"

"Simon! He's the owner of the Greystone next door! He wanted exposed brick like ours. He can only do that by sanding the walls to expose the brick. I told him to let me know so he could come over and put plastic on our wall so this shit wouldn't happen. Let me call his ass!"

I walked into the sunroom before walking downstairs. All of our furniture was covered in dust.

"It's everywhere."

"Damn it!" Mona yelled. "He didn't pick up. Let me call him again."

I waited on the balcony as she paced back and forth.

"Simon! This is Mona. You need to get over here as soon as possible. I asked you to let me know when you'd be sanding the walls. The dust came through the walls and my house is covered in dust."

"I can't breathe," I said. "I'm going to sit on the balcony."

"Go ahead, babe. This is a fuckin' mess!"

I stayed on the balcony until I heard Simon's Russian accent.

"Mona, I so sorry. I not think this could happen."

"I told you this would happen because you were sanding a shared wall. I'm going to have to have everything cleaned. This is fucked up! You're going to have to fix this. Come look at the damage."

"Mona…Mona…I fix it. I sorry. I call my insurance company and call you back." She basically pushed him out of the door.

"I don't believe this shit. We can't stay here."

"But where are we going to go?" She shook her head.

"Either he or his insurance company is going to have to put us up in a hotel. We can't inhale this."

That was the last thing we needed as Mona continued to grieve over Miss Lillian's passing. I went upstairs to change my clothes and begin coughing again. I was stunned when I saw that all our clothes had dust on them. The brick wall extended the length of Simon's rental unit. I couldn't imagine how much this was going to cost to clean. How were we going to live out of a hotel with work and Karlos's multiple activities?

I called our neighbor Babette and explained what happened. I asked if Karlos could spend the night with her and Ale until we figured things out. She calmed my nerves when she said Karlos could stay as long as we needed him to. I left a message at school for Karlos to go home with Ale. I walked outside and joined Mona on the balcony.

"All of our clothes have to be put in the cleaners," I said.

"This is really fucked up. I can't believe I didn't see it or smell it."

"You wouldn't have, working from the bedroom. I asked Babette if Karlos could stay with them tonight. She said he can stay as long as we need him to."

"Thank God. I'm waiting for the insurance company to call me back."

The insurance company called back shortly and authorized our stay at a hotel until they could send an adjustor out. We just made the cutoff to take Misty to the doggy hotel before they closed. We packed a suitcase and grabbed a couple of work outfits to put in the cleaners.

I called in sick the next day so I could help Mona sort things out. We lived out of a hotel downtown for a month before we could move back home.

I don't know how we juggled our work schedule as well as Karlos's, but we did. We agreed to do something nice for Babette to thank her for taking care of him.

We were approaching the end of the SDK production schedule. Most of his character scenes had been shot in the evenings. We spoke with him every day to ensure he was staying on top of his schoolwork. I missed him so much while we were apart. And yet, I was happy he could just focus on being a kid.

CHAPTER TWENTY-NINE

The total cost to clean all three levels of our home was over eighty thousand dollars. We laughed at how Misty probably thought we had given her away. After being out of the house a month, she went crazy the day we brought her home. We tried to get back to a sense of normalcy as fall set in. We resumed our challenge to get in shape for Mona's fall fundraiser. I found a trainer who made house calls.

One day, I was running on the treadmill, and he increased the speed. I huffed and puffed. "You're too young to be breathing that hard," he said. "Do you have asthma?"

When I said I didn't, he suggested I have my primary care physician check it out. I noticed that my breathing became labored whenever I walked for extended periods of time, but I didn't think much of it. I made an appointment with our doctor, Dr. Khassi, who said she needed to recommend me to a doctor who specialized in internal medicine. Anxiety set in when the internist ordered a biopsy.

He conferred with Dr. Khassi before scheduling the biopsy. After reading his notes, she called him while I was in her office.

"I'm looking at your notes. Miss Blue is a relatively young woman, so I recommend the biopsy incision be mid-cleavage and not on her neck."

My neck? Oh no! I'd seen people with dark scars on their necks due to a biopsy and I was thankful Dr. Khassi provided a woman's perspective.

I received her phone call a few days later. I was stunned when she asked if I was familiar with sarcoidosis. Her words ran together in my ears as she confirmed the diagnosis. She attempted to soothe my fears by stating that sarcoidosis could be managed with medication. My heart sank when she said there was no cure and requested a follow-up appointment.

I dialed Mona and broke down at the sound of her voice.

"I have sarcoidosis," I explained. "It's inflammation in my lungs, eyes, and lymph nodes. There's no cure. Dr. Khassi said I'll be on medication for the rest of my life."

"Don't cry, babe. We will get through this like we always do."

I was relieved when Mona said she would pick up Karlos from school. I drove home and got into bed. I pulled the cover further over my head when I heard the alarm sensor.

"Babe, Karlos and I stopped to get sushi. Come down for dinner?" She came upstairs when I didn't answer. "Babe?"

"I'm not hungry," I said.

She gently pulled the cover from over my head and kissed me on the forehead. "We'll get through this."

I got up and washed my face. My eyes were red and puffy from crying. I walked into the kitchen and tried not to look how I felt.

"Were you crying, Mom?" Karlos asked.

"Mommy is tired. Why don't you say the grace?" We all held hands and I felt his hand grip mine harder.

I became obsessed with researching the symptoms and prognosis of sarcoidosis. I calmed down after reading it was manageable with steroids. Maybe it wouldn't so bad, after all. Dr. Khassi prescribed a high dose of prednisone during my follow-up appointment. I was ashamed to admit that my greatest concern was one of the biggest side effects: weight gain. After a week on prednisone, insecurity set in when my face swelled to twice its normal size. I became self-conscious and wondered if Mona was still attracted to me.

Karlos's auditions made me focus on something other than myself. We prepared to attend the premiere of the short film at a local theater. *Secrets* highlighted the lives of five students who were secretly dealing with issues such as homelessness, poverty, illiteracy, and molestation. Karlos was excited that Mona and I would be there to support him. I couldn't believe how much of a natural he was. His character drew you in with his story of illiteracy. I wanted to cry as the credits rolled and actors bowed. I dreaded waiting for him as we stood near the exit doors. I prayed no one recognized Mona and approached us as we waited for our son. We simply wanted to bask in the glow of being proud parents.

Karlos glowed as he walked toward us. He embraced us as we wrapped our arms around him.

"You were amazing," I said.

He kissed me and then Mona on the cheek. "It felt like I was someone else. Could you believe that was your son up there?"

Mona kissed him on the cheek. "I was looking at the screen like, is that our son?" she said. We laughed as guests congratulated him.

"Look at you with fans," I said.

I was more tired than usual when I woke up with a headache the next morning. I began to blink as things seemed to become blurry. I called and made an appointment with Dr. Khassi before leaving for work.

I was on track to close two new accounts. I was looking forward to my commission checks as I thought of Christmas. I wanted to do something special for Mona and for Karlos. She'd given us the life I had always dreamed of, and I wanted to show Karlos what unconditional love looked like. I remembered Char's fabulous fur coat in a trailer for her upcoming movie.

Char picked up the phone on the second ring.

"Hey, suga. How are you and that beautiful family of yours?"

"We're well. Karlos just starred in his first short film."

"I'm not surprised. He is some kind of handsome. How's my Mona?"

"She's taking one day at a time. Each day is different. But listen, I don't want to keep you long, but remember when I asked you about that fur coat you had on in your movie trailer? You said when I was ready to surprise my baby, you would refer me to your contact in New York."

"Chile, Natalia can get you whatever kind of fur you want," she declared. "Let me grab her number. Tell her I referred you. She should give you a nice price given all the furs I've bought from her. You know, I just want to tell you that what you two have is special. I love you for each other."

"Thank you, Char. That means a lot coming from you."

I couldn't wait to call Natalia on my lunch break. She had a deep Russian accent. I explained to her that I was looking for a one-of-a-kind fur coat. She asked questions about Mona's style as well as her height. I was shocked that she never asked how much I wanted to spend. She asked for an email so she could send a couple of images for me to choose from. I was excited when I hung up. Mona would finally be on the receiving end of everything she deserved.

Once again, I began to eat lunch at my desk to stay ahead of my revenue goals. I cold-called new leads at a dizzying pace. I thought I was overworking myself when my eyes became blurry again. I took a break and checked my personal email. I was surprised when I opened an attachment and saw a sable stroller and a black swing coat. I opened the third attachment and my mouth dropped. There was a blond and chocolate mink swing coat with an oversized, shawl collar. I responded to Natalia and informed her of my decision. I finally inquired about the price for each coat. I prayed that at least one of the furs was within my budget.

I left work early that day as my head continued to throb. I pulled out of the parking garage when suddenly the traffic lights became hazy. I rubbed my left eye and it got worse. I rubbed my right eye only to have the same effect. I panicked when I drove through a light and couldn't make out the color. Drivers began to honk their horns. Did I just run a red light? I gently applied the brakes and pulled up to another light as several cars sped around me. I rummaged through my purse for my phone. I felt like I couldn't breathe when I looked up and couldn't read the street signs. My vision in both eyes got progressively worse until I realized I was under a viaduct. I turned on my hazard lights in hopes that drivers would go around me. To no avail, they kept honking their horns. I took a risk and stopped the car. I couldn't see the numbers, so I held the phone closer to my face. I took a chance and pressed a key hoping the last number I dialed was Mona's.

"Honey, I'm driving and I can't see!"

"Where are you?"

My voice quivered. "I don't know but it's dark. I can barely see the tail-lights of the cars in front of me."

"Listen to me. Try to calm down. I don't want you to have an accident."

"Everyone is honking at me!"

"Put your hazards on," she said.

"They're on. I think I'm under Emerald City."

"I want you to follow the lights of the cars in front of you."

"But I can't see the colors of the traffic lights."

"Stay close enough behind them until you see the natural light. If you're in Emerald City, stay west and that should bring you out on Lake Shore. If you still can't see when you get to Lake Shore, pull over and I'll come and get you. Stay on the phone. Try to relax. Did you call Dr. Khassi?"

"Yes, but she referred me to an ophthalmologist."

"Okay, call them when you get home to see if you can be seen first thing in the morning. I'll move my meetings so I can take you."

"I think I see the exit."

"Good. Do you think you can make it home?"

"I think I can. I'll drive slow. Thank you, honey. I love you."

"I love you, too. I'll be home shortly."

I drove in the right lane all the way home. I pulled into the garage and sobbed uncontrollably. I sat there until my heartbeat slowed. I was happy to see Misty waiting for me at the door. I walked upstairs and strained my eyes to find the ophthalmologist's number in my phone. I made an emergency appointment with Dr. Levinstein for the next morning. Mona consoled me that evening as I prepared for the worst.

We held hands as we drove to Dr. Levinstein's office the next day. Mona waited in the reception area when the assistant called my name. I explained to Dr. Levinstein what happened the day before. He completed a few exams before pushing his stool back.

"Miss Blue, you have uveitis, which is basically inflammation of the middle part of the eye, the uvea. You will need steroid shots to slow the progression."

"Steroid shots? In my eyes?"

"I know it's alarming, but I will place a numbing solution on a cotton ball before injecting the steroids beneath your eyelids."

I felt sick to my stomach.

"Will I be able to feel the needle?"

"You will feel pressure." He reached over and handed me a tissue as I wiped tears from my eyes.

"Am I losing my vision?"

"You may experience some temporary loss but I'm recommending a rigorous treatment plan with my colleague. I'll start you on the steroid shots today, but I want you to follow up with him as soon possible." He left the room and returned with a hand full of medical supplies. He adjusted my seat and put on a pair of rubber gloves.

"I'm going to tell you exactly what I'm doing before I do it. I'm going to pull your upper eyelid back and insert a cotton ball." He squirted a solution onto a cotton ball and stood over me. He pulled my eyelid back and I flinched.

"Try to relax." I willed myself not to move as he inserted the cotton ball beneath my eyelid. I felt nauseous as he plucked the end of a long needle and a drop squirted into the air.

"I'm going to inject the steroids, now. Look up, for me." I looked up and felt pressure as the needle moved deeper into my eye lid.

I felt queasy when I walked into the waiting room.

"What did he say, babe?" Mona asked.

"I'll tell you when we get in the car."

We spent the next week going to ophthalmology appointments. I scheduled the appointments around my lunch hour. I didn't want Grace or my team members to know I was having health issues.

CHAPTER THIRTY

Things took a turn for the worse when I was assigned to a huge account. Grace offered to have another manager assist me given the potential revenue. I was confident I could manage the account on my own. The numbers didn't balance when Grace reviewed my report as the deadline neared. I was anxious when she summoned me into the conference room. Ron and two other senior managers were seated. Ron stated that the client was too important to lose. I was embarrassed when he asked Grace to manage the account. I called Mona, who'd been waiting outside for two hours. I was humiliated when I looked at the clock. It read eleven o'clock pm. Although Grace managed the account, the entire team sat in the conference room as she pulled data from various departments. I could barely look at my team members as we exited the room. I called Mona to let her know I was on my way down.

"What's going on, babe?"

"I think I'm going to get fired."

She tried to console me. "I'm sure you're not going to get fired. Do you want me to call Lewis to see if he can find out anything from Grace?"

"Please, don't. I'm so embarrassed."

I was so exhausted that I went to bed without eating that night.

I squared my shoulders as I made a walk of shame into the office the following morning. I was sure everyone knew what had happened the night before. I was taken off one of our largest accounts in history. It was nine o'clock on the dot when Ron's assistant buzzed me.

"Good morning, Nikki. Ron would like to see you in his office." I took a deep breath before walking into his office. He leaned forward in his chair.

"Please, close the door," he said. "You've made some significant contributions to our department. However, last night was an indication that the responsibilities of sales manager may be too much. We could have missed the opportunity to land a substantial contract. I think you're in over your head and that was an oversight on my part. Effective immediately, Heather will assume responsibilities as Midwest sales manager. You'll resume your duties as account executive. Do you have any questions?"

"No, I understand."

I was in a fog for the rest of the day. I was sure everyone knew I'd been demoted. And yet, I was grateful I wasn't fired. I was glad it was Friday. I needed the weekend to regroup. I tried to put on a happy face when I picked Karlos up from soccer practice.

"You look tired, Mom."

"I am, Breezy."

"Will you be too tired to come to my game tomorrow?"

"I'm never too tired to come to your game." We picked up some take-out while I listened to him talk about his day. I was in the bed by the time Mona got home.

"Babe, why are you in the bed so early?"

I painstakingly rehashed my day before rolling over and falling asleep.

I was surprised when my phone rang early that morning. It was my aunt. "Hi, Ros. What are you doing up this early, Auntie?"

"I haven't talked to you in a minute, niece," she said. "My spirit told me to check on you." We spent the next thirty minutes catching up and laughing. She said she was having a hard time after a biopsy scare.

"Why didn't you call me?"

"I didn't want you to worry."

"Please, don't ever do that again. I want to know if you're not feeling well."

We ended our call with a promise to check in more often. Mona was lying beside me, checking her email.

"We better get ready for Karlos's game," I said. Before she could answer, I got out of bed and fell to my knees.

"Babe?"

I felt nauseated as the room began to spin. My head felt like someone had hit me with a sledgehammer. I tried to stand up and fell again.

"Honey! What's wrong?"

I couldn't speak as I squeezed my legs together to keep from losing my bowels. I heard the fear in her voice.

"Karlos! Call 911! You're mom's sick."

I crawled to the bathroom while trying not to vomit as she walked beside me. The room continued to spin out of control.

"I need to lie down."

Mona pulled me to my feet and guided me to the bed in the guest room. The pain was excruciating. It seemed like it took forever before the medics arrived.

"My head is killing me," I croaked out.

"Hold on, babe…hold on." I heard footsteps bounding up the stairs as Mona yelled out.

"She's in here."

A female EMT leaned over me.

"Can you hear me, hon?"

"Yes. My head."

She turned to Mona. "Did she fall or hit her head?"

"No, she was talking on the phone with her aunt and went to get out of bed and fell."

"Okay, let's get her dressed. Do you have any sweats or pajama bottoms you can slip on her?"

I began to massage my temples. "Maybe I ate something that was bad."

The EMT felt my wrist for a pulse. "No, dear, nothing you ate would cause this. Tony, she's ready."

A burly male EMT walked into the room. "What's her name, miss?"

Mona's voice quivered. "Nikki."

"Can you hear me, Nikki?"

"Yes."

"Do you think you can sit up for me?"

"I feel like I'm going to throw up."

"I want you to listen to me," the burly medic said. "I'm going to kneel in front of you. I want you to wrap your arms around my neck." I felt his back against my legs and realized he wanted me to climb onto his back.

"I'm going to count to three and I want you to hold on as tight as you can. One…two…three." I felt like a ragdoll as he hoisted me onto his back and gripped my legs.

Mona called out to Karlos. "Get dressed, Breezy." I couldn't see Karlos's face, but I knew he was scared as the EMT carried me down the spiral staircase on his back.

"Hold on, now." Something moved through me as we approached the second-floor landing. My eyes rolled in the back of my head before refocusing. Misty was standing at the bottom of the staircase. There was a stillness I'd never felt before. She never barked as the EMT carried me down the steps.

"Babe, Karlos and I are going to follow the ambulance. We'll be right behind you."

Two EMTs lowered me onto a stretcher and into the back of an ambulance. I managed to murmur a few words before passing out.

"Where's my son?"

My head was spinning when I saw the bright lights as the EMTs wheeled me into the Chicago MedStar emergency room. They stationed me in an ER bay just as Mona and Karlos appeared beside the bed. Karlos wiped his tears as I held my hand out.

"Mommy's going to be okay."

A nurse came over and I heard Mona tell her that I had sarcoidosis and explained what had happened. The nurse ran an IV and came back shortly with what she told Mona was morphine. Slowly, the stabbing pains in my head begin to subside. I'd been in the ER for more than six hours when Mona turned to Karlos.

"I'm going to go home, take a shower and change. Stay with your mom. Ask to use a phone if you need me."

When I opened my eyes, Karlos was leaning against the wall staring at me.

"I'm scared, Mom."

"Don't be. I'm right here."

Each time I opened my eyes he was staring at me. It was as though he was afraid to close them for fear I would be gone when he opened them. I fell back asleep and when I opened my eyes, the clock read one o'clock. We had been in the hospital for five hours. When I didn't see Mona, I assumed she had taken the time to reschedule her meetings. The hustle and bustle of the ER room came to a complete stop when her voice rang out.

"Who's in charge here?" The beeping monitors resonated through the silence.

"Who...is...in...charge...here?" Her words were firm the second time. I opened my eyes and Mona was standing in the middle of the ER room. She stood out in a black turtleneck and matching black pants covered by a camel-colored cashmere coat. Her makeup was immaculate. A tall white woman timidly approached her.

"I am the attending ER doctor, tonight." Mona's glare pierced through her.

"My significant other was brought into this emergency room at nine o'clock this morning. It is now one o'clock. She has been laying in the same position for eight hours. Our son is a minor and he's been by her side without food or water. When is she going to be seen by a doctor?"

"Ma'am, I'm sorry but I didn't get your name."

"Mona Hatchett."

"Thank you, Miss Hatchett. We are waiting for a doctor for Miss...Miss..."

"You don't even know her name!" Mona took out her cellphone and began dialing a number. The doctor walked away red faced. I looked at Karlos and he no longer had a look of fear on his face. He tried to stifle a look of amusement. He'd seen that look on his other mother's face before and the situation usually didn't end well. We listened as Mona stood beside my bed.

"Hello, Carrie. It's Mona. I'm sorry to bother you on a Saturday but my partner was rushed to the hospital at nine o'clock this morning. She and our son have been waiting in the emergency room for eight hours without seeing a doctor." Karlos lowered his head when Mona turned around and held the phone up in the air.

"Who's really in charge here?" The same doctor walked over and Mona handed her the phone. I watched the blood drain from the doctor's face.

"Yes, I understand, Provost Miller. I'll ensure that she receives the utmost care." The doctor handed Mona the phone and walked away. Within minutes, there was a flurry of activity. A different doctor introduced himself as Mona stood at the foot of my bed.

"Miss Blue, I'm Doctor Foster. I apologize for the delay. We're waiting on your blood test results. Until then, we're going to get you into a room so that you're more comfortable." I acknowledged him with a nod. I looked at Mona as she caressed my leg.

"Thank you, honey," I said.

She rubbed Karlos's back. "Thank you for taking care of your mom while I was gone."

In that moment, our relationship changed in a way that I'd longed for. We'd been together for five years when Mona finally came out to one of her business associates. I loved her more for making that sacrifice.

Ten minutes later, a technician steered my bed into a private corner room with a view of the university courtyard. Mona and I made eye contact. We watched the technician make every possible accommodation to make me comfortable. Karlos watched as the technician swaddled me in a warm blanket before leaving the room. I raised my eyebrow as Mona closed the door.

"Who in the hell did you call, honey?"

"Carrie, one of my funders, just happened to be at a play with the provost of the university."

I shook my head. "You're bad as shit!"

Karlos finally smiled. "What's a provost, Mom?"

"A provost is the second in charge, next to the president of the university."

"Whoa, Mom."

"But do you see how we, Black people, are treated when they think we're poor?" Mona explained. "They left your mom laying in a cold emergency room with no blanket because we probably looked crazy when we came in. We had on pajamas. Our hair wasn't done and they thought they could treat us any kind of way because we're Black. They assumed we were poor based on the way we looked."

I shook my head. "And you came back in here looking like the Matrix."

CHAPTER THIRTY-ONE

I was at Chicago MedStar for two days before I was diagnosed with neurosarcoidosis. I was thankful Karlos was in school when Mona and I received the diagnosis. The sarcoidosis had spread from my lungs to my eyes and finally to my brain. Mona held me as I sobbed. My life would never be the same.

The short-term diagnosis was just as devastating. Due to the inflammation in my brain, I'd suffered a stroke. I was so consumed with my headaches that I failed to notice that I couldn't move my legs. My world was crashing down around me. Mona called my mother and sister to inform them of what had happened. This would change our lives forever.

I felt like a little girl when my mother called later that evening. I just wanted my mother.

"I'm on my way," she said. "Everything is going to be all right. God is still on the throne."

I told her they would soon be moving me to one of the best rehabilitation centers in the country. It just happened to be located downtown. I was comforted knowing she would take care of Karlos and Mona while I was in rehab.

One morning, I asked the nurse for a mirror and burst into tears when I saw my reflection. I didn't recognize myself from all the swelling. I saw the fear in Karlos's eyes when Mona brought him to visit. I tried to make him laugh to keep him from crying. I didn't know if that was more for me or for him.

"Look at my face, Breezy! I look like those little M&Ms with legs."

"Don't say that, Mom. You're gonna be rocking your heels again after you get out of rehab."

"I may not ever be able to wear heels again. But tell the truth: Which M&M do I look like?"

He laughed. "The chocolate one is the cutest."

Three days after suffering a stroke, I was transferred to the Rehabilitation Center of Chicago. My mother flew in the first day of rehab. She arrived after visiting hours, so I had to wait until the next morning to see her. I heard the excitement in her voice when she recalled Mona taking her grocery shopping. She was determined that Karlos and Mona would have home-cooked meals and said she wasn't leaving until I was discharged.

I felt like a kid when I told food services that I wouldn't be ordering dinner that night because my mother was bringing me a home-cooked meal. Mona was going to bring Karlos and my mother to visit after she got off work. I'd fallen asleep after my afternoon rehab session. I opened my eyes when I heard a knock at the door. My mother danced into the room holding a plate wrapped in aluminum foil.

I couldn't help but smile. "Hi, Mom."

She continued to dance while holding up the plate. "You got salmon cakes, spinach and rice."

"Thanks, Mom. I'm so happy you're here."

"Me too, but Misty won't let me cook. She follows me all over the kitchen, waiting for me to drop something." We laughed about Misty's antics.

My mother had been in my room for two hours before she asked about my diagnosis. She never did handle confrontation or trauma well.

I was more determined to make progress in therapy, knowing my mother was waiting in my room. After two weeks, I was strong enough to walk around the nurse's station with a walker. My physical therapist followed close behind with a wheelchair in case I got tired or fell. A nurse yelled out to me as I circled the nurses' station for the second time.

"Okay now, slow down, Miss Blue."

"I love y'all, but I got to get the hell out of here!" I said.

I was discharged from rehab the first week in November. Although it was bitter cold in Chicago, we would have to manage six weeks of outpatient therapy. Mona and I discussed what my future work life looked like. I was sad when colleagues sent flowers and a teddy bear to the house. When I informed Grace that I would have to take a medical leave of absence, I broke down. The realization that I wasn't the same person I'd been, and probably never would be, caused me to fall into a slight depression.

I didn't want to be a burden to Mona; it was important to me that I still contribute to our household. I had no other option other than to draw down on my 403(b) account. I felt defeated when I made the withdrawal but was happy I could still contribute. I withdrew forty thousand dollars and transferred twenty thousand to Mona's account. I told her to use the money to catch up on the mortgages in Chicago and Michigan. All of our bills, including both mortgages, were in arrears since I'd had my stroke.

After being treated so poorly at Chicago MedStar, Mona and I decided to take advantage of the civil union law and get married. I printed the paperwork and searched for a minister who would marry us in the privacy of our home. There was nothing spectacular about the moment as the minister married us that day, yet we found comfort in knowing we would be afforded similar rights as heterosexual married couples.

I felt an urgency to re-create myself, but I wasn't recuperating as quickly as I'd hoped. I was determined to walk again. My neurologist reiterated that I would have residual nerve damage for the rest of my life, but I was determined to beat the odds. After all, I had an MBA from Johns Hopkins! I couldn't imagine spending the rest of my days as a disabled housewife. But once we realized that I may not ever have the same earning potential prior to suffering a stroke, we fought tirelessly to secure disability benefits. I was denied benefits several times before searching for a disability attorney. I began journaling to keep my mind alert. The process became therapeutic as I wrote from the view of my five-year-old self. I had an epiphany when I decided exactly how to re-create myself.

I am going to write a book. I am going to become a bestselling author.

I was excited to share my revelation with Mona. She was supportive, as usual. I shared how my work would be fiction. I thought it would be more freeing and imaginative. I wanted to craft a story of courage and resilience, yet my imagination got the best of me. I was hesitant to share one of the most salacious chapters I'd written. Based on the lustful passages I'd penned, I was sure the book would fall under the erotica genre.

Adjusting to being housebound was challenging. The bitter-cold Chicago winters didn't help. Not only did I want to contribute financially, but I also wanted to show Mona how much I appreciated her. No matter how tired she was after work, she would call me before she left the office.

"Babe, do you need some air?"

I couldn't put my clothes on fast enough. She would pull in front of the house and patiently help me down the steps. I would roll down my window and stick my head out of the gap like a puppy as she drove around the neighborhood.

I was looking forward to the holiday season. Deacon and the boys were coming to spend Thanksgiving with us. It would be the first time they'd be together since Miss Lillian's passing. Karlos was ecstatic when we told him his cousins were coming.

Meanwhile, after everything that had happened because of my stroke, I'd almost forgotten about Mona's fur coat. I checked my email and was relieved to see that I had only missed one message from Natalia. I was thrilled when she gave me a price of ten thousand dollars for the blond fur coat and fifteen for the other two. She agreed to three payment installments. She would send me a sample to help me decide. I gave her the Hollings office address to prevent the box from being delivered to the house. I called Poppy and told her about Mona's surprise, and she agreed to bring the box over when it arrived. I was surprised when she called the next day.

"Did you order something other than Mona's surprise?"

"No, why?"

"A small box just arrived. What do you want me to do?"

"Open it." I waited as she opened the box.

"Oh my God, Nikki!"

"What?"

"Girl…there are three full-length fur coats in this box."

"You're lying! I thought you said the box was small."

"It is, but they packed the hell out of this box. What do you want me to do?"

"Can you bring them over after work tomorrow?"

"I'm working a half-day today. I have a doctor's appointment, but I can swing by."

"Are there a lot of people in the office?"

"Not really."

"Good. I need you to send the black and the sable one back before you leave today. They came from a Russian dealer in New York. I don't want no Russian dealer looking for me."

I couldn't wait to see Mona's face on Christmas morning. I had to think of a way to surprise her.

My 403(b) dwindled as Thanksgiving approached. I threw myself into writing as I began to feel like a burden. I woke up one morning with an idea. I remembered working with a consultant for one of Hollings's nonprofit clients. Her name was Fatima, and she worked with several nonprofits in the community. I called and invited her over for lunch. I ordered takeout and she picked it up on the way to the house. Fatima was loud with a vibrant personality. She couldn't be in a room without you knowing she was there. She was witty and unapologetically Black. When she arrived, I put Misty behind the gate before answering the door.

"Girl! You saved me. I'm working on a piece for a magazine, and I have writer's block," she exclaimed. She marveled at how beautiful the house was as we walked upstairs. "Damn! You need a second wife? I can cook and clean. Shit...both y'all fine."

I laughed. "You got a big ass and all, but please don't make me slash your tires."

We spent an hour eating and catching up before I pulled out an outline. "I'm writing a book and I want to hire you as a consultant."

"You better do it! I've been wanting to write a book for years, but I'm always working on everyone else's shit. Is it fiction or nonfiction?"

"Fiction. I think fiction is more intriguing. If you're a good writer, the reader won't know what's true or not."

She scribbled a few notes on her pad. "Are you going to write one or two books?"

"One, why?"

"Someone once told me that if you are trying to create a brand or legacy, you should always think in threes." I saw a twinkle in her eyes.

"What do you mean?"

"Write a trilogy. Write each book leaving the reader wanting more."

"I never thought of that."

"Well, there you have it! Write an outline based on three novels instead of one."

We made an agreement that would allow me to pay on a per-project basis. I would take her payments out of my short-term disability checks. I wanted to do this on my own. Mona was already stressed with the responsibility of paying two mortgages. I tried to help by paying the utilities, but in my eyes, it was never enough. Still, Mona tried to give me something to do. "So, babe, you know I haven't found a salesperson yet," she said one day as we were decorating just before the holiday.

"I thought you interviewed someone," I said.

"She took another job that paid more."

"What are you going to do?"

"Have you seen any shoes you want?"

Karlos laughed. "Dang, Mom. You working for shoes now?"

I threw a roll of ribbon at him. "Don't judge me."

CHAPTER THIRTY-TWO

There was a shift in Mona's energy as Thanksgiving neared. She became quieter after Deacon called to say they would arrive in two days. She said she wanted to put the tree up over Thanksgiving before Deacon and the boys left. I was surprised when Mona said she'd be taking a few days off before and after Thanksgiving. She promised that she wasn't going to work. But I knew working kept her mind off missing Miss Lillian, and this holiday would be tough, but I didn't push it. We tried to get into the holiday spirit by playing Christmas music in the house.

Mona's mood was lifted when Char called to wish us happy holidays.

"I was just thinking about you." Mona placed Char on speaker.

"It's good to be thought of."

"I know you won't be able to host our spring gala," Mona began, "but who's hot right now? It could be a seasoned entertainer or an up-and-coming artist."

"Let me think about it. I'll call around and get back to you. Tell that handsome son and that sexy wife of yours I said Happy Holidays."

As promised, Char called two days later. "What about Isabelle White?"

She's kind of earthy, but she has a voice like an angel. I'll text you her manager's number." Mona searched online for Isabelle White as soon as she hung up. We listened to a few of her songs.

"Her voice is crazy."

"You think my audience can appreciate her?"

"I think so. You can introduce them to something new." I continued to read her bio.

"Oh, wow. She's a preacher's kid from Georgia. Look at this album cover. I wonder if she has a lesbian following."

"Probably not with her jazz and gospel following," Mona said.

It was bittersweet as we prepared for Thanksgiving dinner. Mona was quiet and I tried to give her space. Karlos could barely contain himself as Deacon provided updates from the road. Mona's attitude changed when Deacon said they were close to the house. Karlos ran downstairs and waited in the foyer.

"Which one of y'all about to get spanked in Grand Theft Auto?" He couldn't stop smiling as he helped Jacob and Jordan carry their bags inside. Mona and I hugged each of them as they trudged up the steps. They dropped their bags and raced to the basement. I saw a look on Mona's face that I hadn't seen in a long time. Deacon lugged his suitcase up and hugged Mona.

"It smells like Mama's kitchen up in here," he said.

"No one's kitchen smells like Mama's."

The boys spent that first night challenging each other in video game championships. I went to bed early to allow Mona and Deacon some quality time as they tried to replicate Miss Lillian's signature broccoli and cheese casserole. The syrupy scents of candied yams and sweet potato pie wafted through the vents. Her body felt warm when she finally lay down and wrapped her arms around me.

"I miss her."

"I know you do, honey," I said.

We heard the alarm deactivate and reset early the next morning. We were in the kitchen when Deacon and the boys returned.

"Where did y'all go that early?" asked Mona.

Jacob stepped closer to Mona, pulled up his sleeve. and slowly peeled back a piece of gauze. I moved closer as he revealed a heart with a ribbon that read "Mema." Mona's eyes welled with tears as Jordan and Karlos followed suit. She moved the frying pan off the hot stove and began to cry.

"We all got the same tattoo. Do you think Grandma would like it, Mom?" Karlos asked.

"She would love it," Mona managed.

He stood back and raised his other sleeve. "I hope you and Mom like this one too." He pulled back a piece of gauze on his opposite shoulder to reveal a tattoo that read, "First Ladies."

We woke up Thanksgiving morning to Deacon making breakfast. "Okay, now," he announced. "Mama would not want us to be sad on Thanksgiving, so there'll be no crying today."

We sat down for breakfast and laughed at their childhood stories. I baked cookies while Deacon and the boys drove to a nearby lot and bought a Christmas tree. Mona busied herself unwrapping Miss Lillian's Christmas ornaments.

"This was her favorite angel set. She bought a collection every year."

I gently held the Black angel. "They look so regal." It was as if the boys knew how special the ornaments were as they carefully placed them on the tree. We didn't cry that night, but I felt everyone's grief.

The boys were already dressed by the time we got downstairs the next morning. Karlos tried to hide his sadness as we walked them downstairs and waved as they drove off.

Mona threw herself into work as Christmas neared. I continued to struggle with finding my passion. I masked my frustration by helping her secure corporate sponsors for her spring gala. I was overwhelmed with trying to be a good mother and wife.

Although *Secrets* was shown at an international film festival, I wasn't physically able to support Karlos in his acting endeavors any longer. But he could still work as a model. A new opportunity for him to become the face of a local retailer's campaign was a welcome surprise. Unfortunately, I was more excited than Karlos. I called to him through the vent when I didn't hear him moving around. I walked downstairs when he didn't answer. He was half-dressed.

"Why aren't you dressed? Did you iron those pants? Your Mom is almost ready."

"This is ironed, Mom."

My temples began to throb. "I told you a thousand times. Modeling is not just about having a pretty face. You gotta have the right attitude. Do you even want to do this? Because we're not wasting our damned time."

He casually brushed his hair. "You're stressing me out, Mom."

"I'm stressing you out? Do you know how many kids would kill for this opportunity?"

"Mom, you're acting like Joe Jackson."

If I wasn't so pissed, I would've laughed. Joe Jackson? I wanted to drag him by his collar. His heart wasn't in it, and it showed when he didn't get the job. That day was the end of Karlos's acting and modeling career.

We were grateful Karlos hadn't given us any problems in high school we couldn't fix. He began spending more time in his room on his phone. It all made sense when he asked if he could go to a party at Johnson College Prep. He told us that Kiya Spalding was going to be there. Kiya Spalding's reputation preceded her; during his sophomore year in high school, Karlos had spoken occasionally of a young lady that all the boys liked. He smiled dreamily whenever he talked about her.

Although he and this young lady had the commonality of both African American and Italian heritage, he dejectedly mentioned that everyone knew Kiya preferred "bad" boys. In his mind, she would never notice a good guy like himself. He was determined to win her affection. We knew he really liked Kiya when he said he wanted us to meet her. Now that he was dating, Mona and I knew it was time we had "the conversation" with him.

"Did you tell her you have two moms?" I asked. "Because we're not de-dyking our home for anyone. We will not be taking down family photos. I'm not calling your mother by any other name than 'honey.'" He simply smirked and shook his head.

Shortly thereafter, he nervously confessed that she was the single mother of a three-year-old son. I asked why he'd failed to mention she had a child. He said he thought we wouldn't want him to date her if we knew she was a single mother. I reminded him that I was a single mother and his other mother had chosen not just me but him. However, I stated, we weren't interested in meeting her son at such an early stage in all their lives.

I didn't give it much thought until they went on their first date. Karlos brought Kiya home to meet us before heading to a comedy show. I had just finished cleaning up the dishes from dinner when they walked up the steps.

"These are my two moms," he announced. "This is Kiya."

Behind him stood a beautiful young lady who looked just as nervous. She smiled and nervously tossed her long auburn mane. We chatted before they left for their date. That night was the beginning of their relationship.

CHAPTER THIRTY-THREE

As Christmas approached, Mona and I took turns sneaking around town with Karlos while we shopped for each other's presents. Mona and I had lovingly created a game where we tried to outdo each other with gifts. I wanted to buy her things she would never buy herself. It was nice to see her smile again. I was happiest when we were all together. Sitting in the den in front of the fireplace and watching old movies while Misty sat at our feet felt like heaven. Karlos couldn't wait to go to bed on Christmas Eve so he could wake up early and open his gifts.

I turned over when I heard him running down the hallway to our bedroom Christmas morning. "Merry Christmas!"

We giggled as he jumped between us.

"Get out of our bed with your big self!" I playfully pinched his butt before following him downstairs to the Christmas tree.

We took turns calling out name tags and opening our gifts. I saved the best gift for last. Karlos didn't know that I'd hidden Mona's fur coat under his bed, so I whispered to him to bring the box up from under his bed when Mona went upstairs to call Deacon. Then I told her not to come into the guest room until we called her.

Karlos had never seen her gift. I wanted him to be just as surprised. I whispered, "Open it." He opened the box and dramatically placed his hand over his mouth. "Y'all be going hard, Mom."

"You're supposed to when you love someone," I said.

Mona yelled from our bedroom. "What y'all doing in there?"

"Don't come in yet, Mom."

Thankful for Karlos's help, I pulled out a big red bow with ribbons and draped it around the coat before hanging it from the railing of the guest bed.

"Okay, you can call her."

"Come in, Mom."

Mona playfully peeked around the corner and stood in the doorway.

"Whoaaa…!"

Karlos and I laughed, as we knew that was her way of showing excitement. She walked over and ran her hand along the fur as Karlos jumped on the bed.

"Try it on, Mom."

She slowly tried on the coat and looked in the full-length mirror. "I'm never taking it off!"

"You look like a million dollars," I said.

She kissed me and then Karlos. "Thank you, guys. I feel like a million dollars."

My life was on autopilot as I secured corporate sponsorships for Mona's spring gala. I was also committed to working on my book each night. The more I wrote, the more I began to think I could write a bestseller. I was beginning to regain my independence and my confidence. I'd managed to make it through the winter without having another health crisis. I still had difficulty walking, but, thanks to my outpatient therapy, my mobility was slowly returning. I was grateful for the big and the small wins.

I didn't want to depend on Mona to finance my dreams of becoming a bestselling author, so I fell back on my marketing and sales experience for ideas. What could I give supporters in exchange for donating to a GoFundMe campaign? A lightbulb came on. In exchange for a donation of any amount, each donor would receive the most lustful chapter of my novel. I edited a rough draft of the "donor chapter" for Mona to read. I was happy when she said it was good. And yet, I saw something in her eyes that was unfamiliar.

I decided to conduct a focus group with the readers who'd read the donor chapter. I reached out to Fatima for a caterer referral and asked Mona to create a signature cocktail drink for the event. Everyone knows that alcohol is a "truth serum." My plan was to gain valuable feedback from my readers. It was important that the focus group be diverse; the group would consist of straight women, married women, lesbians, bisexual women, and women who were only lesbians on girls' trips.

I called my sister to pump me up. "What do you think about the focus group, Ce?"

"Oh, that's going to be fun."

"I want you to come."

"Of course, I'll come. This is huge."

"I'm going to call Toni, Morgan, and some of Mona's friends here in Chicago." We cackled as we came up with more ideas.

I called Toni and Morgan and they were immediately on board. In that moment, I realized how much I missed them. It was hard being away from my family and friends. Mona's life had become mine and I desperately needed to change that.

I switched gears and put on my CAPA hat. Char agreed to host the spring gala when Mona was successful in rebooking Isabelle White. The event would also include iconic R&B singer Avis Banks as the headliner.

I always knew when Mona wanted to ask for something she was unsure of. She often began the conversation with, "So..."

"So, babe, since she's only going to be here for two days, Char wanted to know if she could stay with us."

"I don't mind. I just need to call Karina to clean the house."

"She also wanted to know if Isabelle can stay as well."

I hesitated. "Wouldn't that be awkward? We've never met her. Is Char having her?"

"She said she's straight," Mona replied.

"That's what they all say."

I remember the first time I met Isabelle White. I had been running errands, making sure the wine bar and refrigerator was stocked for our guests. Mona said she would pick me up later so I could sit in on the sound check for the entertainers. When I arrived. all the artists were seated in the lounge area at

CAPA. There was a woman with dreadlocks sitting on the couch with her legs stretched out. It was interesting to see entertainers or actors in their natural state versus being onstage or on screen in all their glory. They behaved differently when the world adored them. But, offstage? Oftentimes, it was the complete opposite.

The spring gala was a success. The CAPA audience loved the diverse lineup of entertainers. I left the event early to make sure the house was ready for our guests. I had an adrenaline rush when I remembered my focus group was the next day. My girls were flying in that morning. Approximately thirty women had RSVPed for my focus group.

After the gala, I sat up with Mona, Char, and Isabelle at the house for as long as I could. Char was her usual dramatic self, but there was something almost child-like about Isabelle. The sound was muted on the TV while they drank cocktails, but Isabelle was glued to the screen. Her eyes looked dilated as she stared at the soundless images. It was off-putting, but I was too tired to care. I kissed Mona goodnight and excused myself.

"I know you're tired, babe," she said. "Thank you. Everyone was talking about the corporate VIP section."

Char smirked. "Where'd you find her, Miss Mona? Do you have a sister, Nikki?"

"I do, but she's strictly dickly!"

"Me too, but sometimes I'm crooked."

I left them downstairs to have industry talk. Mona slid into bed a few hours later.

"That was an amazing show, honey."

She snuggled beside me. "Char and Isabelle are still downstairs talking."

"Did you see how she zoomed into the TV like she was in a trance? That was kind of weird."

"I know," Mona said. "Both her parents are pastors. She, her sister, and brother were never allowed to watch TV."

"What?"

"And she said her father used to make them pray in the closet for hours."

"In the closet? Didn't they say Marvin Gaye's father used to do that?"

"I think so."

"I guess you can't have everything."

"I guess not."

Could I have everything? At this point, I had begun to feel a shift in our marriage. It was like a secret I was hiding; I was afraid to admit it, even to myself. I couldn't help feeling like a burden to Mona. She told me she'd take care of our family until I could get back to myself. But I felt self-conscious when we were introduced to strangers, as we had at the gala. People's eyes lit up when Mona explained what she did for a living. To not feel less than, I boldly stated that I was a "well-kept" housewife. Outwardly, I laughed along with them. Inside, I shrank in despair.

The morning of my focus group, I got up early for my hair appointment. Audrey, my hairstylist, had agreed to let Jon Hayward apply my makeup at the salon. Jon was one of the best makeup artists in the industry. He did the faces of local and national celebrities. I felt like a million dollars as he applied the finishing touches. I drove straight to the airport to pick up my sister, Toni, and Morgan. I enjoyed having a minute to myself, driving down Lake Shore Drive. *I'm really doing this. I'm going to re-create myself.* My life was coming full circle. I'd wanted to study journalism before dropping out of Norfolk State, but look at me now.

I parked in the visitor's lot and waited for my sister's call. I'd been there no more than ten minutes before my phone rang. My face lit up when I saw all three of them. I popped the trunk and jumped out.

"We must love you, shawty. Ain't nothing cute about Chicago weather and this is spring." Toni kissed me on my cheek.

Before I could hug my sister, someone grabbed me from behind. I spun around to see Dean's smiling face.

"What?"

She squeezed me more tightly. "You know I wasn't going to let you make your debut and I not be here."

It felt like old times.

CHAPTER THIRTY-FOUR

Char and Isabelle had left early that morning. Mona caught up with my girls while I napped before my other guests arrived. I woke up an hour later and pulled out my favorite stove-pipe jeans. I paired them with a simple long- sleeved T-shirt. A pair of blue suede flats completed my debut outfit. I sat at my desk and flipped through the pages of the chapter I was going to read during the focus group. I turned around when I heard footsteps.

"What are you doing here?" I was surprised to see Karlos.

"I bought you something." He pulled a bouquet of flowers from behind his back.

"Aww, thank you."

"You ready?" he asked.

"You know who your mama is."

He walked down the steps and stopped to kiss Kiya on her way up. I smiled as I thought about how quickly time had passed. Upon graduating from high school, Karlos seemingly breezed through four years of college. My dreams of becoming a Division I soccer mom were dashed when he majored in Business. After many years of soccer, he warily informed us that his grades would suffer if he played D1 soccer. Our decision was unanimous, his grades came first. So, he partied like a rock star once he pledged Kappa Alpha Psi fraternity. We were grateful that he never gave us any problems that we couldn't solve. And like a moth to a flame, he and Kiya picked up where they left off in high school. We were adamant about him not moving in with Kiya and Connor so soon after graduation but he was no longer a child. Kiya's embrace brought me back to reality.

"Thank you," I said. "I knew those flowers were your idea."

She smiled and bent over to kiss me on the cheek.

"I'm so proud of you. Are you ready?"

"I'm nervous but a good nervous."

"I brought a friend with me," she said. "We went to high school together."

"That's fine but listen…you've been in my life for three years, but your future mother-in-law and the author are two different people. Cover your ears when I read the juicy parts."

Our basement was packed by the time I made my grand entrance. I walked to the chair in the center of the room and motioned for the ladies to sit as they clapped. For the next three hours, I fielded questions about the book and what led me to write it. Mona looked uneasy when I pulled her seat closer to mine.

"I need some motivation," I stated. "I'm going to read the excerpt y'all been texting me about. Y'all nasty." The ladies roared with laughter.

One of Mona's straight girlfriends held up her cup. "I think I'm a lesbian after reading that chapter."

Mona blushed.

"Oh, please, honey. These are our friends. They know you ain't marry me for my cooking."

As I began to read, my spirit told me she was happy for me but not for us. She was uncomfortable with who I was becoming.

Mona's budding friendship with Isabelle began to take a toll on our marriage. I was perplexed when she insisted that we attend Isabelle's performances whenever she was in Chicago. I was even more baffled when she invited her to stay in our home versus a hotel to save money. The shift in our marriage began to feel like salt on an open wound. I would enter a room, or her studio and she would be on the phone. She was always transparent about her friendships, but there was something different about her newfound friendship with Isabelle. About a month after Isabelle stayed at our house, I addressed what I was feeling.

"Who were you talking to, honey?"

"Isabelle. She's going through some things with her boyfriend and she didn't have anyone to confide in."

"Oh, and she just happened to confide in you?"

"She lives in Ashford and she's usually the only Black person in a restaurant or coffee shop. Her boyfriend is a drummer with Connie James. She told me he gave her an STD."

"Why are you having such personal conversations? We just met her. But an STD? Like what?"

"She didn't say, but she said she has to take medication for the rest of her life. She told me he called her the 'N' word."

"Here we go."

She stopped painting. "What are you talking about?"

"Why do you surround yourself with broken people?" I asked. "You can't fix everyone. All your friends either want you or want to be you. Either way, it's dysfunctional."

"Maybe you're right."

"I know she better stop calling my house thinking she's going to talk to my wife all times of the night."

The need to re-create myself intensified. I was beginning to think Mona was tired of taking care of me. I realized that calling myself a "well-kept housewife" reflected my own insecurities. I asked God to send me a sign because I didn't know how I would raise the rest of the money to self-publish my book. That sign came when Fatima called one morning to ask if I'd checked the balance on my GoFundMe page. I had lost count of the number of chapters I sent out. I went online and checked the balance. I was surprised to see a balance of four thousand dollars. I was in awe when I tapped the link to review individual donors. Some donors left messages while others remained anonymous. The donations ranged from fifteen to five hundred dollars. It still wasn't enough to reaffirm my financial independence, but little did I know that would be the least of my worries.

I remembered Mona staring at me one day. "Babe, you're walking sideways."

"Sideways?"

"Walk over there and walk back."

I squared my shoulders and attempted to walk toward her. I felt fine before stumbling.

I called Dr. Khassi's office and made an appointment for that afternoon. I was anxious as her assistant drew blood. Dr. Khassi said I could have an infection. It was a rainy day but afterwards I didn't want to go home. I drove around aimlessly until I parked in a lot overlooking Lake Michigan. I called Mona several times throughout the afternoon, but she never picked up. I had made a habit of carrying a notebook that I wrote in every day, and I took it out and scribbled down my feelings.

I was dialing Mona again when Dr. Khassi called. She confirmed that I was having a flare-up due to an infection. She called in a prescription for vertigo. I was thrown for a loop when she said she would have to increase my steroids. She said it was temporary, but that it was the best course to fight the infection. I knew it was only temporary, but my face had just returned to its normal size. I saw the way people looked at me. I knew I was blessed to not have a terminal disease, but having a chronic illness was taking its toll, physically and mentally. Again, I called Mona and she didn't pick up. I sat in the parking lot until the lampposts came on.

I drove past CAPA and looked up at her office window. It was dark, which meant she'd gone for the day. I drove home and was surprised to see her truck in the garage. I heard her voice from upstairs as I deactivated the alarm. She motioned with her finger for me to wait as she finished a call. I sat on the edge of the bed.

"Hey, babe," she said, finally.

"I've called you all day. Why haven't you answered my calls?"

She nervously began folding clothes. "I came home early to work on this donor presentation for the mayor's event."

"Who were you talking to? I just called and you didn't pick up."

"Isabelle, she was in crisis."

I spat my words out. "Crisis? You're not a damned therapist! I'm in crisis! Why are you so drawn to her?"

"She's my friend."

"Your friend? We just met this bitch!"

I was furious and hurt. I took off my clothes, showered, and got into bed. I tortured myself, wondering what Mona saw in her. Isabelle had a nondescript body with wide shoulders. She was rather plain when she was offstage. Was Mona drawn to the commonality of their southern upbringing? Was it her lifestyle? After all, she was twelve years younger and she had resources that I didn't have. No, she couldn't be attracted to her. Could she?

My deepest fears were confirmed when we spent that weekend at our house in Michigan. Mona was installing a wooden wall in the bathroom. I was sitting on the bed, writing. The sound of her laughter as she talked on the phone was unnerving. She often talked to me or to no one at all as she completed home projects. The joy that was once reserved for me was no longer mine. I was incensed as I listened to her cautiously answer Isabelle's questions. It was obvious she didn't feel comfortable talking in front of me. I met her gaze with disdain each time she glanced at me. She finally hung up the phone two hours later and stepped into the doorway.

"I bought the wrong screws. I need to run to the hardware store before they close. Do you want to ride with me?"

I couldn't hide my sadness. She never asked if I wanted to ride with her. It was unspoken that I always would. "I'll ride with you."

I threw on some tennis shoes and we drove in silence. After fifteen years together, not communicating openly with each other was something new.

She finally spoke. "This jealousy thing is not cute. You don't want me to have any friends." Her jawline tightened.

"Jealousy? I've never been jealous of anyone because you never gave me reason to be. You're changing."

"I'm changing? I want to change! I don't need this right now! I'm stressed at work, and now I can't have friends?"

"You have friends who've been in your life since you were eighteen," I noted. "You don't spend that kind of time with any of them on the phone. You don't even like talking on the phone! I feel like I'm losing my best friend."

She rarely cried, so I was shocked when her eyes welled with tears. In my mind, I dared her to shed a tear over someone we both just met.

"I thought I was your best friend," I said softly.

She stared straight ahead. "You are my best friend, but she's my next closest best friend."

"How is she your best friend after me? We just met her three months ago," I said, before adding, "You need people to need you. I want you, but I don't need you."

That was the moment I realized I was losing my best friend and my wife. The pain was unbearable. I felt sick to my stomach, knowing that infidelity doesn't start with physical or sexual interactions. It starts when one partner hides conversations and feelings from the other. But…she always told me that I would be the first to know if she wanted something or someone else. Was it my ego talking? This was the first time in fifteen years that I didn't know what to do.

I was ashamed to tell my sister. I could hear her now: *See, that's why I can't be around a lot of bitches.*

Mona and I went to sleep that night without kissing goodnight.

I woke up the next morning with a renewed sense of unconditional love. If Isabelle was her friend, then I would support their friendship. I loved Mona. I prayed and asked God to give me strength and guidance because I didn't understand this journey we were on. My prayers were answered when she pulled me closer.

"I love you and I hate when we're not getting along," she said. "I don't know how to function. There is no one that I love more than you."

"I love you too, but please, if you ever want someone or something else, love me enough to tell me. It would break my heart knowing you weren't the person I thought you were. Love me enough to be honest. I deserve that much."

She kissed the nape of my neck. "I will. I promise."

Her words were soothing to my heart, but my head told me that weekend was the beginning of the end.

CHAPTER THIRTY-FIVE

The urgency to re-create myself welled up inside of me like a phoenix rising from the ashes. I was grateful when Char referred me to a self-publishing company for my book. Level Up Publishing was run by Devon Brooks, who had the voice of a young Geoffrey Holder.

"Nikki, thank you for considering Level Up for your first manuscript. I read your excerpt and couldn't put it down," he said. We spent the next hour creating a production timeline. Finally, my book was closer to becoming a reality. Still, I continued to ignore the signs for clarity that I asked God to send me.

Mona came home that evening with a smile on her face.

"Babe, the mayor chose CAPA as one of the nonprofits to highlight to a private group of donors."

"That's cool. When will that be?"

She opened a folder and we went over the agenda for the event. I wondered when she was going to ask for my help.

"I know you're working on your book, but I don't have anyone else who can secure donors."

"What's your hard deadline?"

"Three weeks," she said.

"That's tight, but it's doable. I'll have to throw the mayor's name around." I felt needed by her until she flipped through the folder and took out a magazine mock-up with Isabelle on the cover. My eyebrows furrowed.

"I knew you were going to react that way," Mona said.

"Why are you so enamored with her?"

"Miguel suggested we put her on the cover since she will be performing at the event. Babe, work with me on this. There'll be a lot of private donors who the mayor will personally ask to donate to CAPA."

I didn't know what to do, so I didn't do anything. I spent the next three weeks juggling CAPA goals and writing. The more I wrote, the more cathartic the process became. The story began to take on a life of its own. Contributions of Black lesbians are rarely told. I wanted to change that narrative by offering a glimpse into a world that's seldom celebrated.

My writing became an escape from my reality. And yet, I continued to give Mona the benefit of the doubt. I thought I owed it to her for taking such good care of our family when I couldn't. Yet, I felt foolish for loving so hard. Was I not enough? Was our life together not enough? I felt as though I was drowning and no one could save me.

I braced myself to feel invisible as I got dressed for the mayor's event. I decided on a vintage, floral sleeveless dress I bought when we were in Martha's Vineyard. I may have felt invisible, but I damned sure wasn't going to look invisible.

Mona picked me up and gave me a rundown of the agenda. We were escorted through a private club downtown. Mona sat me at a table with Marisol Abanto, a wealthy CAPA donor who was the chair of the Chicago Arts Endowment. We had crossed paths at previous events. We listened intently as Mona shared the mission of CAPA. I was floored when she introduced Isabelle as the newest CAPA board member. My eyes pierced through her as Isabelle took a bow before performing. As she sang, the audience was captivated. I had to admit, she had one of the most beautiful voices I'd ever heard. I tried to adjust my attitude as the program ended. I got up to thank the donors I'd secured. Suddenly, Marisol placed her hand on my elbow and guided me toward the mayor's receiving line.

I hesitated. "I'm not interested in all that."

Marisol tossed her perfectly coiffed bob. "Others may not realize it, but I know you hold Mona down, at work and at home. My staff said you were relentless in getting past my assistant." Before I could resist, she gently nudged me and I was face to face with the mayor.

"Mr. Mayor, this is Mona's better half, Nikki Blue."

He couldn't hide the surprise on his face, but he quickly recovered by cupping my hands in his. "It's a pleasure to meet you...and that dress! That looks like a work of art."

I smiled and thanked him before looking for an exit. I asked Yani where Mona's things were and she guided me to a door off to the side of the room. I sat next to her garment bag and her purse. I couldn't hide my annoyance when the door opened and in walked Mona and Isabelle.

"That was amazing! Yani said she totaled checks for almost fifty thousand dollars," Mona announced. Isabelle was preoccupied with her phone.

"So, babe. You know how you've been saying I need a break?" Mona said to me. I looked at her and nodded.

"Well, do you mind if I fly back to Ashford with Isabelle for the weekend? She said the golf course there is amazing."

Was she really doing this? Why would she put me on the spot like that? I willed myself not to react.

"If that's what you want to do."

Why didn't I say no? Anyone in their right mind would have said no.

Her face lit up. "Good! Belle, I'm going to run home, throw some clothes together, and grab my golf clubs."

I wanted to cry as she talked constantly about the event as we drove home. I went upstairs and lay across the bed as she packed.

"I'm just going to jump in a cab to the airport." She stopped and stood at the foot of the bed. "If you don't want me to go, I won't."

"I just thought you'd want to celebrate with me."

Mona sat on the bed. "I just need to get away. I haven't played golf all year."

"Do what you want, Mona."

She leaned over and kissed me on the lips. "I'll call you when I get there."

I never responded and sadly, I knew it didn't matter. I fed Misty, secured the house, and went to bed. Karlos's call woke me up.

"Hey Mom, what're you doing?"

"Taking a nap."

"Where's Mom?"

"She went to North Carolina with Isabelle."

"What? Who's this Isabelle person?"

"A friend of your mother's."

"Why do you sound so sad?"

"I'm just tired, Breezy."

"Okay, I'll check on you later."

I cried myself to sleep, wondering how I was going to handle losing my best friend and my wife.

Mona finally called that evening. She apologized for not calling sooner, but Isabelle lived deep in the mountains and she didn't have cellphone reception. I cringed at hearing the excitement in her voice as she described the waterfall on Isabelle's twenty-three acres. I told her to have a good time and that I would talk to her later. I lay in the bed and wondered if she'd already slept with her. If she hadn't, it was just a matter of time.

My questions were answered the night she returned and we had dinner at our favorite sushi restaurant. We had surface conversations on our way from the airport to the restaurant. She was detached as we ordered. I decided to break the ice.

"I'm not happy. I feel like me and Karlos, our family, isn't enough for you anymore. Are you sleeping with her?"

Mona feigned disgust. "That is so shallow! She's my friend."

I fidgeted in my seat as our waiter placed our dishes in front of us. I lost my appetite as Mona picked over her food.

"This has nothing to do with you," she said. "I used to travel at least twice a year, nationally and internationally. I haven't stamped my passport in two years."

"This has everything to do with me."

"I feel like I'm running out of time. I have this urgency to do things before I die."

"Say it. Admit we're not enough for you anymore. Is our season over?"

"If you can ask me that, then maybe it is. I need space."

"If you need space after fifteen years together, then you don't want this anymore."

"I want to travel and explore places I've never been."

"It sounds like you're having a mid-life crisis. Not in a bad way, but in a way that doesn't include me and Karlos. If that's the case, I love you enough to let you go. All I ask is that you be honest with me. I cannot imagine living my life without you. But I don't want you if you don't want me."

"I just need space." Her words hung in the air, like a stench overpowering the sweetness of the love we once shared.

"I'm going to go home and spend some time with my mother and sister. What are we going to tell Karlos?"

She lowered her head. "I don't know."

I didn't know how to feel. Early in our relationship, we made a commitment to always communicate, even when it was uncomfortable. My heart ached for our family. I hesitantly called my mother. I would have to be in a totally different headspace before I called my sister. I swallowed hard to suppress the shame that engulfed me.

"Hi, Mom."

"What's wrong?"

"Can I come and stay with you for a while?"

"Now you know, you always have a place to stay if I got a place. When are you coming?"

"As soon as possible. I have to book a flight." I was glad she didn't probe further because I wasn't ready to tell her the truth. I would call my sister when I got there. Sadness and reality overwhelmed me as I threw my clothes in a duffel bag. How was I going to start over at fifty years old? In that moment, I knew that this was no longer our home. This was Mona's home and I had to leave.

I sat on the bed and scrolled through flight schedules on my phone. I found an early flight for first thing in the morning and booked it. My chest felt heavy as I called Karlos.

"Hey, Breezy."

"Hi, Mom. What are you doing up so early?"

"I couldn't sleep, but I wanted to let you know that I'm going to stay with Grandma for a while."

He paused. "Where's Mom? Is everything okay?"

"No, it's not, but it will be."

"I stopped by Mom's studio the other day and she seemed different."

"She is different. She wants a life that doesn't include us, but she's not courageous enough to say it."

"She was saying stuff like she doesn't need someone to just make her lunch every day. She wants to travel and stuff."

"Like I said, she's not telling me or you the truth. But we, as in me and you, will be fine. We've been through worse. I'm leaving early in the morning, but I'll call you when I get to Grandma's. I love you."

"I love you, too."

I wanted to be honest with him, but I was embarrassed with my own son. I tried to maintain decency and left Mona a voice message before leaving that morning.

"I'm leaving. I'll be at my mother's if you need me."

I finally allowed myself to fall apart on the plane. I had no idea when I would return. I pulled my notebook out and began to write. I was determined not to miss any deadlines for my manuscript.

CHAPTER THIRTY-SIX

Seeing the Capitol building in the far distance brought back memories of growing up in the DMV.

I pulled out my phone. "I just landed, Mom. Give me about fifteen minutes. I have one bag, but I'm waiting for a wheelchair."

When I spotted my mother, I forgot about everything that was going on for a minute. As usual, she started dancing and hunching her shoulders.

"Hi, Mom."

"I thought I was going to have to fight those parking people. You came out just in time."

We spent the twenty-minute ride to her house catching up. She couldn't ignore my sadness any longer.

"What's wrong?"

"I think Mona is seeing someone."

"Well, fuck all that! Just come home," she said. "You don't have any family or friends there anyway. You're writing your book and who knows where that'll take you. Don't be all sad and shit."

Little did either of us know that what I was feeling was just the beginning of the heartache I would come to know.

I felt humiliated having to sleep on my mother's couch at forty-nine years old. I watched the clock on my mother's wall. I didn't know how much longer I could keep up the facade of being okay.

My mother made up the couch with sheets and a blanket. "Everything happens in God's time."

"I know, Mom." I waited for her to close her door before I lay on the couch. I placed the pillow over my face and sobbed uncontrollably.

Father God, give me the strength and guidance I need to endure. I don't know what I did to deserve this, but I surrender. I surrender to your will and not my own.

I cried until I began to gag. I lay there in the dark until my breathing slowed. I thought of being a sexual abuse survivor. I thought of being bullied in high school. I thought of the women who broke my heart. I sat up and went to the bathroom and looked in the mirror before grabbing a washcloth. I hadn't realized how much weight I'd lost. I ran the cold water over the washcloth and placed it over my face. *Remember who you are, Nikki.* My tears mixed with the cold droplets of water. *Remember. Who. You. Are.*

And at that moment, I did. I returned to the living room, turned on the light, pulled out my notebook, and began to write. I thought of Mona and who I thought she was. She may have broken my heart, but she wouldn't break my spirit.

That was the first time I pulled an all-nighter. My mother looked confused when she walked into the living room and found me awake.

"What time is it?"

"It's 3:30, Mom."

She shook her head. "You gotta get some rest."

"I can rest when I'm dead. I can't miss this deadline."

I finally got up the nerve to call my sister the next morning. "Hey, Ce."

"I was like, where is my sister?"

"I got in last night," I said.

"You sound so sad. What's going on?"

I wiped the tears from my eyes. "Me and Mona are going through something and I needed to get away."

"I'm sorry," she said. "I thought her energy was different the last time I was there."

"I don't want to talk about it right now. I just wanted to let you know I'm here."

"How's Karlos?"

"Confused and afraid."

"Well, take the time you need to figure it all out."

For the next month, I found shelter in my mother's apartment. My stepfather was his usual soft-spoken self as he tried to get me out of the house. He and my mother had ended their common-law marriage years ago and yet they still took care of each other. She cooked Sunday dinners for him, and he did whatever she needed him to do. He lived ten minutes away from the senior community building where my mother lived.

I finally broke down and told Toni and Morgan. They were disappointed when they couldn't get me to go out. I confessed that I was ashamed and didn't want to be seen. I wasn't prepared to answer questions from anyone in our circle of acquaintances. My best friends allowed me to cry and vent as best friends do, without judgement. They allowed me to rationalize her behavior. I professed that everyone had the right to move on and find happiness, but it's not what you, do it's how you do it. For fifteen years, Mona was an amazing partner and co-parent to my child. And yet, I had to question myself. Did she change? Or was this who she really was the whole time? Each night I cried myself to sleep, realizing that it was the latter.

I became obsessed with finishing my first novel. If I wasn't working on it, the days were easier as I slept them away. My mother saw right through that. She would burst through the door after work.

"You've got to get up. Open these blinds! I'm going to make you some chicken noodle soup." I dragged myself into a seated position and gave in to her demands until she went to bed.

I desperately needed something or someone to let me know that this too shall pass. *Order my steps, Father God, because I don't know what to do. I surrender to your will.*

Determination carried me through the days and grief consumed me at night. Mona would call intermittently to tell me about the mail I received, or ask me to pay bills using her debit card. She continued to deposit money into my account to supplement my disability benefits. I learned to live off seven hundred and fifty dollars a month.

Mona had a meeting in D.C. before traveling to a conference in Virginia. She invited me to stay with her at her hotel in D.C. I agreed to spend the one day she had in D.C. I packed my bag and told my mother that I'd be staying at Morgan's house to be closer to Mona's hotel. My thoughts were all over the place on the cab ride across the Fourteenth Street bridge. I was happy to see Morgan's smiling face.

"Look at you, Skinny Minnie. You ain't gonna have a problem eating, hanging with me." Morgan was tiny but she had the appetite of a man. We ordered pizza from her favorite spot. It's amazing how you can feel at peace in the presence of someone who loves you. We sat down to eat in the guest room where I would sleep.

"Mona is having an affair with Isabelle," I said.

She stopped eating.

"No…are you sure?" I brought her up to speed on all the incidents, but most importantly, what my gut instinct told me.

"Remember when I asked you to visit the same weekend Isabelle was there? Did you not feel the energy between me and Mona? Everything was about Isabelle. I asked you to come only after Mona said Isabelle had a show in Chicago and asked if she could stay with us. I needed you there for support, but I was too ashamed to tell you why."

I broke down in tears as Morgan hugged me.

"Oh, baby. I'm so sorry. Why didn't you feel you could tell me?"

"I'm so embarrassed."

Morgan pulled away and looked me in the eye. "You don't have anything to be embarrassed about. That 'B' should be embarrassed. You welcomed her into your son's life. You left your support system and had no one in Chicago but her. What a disappointment. I would've never imagined she would do this. Y'all seemed so happy."

We called Toni. I explained my situation.

"I felt the difference the last time we were there," she said. "She wasn't as talkative and she couldn't look me in the eye. I'm so sorry, Blue, but God has something better in store. We just don't know what or who it is."

I was nervous the next morning as I threw on a pair of jeans and a long-sleeved T-shirt. Why was I nervous when I'd spent the last fifteen years with this woman? I walked into the lobby of the Drexel Hotel and told them I was there to see a guest. They called Mona's room and informed her I was there. My chest tightened as I walked to her room. I took a deep breath before knocking on her door. She opened it and immediately grabbed my bag before pecking me on the lips.

"Hey."

"Hey. The hotel is nice. When did you get here?"

"I checked in about two hours ago." I could no longer believe anything that came out of her mouth. "You hungry?"

"Kind of. I haven't had much of an appetite lately."

"You look great. I can tell you've lost weight."

We ordered room service and watched a movie in bed and talked about Karlos and Misty. I couldn't take it anymore.

"Are we really going to talk about everything but us?"

She sucked her teeth. "Are you really doing this? You're going to stress me out before my presentation? I can't do this. I thought it would be nice if you stayed with me the one night I'm in D.C."

"Who *are* you?" I yelled. "I don't even know you anymore. Maybe I never did. I'm not stupid. You only invited me to stay with you because you'd feel like shit if you didn't. I can't believe you're just walking away from our family after fifteen years because you want to travel the world."

Mona turned off the TV, fluffed her pillow, and turned her back to me. "I'm not doing this with you. I have to check out early in the morning."

I grabbed my pillow and turned toward the opposite wall.

Daylight took forever to come. The alarm rang at five a.m. I reached over and hit the off button.

"I gotta leave at six o'clock to make an eight o'clock meeting," she said. "You can order breakfast. Check out isn't until noon."

"Yeah, okay."

I listened as she got ready. How did we get here? How did I let this happen? So much of my identity was tied to hers. How did I lose myself? I knew she was ready to leave when I heard her put on her jewelry. That was always the thing that completed her morning ritual.

"Thank you for staying the night. I'll call you later." She gave me a peck on my lips and walked out. I willed myself not to cry as I showered, got dressed, and hailed a cab back to Morgan's.

"Hey, sweetie. How was last night?" Morgan asked.

"What a fuckin' coward. She wouldn't even talk about us. I don't want anyone who doesn't want me, but just be honest." The sadness in my best friend's eyes made me feel sorry for myself.

Pull yourself together, Nikki! She's not the person you thought she was.

I tried to rationalize the pain away. But why did God allow our paths to cross? I'm a good person. Was this some kind of karmic debt I hadn't resolved? I stopped crying and thought about my promise to God to surrender to His will. Suddenly I felt as though I'd been hit with a lightning bolt hit. Everything was now clear. *Oh, my God…*

Mona was my blessing from God for taking care of Valencia when she was sick. Mona was my blessing in that season, and now our season was over. I got on my knees and thanked God. Mona had taken care of me and Karlos when I couldn't. No matter how unkind she was being to me at this moment, I could never take that away from her nor would I allow anyone else to.

I woke up the next morning after writing most of the night. My mother's voice echoed in my head: *If you go looking for something, you'll find it.* I opened my laptop and searched the Internet for the conference Mona said she was attending. I was relieved when it popped up. Maybe she wasn't lying after all. For some reason, I scrolled through the agenda. When Isabelle's image appeared, I immediately felt nauseated. The disappointment was worse than the deceit.

I checked on Karlos whenever I took breaks from writing. He told me that Mona said I had mail at the house and thought he should tell me. I told him to open a letter from Dr. Khassi; I had a follow-up appointment. I called Mona and left her a message letting her know I would need to stay at the house the weekend of my appointment. She didn't return my call until early the next morning.

"Sorry, I didn't have a chance to return your call. I had a full day at work. Of course, you can stay at the house, but I will be on a business trip until Monday night. Should I take Misty to the doggy hotel?"

"Thank you and no. I'd like to see her."

I was anxious as I approached the deadline for my book release. The self-publishing company I selected offered a publishing package for seven thousand dollars. I had raised four thousand with my GoFundMe campaign, but I was short three thousand. I had to find a way to come up with the rest. I had no other choice but to turn to the one person who could help me. I set my pride aside and asked my stepfather to invest in my dream. He loaned me the money to purchase my publishing package in installments.

My anxiety increased as my mother drove me to the airport. I sensed her apprehension.

"Is Mona going to be there the whole time you're there?"

"No, she said she'll be on a business trip, but she's lying. It's better for both of us if she's not there."

Once I arrived back in Chicago, I walked out of the airport into Karlos's waiting car. His radiant smile was everything I needed.

"Okay, Mom Dukes! You looking fly."

"You so crazy. Where's Kiya and Connor? She's such a good mother."

"You'll see them tomorrow. She's working late and he's spending the night over her mother's house. Kiya and I are taking you to a new sushi spot tonight."

"Yummy! How've you been?" We chatted on the way to Mona's house. I caught my breath at the sight of the house, but I had to be strong in front of Karlos.

"You have your keys, right Mom?"

"Yeah, I have them, but you know you gotta come in and check the house for me."

"You are such a scaredy-cat, Mom, but okay." My heart raced as he unlocked the door. Misty jumped on us as soon he opened the door.

"Hey, girl. What you doing?" Her tail wagged as she jumped up and licked me.

I sat on the bench in the foyer and began to sort through the mail. My eyebrows furrowed when I picked up a letter addressed to Isabelle White. At this address. *Wow, Mona. You didn't waste any time.*

I braced myself as Karlos walked me upstairs. I waited in the kitchen as he checked the house. Although I knew this was no longer my home, I did what any other woman would do. I opened the refrigerator and saw food that we didn't eat. I looked through the cabinets and saw a set of teacups. Mona didn't drink coffee or tea, but I remembered buying organic tea for Isabelle the first time she stayed with us.

"What are you doing, Mom?"

"A woman knows when another woman has taken her place."

He looked confused. "Wait…are you and Mom getting a divorce?"

"I'm sorry. I should have talked to you sooner. We'll probably get a divorce."

He wiped his eyes. "Is it Isabelle?"

"Yes, honey."

"I hate her! She was always here too much. Why did she have to stay at our house whenever she performed in Chicago? And who comes to visit on your anniversary?" Yes, Isabelle had even inserted herself into a celebration that was supposed to be for Mona and me alone. Even Karlos had thought it was strange.

I took off my coat and hugged him. "I'm sorry I didn't tell you sooner, but I've been so sad."

"But what are you going to do, Mom? You sold our house and left our family for us to be a family with Mom."

"I know, but it's going to be okay. She's not telling me the truth, but I know what I feel."

He lowered his head. "I didn't want to tell you, but I was so mad at Mom. I needed something out of the closet from my old room and I just came in with my keys. Mom went crazy, talking about I had to call before I came over. I was like, why? This is my damned home. Isabelle was half-dressed and I guess I surprised her. This is crazy."

"I know you're sad, but we'll be okay. We always are. Thank you for checking the house." He held me longer and tighter that time.

I felt like I was walking in quicksand as I walked to our bedroom level. I exhaled when I entered the guest room and didn't see anything out of order. I knew it was only a matter of time.

I took off my shoes and headed toward our bedroom. It broke my heart to see a picture frame was placed face down on her nightstand. Dean had taken a black-and-white photo of me and Mona embracing at our Michigan house. Only my face was visible, and what stood out was my hand on the nape of Mona's neck. We had been so in love. But now I felt as though someone had punched me in the stomach. I looked at the replica painting on my side of the room. It took up half the wall. I knew her better than any-one – she was struggling with her decision to take it down. She couldn't bear looking at our photo before going to bed each night. Laying it flat would give her some relief from the guilt. She hadn't gotten around to taking the painting off the wall. It confirmed for me that Isabelle hadn't slept in our bed…yet. I assumed they slept in the guest room downstairs, because what woman would want to see an image of her lover's wife before she closed her eyes each night?

Memories resurfaced as I sat on my side of the bed. I remembered when Isabelle was in Chicago for a gig. It was our anniversary weekend. Isabelle and I waited in the car while Mona ran into Nordstrom's to buy some makeup. I tried having a conversation with Isabelle, but it was like pulling teeth. She perked up when Mona got back into the car. Mona pulled a box out of the bag and handed it to me.

"What is this, honey?"

Her dimples deepened. "It's an early anniversary present. Open it."

I opened the box and squealed. "Oh my God! We can't afford this right now. Aww…I love you so much." I took the sparkling watch out of the box and put it on. She looked down at it and we instinctively held hands. I remember Isabelle's words as if it were yesterday.

"I want what you have."

The next day, as I lay on my side of the bed, even more memories engulfed me. I recalled how Mona said she wanted to travel. The issue came to a head when she told me that Isabelle had a concert in Amsterdam and that she'd included Mona's ticket into her budget as a gift. I couldn't help asking if she would have her own room. She said it made sense that they'd share a room. I felt sick. We argued for days. We hit a tipping point when I spat out the obvious.

"You're fucking her!"

"She's my friend!"

"What attracts you to her? She's always talking about having crushes on married men. Didn't she tell you that she had an emotional affair with her guitar player and her drummer? What about that old married white man she wrote a song about?"

Mona got up and walked out of the room. A week later she flat out told me that life was too short and she was accepting Isabelle's gift. I found it odd that she was irritated when I refused to hold her hand as we drove to the airport. We never kissed goodbye. I tried to shake the memories from my mind.

Karlos's call interrupted my new reality. The house felt empty as I sat in the foyer and waited for him and Kiya. I almost ran to the car as Kiya jumped out of the front seat and hugged me hard. She motioned for me to sit in the front seat.

"No, thank you. He ain't killing me by driving and texting."

"I miss you!"

"I miss you, too," I replied.

Having dinner with Karlos and Kiya that evening lifted my spirits, if only for the moment. I was not going to give Mona the pleasure of putting me out. That evening I packed my most cherished belongings. I felt lost as I lay in the guest bed. I tortured myself more, wondering for the millionth time what I had done to deserve this. I had already asked Mona to pack the rest of my things and have Karlos ship them to me at Mom's, and then I began to search for a transportation company to ship my car. I asked Mona to drive it and keep it in the garage so I wouldn't accumulate parking tickets. I'm sure she was happy that I was making it so easy for her.

"Let me know how much it costs to ship and I'll pay for it," she told me. "You can have whatever furniture you want from the house in Michigan."

"Where am I going to put it, Mona? I don't have a place of my own and my mother lives in a one-bedroom apartment in a senior building."

Rehashing those ugly conversations made my stomach turn. I couldn't stay in that house another night. I made the decision to stay with Kiya and Karlos so I could see Connor. I walked down the stairs and waited for Karlos and Kiya to pick me up. I was sad as I patted Misty's head before leaving.

I got into Kiya's Jeep and immediately picked up on her energy. We had surface conversations as we drove to their apartment. Her son, Connor, ran to me and wrapped his arms around my legs as soon as I walked through the door.

"Miss Nikki, do you want to play Connect 4 with me?"

"Okay, but I don't let kids win."

Karlos walked out of their room and put on his coat. "Hey, Mom. I'll be back."

"Where are you going? I just got here."

"I know, I'll be back."

Connor and I played on the living room floor until it was his bedtime. I was caught off guard when Kiya went into the bathroom and started curling her hair. I sat at the kitchen table and we talked through the door.

"Why are y'all fighting on my last night in Chicago?"

"I'm not perfect, but Karlos..." Just then, her phone rang. "Where are you?" she asked. "Your mom's leaving in the morning and you're not here?" She shook her head in disgust and hung up the phone.

"Where is he?"

"Outside, smoking in the car."

Karlos soon walked into the house and slumped on the couch. Kiya left the apartment without saying a word to either of us.

"I'll be right back, Mom."

I was I disbelief as he turned to walk away again. I covered my face with both hands and burst into tears.

"Everyone is leaving me." I sobbed as he walked over and placed his arms around me.

"It's okay, Mom."

"It's not okay. I'm sorry I have to leave you here in Chicago by yourself, but I can't stay here. I need my mother. I just want my mother."

He rocked me in his arms until I stopped crying. He pulled me to my feet and guided me to the couch. He lay me down before pulling a blanket over me. He kissed me on my forehead and lay his head against mine as I fell asleep.

Connor was standing in the hallway when I walked out of the bathroom the next morning.

"Do you have to go, Miss Nikki?"

I walked over and sat on the steps near his room. "I do have to go, punkin, but I will be back to see you as soon as I can. I need to go see my mommy." I opened my arms and he fell into them.

"Go back to sleep until your mommy wakes up. Karlos is going to take me to the airport." Just then, Kiya walked out of their room as Karlos walked toward it.

"Let me wash my face and brush my teeth, Ma."

I sat there while they ignored each other. I put my coat on and kissed Kiya.

"I love you." She hugged me.

"I love you, too."

Karlos held my hand as we drove to the airport.

"I'm just going to say this," I said. "Y'all have got to do better. Connor picks up on all that negative energy. He will remember how you treated his mother. I didn't raise you like that, Karlos!"

"But Mom, you always take her side."

"I'm not taking her side. I don't even know what you're arguing about, and I don't care. But I didn't raise her, I raised you. I know what kind of man I raised you to be. If you don't want to be together, then go your separate ways."

"I don't want to be with anyone but her. She just drives me crazy in a way that no one has."

I tried to lighten the mood. "Y'all need to grow up. You both are still so young. Maybe you need a break to experience life and other people. Shit… I'm surprised y'all haven't killed each other by now." I squeezed his hand as he burst into laughter. "Everything will be fine, honey."

"I don't want you to be sad, Mom."

"This is just the beginning of my sadness, baby, but time heals all wounds. I just need Grandma right now. You'll face hurts and heartaches in life and you won't want anyone but me. This is one of those times for me." I put on a happy face as we pulled up to the airport.

"I love you, Mom."

"I love you, too. I'll text you when I land."

I smiled as he shimmied to his car. I was happy that I was on the first flight out. The flight wasn't crowded. I chose a seat in the back of the plane. I buckled myself in and pulled my collar up over my face as far as I could. I hoped no one heard me crying as we soared over Chicago. The guilt was overwhelming as my heart shattered into a million pieces. I was leaving my baby in this big city without me. I thought about how he was becoming the son I always dreamed of. He would be just fine until I returned. I didn't know when or why, but I would return. My baby was here.

CHAPTER THIRTY-SEVEN

My face lit up when I saw my mother waiting curbside. "Hi, Mom. Thank you for picking me up."

"You don't have to thank me. What were you gonna do, walk to my place?"

We cackled all the way home. I welcomed the distraction of writing early into the mornings. I once read somewhere that writers who write into the wee hours of the morning are called "angel writers." Angel writers are most creative when the world is still. There are no noises, no voices other than the ones that come alive on the pages.

Devon, my publisher, called three weeks before my fiftieth birthday to tell me we were on track for a June 4 release. I couldn't believe how God was working in my life. My first novel would be released on my fiftieth birthday! Once the book was off the presses, Devon and I agreed to meet halfway between New York and D.C. so I could get my copies. My stepfather agreed to drive me the three hours north to the meeting point, since my mother had to work.

In the meantime, I had to finish writing. I pushed myself even harder. I pulled all-nighters for those next three weeks. My first novel was fiction, but it was loosely based on my life. I wanted readers to root for the main protagonist. I wanted them to want her to win as her strength was tested. Little did I know that those words would ring true in my own life. Once I met with Devon, Morgan wanted me to return and spend the night with her. The plan was that I would bring copies of my new book and sign them for some of her friends. Toni would be there as well. I couldn't believe I would become a published author on my fiftieth birthday.

I was asleep on the couch after pulling an all-nighter when my phone rang. It was my son.

"Hey, Mom. What are you doing?"

"Resting. Is everything okay?"

I sat up when Karlos hesitated.

"Mom is getting married."

I shook my head to wake myself up. "Married? To who?"

"To Isabelle…"

I was speechless.

"Mom?"

"How did you find out?"

"She called me. We were talking about me helping her get the CAPA café running until I found a new position."

I stuttered. "What…what did she say?"

"She said, 'Well, it looks like this is happening. I'm getting married.'"

"And what did you say?"

"I asked to who and she said, 'Isabelle.' I asked her if you knew and she said no, but I could tell you if I wanted to. Then, she invited me to their wedding."

I took a deep breath. "I'm sorry she put you in the middle of this. Are you okay, honey?"

"I don't know. This is just so crazy. Where did Isabelle come from? I don't see what Mom sees in her. She's so weird. I hate her!"

"Don't say that, honey. You shouldn't hate anyone."

"But I do. She broke up our family."

"No, she didn't break up our family. Your mother broke up our family. I don't care for Isabelle, but no one can break up a marriage but the two people in it."

Though I tried to sound calm, I felt like someone had punched me in the chest. My stomach was in knots as I thought of her cowardice. *You had my child tell me that you're marrying the woman you denied having an affair with? What a fucking coward! Who does that? You can hurt me, but why hurt him? And besides, in the state of Illinois, we're still legally married. What did I do to deserve this?*

I swallowed to keep from throwing up. After hanging up with Karlos, I dialed my sister's number and fell apart as soon as I heard her voice.

"Mona is marrying Isabelle."

She whispered into the phone, "Oh...my...God. I'm so sorry. How did you find out?"

"This lowlife bitch had my child tell me."

"I'm leaving the office now. I'll call Mommy. I'm on my way."

I rolled up into a ball and cried until my stomach cramped. I couldn't help going over scenarios in my head. I would have respected her if she'd just left me. But to make me feel insecure while she was being deceitful was disappointing. She promised she would never cheat on me. Who was this person I had laid beside every night for fifteen years?

My mother and sister were there within thirty minutes. My sister rushed over to me and held my hands as I sat up.

"This is awful. I am so sorry you're going through this. No one deserves this. I knew that bitch Isabelle had ulterior motives."

"I kept begging Mona to tell me the truth and she continued to lie."

My mother sat beside me and began to rub my back as I fell into her arms. "Oh, Mommy..."

"You're going to be all right. I'm glad you're away from those dirty bitches. Why does she want to be with her? Her shoulders look like a linebacker's!" I gagged as snot flew out of my nose as me and my sister burst into laughter.

"You're so crazy, Mom," I said.

My sister got up to get me some toilet paper to wipe my nose. "I know it hurts, but you've always been in her shadow. Now you don't have to be. I cannot imagine how painful that must have been. You're going to do amazing things and shine in your own light." My sister left, promising to return if I needed her.

My mother tried to soothe my heart the only way she knew how. "I'm going to fry some chicken wings, cabbage, and potatoes. You need to eat."

"I'm not hungry. I need to lie down." I lay back on the couch and pulled the covers over my head. Was God punishing me? Who did I hurt?

A darkness that I hadn't felt since my childhood came over me. I wanted to die. I didn't want to kill myself, but if I could lay down and not wake up, that would stop the pain. Mona was just like everyone else who'd hurt me. I was married to someone for fifteen years whom I didn't even know. What was in me that allowed me to love someone more than I loved myself? I was ashamed and humiliated. I couldn't even say that I was the last to know. I addressed it when I felt it in my gut, but she lied until the very end. I was devastated. I had to find a way to ease the pain.

I felt a sense of accomplishment when I submitted my final draft to Devon. Four days later, I received the layout. I, Nikki Blue, had written a book. I couldn't stop staring at the cover. The model was a young woman based out of New Jersey. She was doing a breast cancer awareness campaign for one of Devon's clients. She agreed to do my cover pro bono to build her portfolio. She was perfect for the image of *Little Girl Blue*. There was a combination of vulnerability and strength in her eyes.

I could finally rest after submitting my manuscript. I thought of the people who assumed I had disappeared to wallow in sadness. I mustered up the strength to call the one person who had to have known what was going on with Mona.

"How long did you know?" I asked.

Dean wasn't a good liar. "I didn't know, boo."

"You had to know. The projects you've done with Mona and Isabelle are all over your social media. You were my friend."

"I didn't know how to tell you. You were so in love."

"We're married! I'm supposed to be in love."

She was silent.

"I hope you know that if you go to this bullshit wedding, I'm done," I declared.

"Come on, Nikki. I'm friends with both of you. Plus, I do projects with her."

"Are you fuckin' kidding me? You were my friend first! You drove me to college. Does loyalty mean anything to you?"

"Don't ask me to choose."

"I want to make myself very clear. If you go to this ceremony, you're dead to me."

I realized that I couldn't become who God was preparing me to become and still be married to her. Our season had ended. She couldn't go where God was taking me. I had several epiphanies and yet, the way she treated me broke my heart. But my midnight sob sessions ended when I stopped feeling sorry for myself. Mona agreed to pay a year-long lease whenever I found an apartment. She scoffed at the seventeen-hundred-dollar-per-month rent on the apartment I wanted. She had the right to change her mind, but she didn't have the right to discard me like trash. I deserved the lifestyle I had before her and with her.

Word got back to me through a mutual friend that she was proudly announcing her partnership with Isabelle. I blocked them both from my social media so I wouldn't have to re-live the hurt. I was embarrassed until I realized that they deserved each other. I decided that they weren't the only ones who were going to tiptoe through the tulips and live happily ever after.

I thought of the time we went to one of Isabelle's shows. Her mother had flown in, and Mona picked her up from her hotel. We sat with Miss Thomasina at the show as she shared hilarious stories with us. She told us that she had the gift of being a medium. In the middle of one of her stories, she stopped and looked at me.

"Spirit put it on my heart to tell you that you are the one." Mona and I looked at each other and back at her.

"What does that mean, ma'am?" I asked. She slowly shook her head.

"I can't tell you that, but it's what spirit put on me to tell you."

I replayed her words over and over in my head. I thought of Mona and the stories she told of her past relationships. I could't recall any of her exes fighting back after being discarded when she no longer wanted them. I thought of Miss Thomasina's words. *Yes, I am the one. I will fight back. This was going to be a battle between David and Goliath.*

At five a.m. the next morning, I picked up my phone and searched the Internet for the top LGBTQ family law firms in Chicago. There were a few with three-star reviews, but there was only one that had a five-star rating:

Judith Katz and Associates. I took a screenshot of their contact page and closed my eyes, knowing that I was in for the fight of my life.

I was anxious when my stepfather picked me up and we headed to meet Devon. We hadn't had a chance to catch up since I left Chicago. I confided in him about hiring an attorney. I was ashamed to tell him that I didn't have the two hundred and fifty dollars for the consultation.

"Damned right!" my stepfather said. "Y'all are married. She can't just leave you with nothing. That's why marriage laws were created."

"I'm so embarrassed."

"Why are you embarrassed? She's the one who cheated."

"I have nothing." I began to cry.

"What are you crying for?"

"I have to retain an attorney. I think I can win, but I don't even have the money for a consultation. She's not expecting me to fight back."

"You have to fight back! You were just as good to her as she was to you."

"But how can I start over at fifty? I feel so broken."

"You're not broken. You have to bend a little, but whatever you set your mind to, you've always done it."

"Thank you for always believing in me. I haven't told anyone but you because I don't want them telling me what I should do. I know in my gut that I can win."

"What do you need to hire the attorney?"

"I'm thinking two to three thousand. I have to pay a two-hundred-and-fifty-dollar consulting fee to see if she'll even take the case."

"Call them. I'll give you my credit card for the consultation. When the time comes, I'll pay her retainer."

We arrived at the halfway point before meeting Devon. We ran inside to get something to drink, and Devon was pulling up when we walked out.

"We did it!" He popped the trunk and stood with his arms open. He was a tall chocolate man with a robust smile.

"Yes, we did it! You told me you would publish my first book and you did."

"You did all the hard work. This is a major accomplishment. Are you ready to see your baby?" He reached into a large box and pulled out my book. I placed my hand on my chest. "Don't do it! Don't start crying. You've worked hard for this. Thank you for choosing Level Up to make your dreams come true."

I couldn't stop looking at the cover and my author photo on the back. I turned to my stepfather. "Look at your daughter!"

My stepfather turned the book over from front to back. "You always do what you say you're going to do."

I told him about my dream of writing a screenplay and turning *Little Girl Blue* into a movie on the ride back home. I felt like a little girl as he nodded in approval. I always wanted to make him proud.

I couldn't wait for my mother to get home. I set all my books up on the kitchen table. I lay on the couch and allowed myself to bask in the joy of becoming a published author. I sat up when I heard my mother's keys in the door.

"Okay, Mom. Look on the table." She walked around the counter and starting dancing when she saw my books.

"All right, now!" She picked up one of the books and turned it over. "This picture looks classy."

"Thank you, Mom. That's the one you said was your favorite."

I smiled as I listened to her call her friends and tell them my books had arrived. I hadn't felt that good in a long time. I packed my duffel bag for the weekend at Morgan's. My mother, sister, and I decided that we would start creating memories and experiences together. Whoever had a birthday, the other two would select a new restaurant and foot the bill for the birthday girl. My birthday fell on a Sunday, so it worked out perfectly. I would spend Friday and Saturday night with my girlfriends and head back to Virginia so we could celebrate my birthday.

I couldn't wait to see my best friends. I was the first to arrive at Morgan's. She buzzed me in and met me the door. She kissed me and grabbed the box.

"My best friend is an author!"

"I know, right?"

"Well, you better get ready because the lesbians are going to be after you."

"I wish the hell they would. I'll bust somebody's head open to the white meat!"

One by one our friends began to arrive. We ordered pizza and one of Morgan's friends made cocktails.

"Okay, y'all. Before we unveil my best friend's first published book, we are going to cut the cake." Morgan opened the oven and took out a home-made chocolate cake. She turned off the lights and lit the candles. I realized how blessed I was to have two of the most kind and loyal friends for the past twenty-seven years. I made a wish and blew out the candles.

Morgan began to cut the cake as I took one of my books out the box.

"Okay, ladies. Allow me to introduce you to *Little Girl Blue*." I slowly turned the book around to reveal the cover. I bent over with laughter at their responses.

"You better do it!"

"Work, bitch!"

"I know that's right!"

I was overwhelmed with gratitude when they asked for my CashApp so they could purchase signed copies. We took selfies and made a live video asking their social media followers to support me as a new author. I couldn't imagine a better way of bringing in my fiftieth birthday.

CHAPTER THIRTY-EIGHT

I woke up that Monday after my birthday weekend and dialed the number for Judith Katz & Associates. I inquired as to whether the firm was accepting new clients. The receptionist confirmed that it was. She instructed me to pay the consultation invoice online before forwarding me to Judith. I waited patiently.

"Nikki?"

"Yes, good morning."

"I'm Judith Katz and I specialize in family law for the firm. Rayna said you were interested in retaining our services. Why don't you tell me more?"

I gave Judith an overview of what was going on in my marriage. She instructed me to access the retainer contract online. Her fee was twenty-five hundred dollars. A five-hundred-dollar security deposit was required. I tried to sound unfazed as we ended the call. My stepfather said he would give me the money, but I didn't feel good about asking for more. And yet, I had no other choice. I knew that to win this battle, I had to have the best representation. I had to strike while the iron was hot.

I couldn't tell anyone about retaining an attorney until I struck the first blow. Silence is the most powerful weapon of all. I called my stepfather and recapped my consultation with Judith. He gave me his credit card number over the phone. Twenty-four hours after retaining Judith, I received a barrage of bank and mortgage statement requests from Rayna. I thought I would feel good about fighting back, but I didn't.

That very next day, my phone rang and Devon's name popped up on my phone.

"Did you get my message?"

"No. What did I miss?"

"You missed the fact that *Little Girl Blue* just became a number one international bestseller for lesbian fiction on Siren!"

"You know what? You gonna stop playing with me."

"You, Nikki Blue, are an international bestselling author."

I lay back on the couch and opened my email. The message regarding my bestseller status on Siren was mind blowing. I didn't have to stand in anyone's shadow ever again. I enlarged the press release and walked into the kitchen where my mother was cooking.

"I got something to show you, Mom."

"Wait, I don't have my glasses on." I took mine off and handed them to her. I watched her eyes adjust to the screen. She looked over the glasses at me and back to the screen.

"What does this mean?"

"It means your daughter is a number one international bestseller on Siren."

She gave me a high five. "I knew you could do it!"

I lay back on the couch and called my stepfather and shared the news. He told me that he didn't expect anything less. Karlos and Kiya were ecstatic when I called. This was just the beginning of my journey as an author.

Reality set in before I could fully enjoy my accomplishment. Three days after my book release, Judith forwarded the contract for representation. Mona had gone on with her life and I deserved to do the same. The last time we spoke was for our birthdays. I sent her a card and she deposited some money into my account. I noticed that she responded to my calls late at night or early in the morning. I knew she was calling me whenever Isabelle wasn't around. I needed my car and had no other choice but to break down and call her. I told her that I'd found a transportation company that would pick up the car and deliver it to Virginia for fifteen hundred dollars. She was more than happy to respond. She told me to use our shared debit card and to let her know before I made the transaction. I took the opportunity to revisit our conversation about my apartment search. All the apartments I was interested in fell into the seventeen-hundred-dollar range. Again, she pushed back.

"You need to find something cheaper."

"This is the apartment I want. I helped furnish the houses in Michigan and Chicago after the brick wall situation. I should be able to live in a safe neighborhood, just like you."

"I can't afford to pay three mortgages."

"You should have thought about that before."

Judith called me three days before Mona and Isabelle's so-called wedding. Karlos had mentioned the October date when Mona had the audacity to invite him. He couldn't comprehend the idea that someone who raised him during the most formative years of his life was manipulating him. Inviting him to their wedding would make their friends and family think that he supported their union. Judith was going to have Mona served with the lawsuit the Tuesday after that long weekend in October. I remembered that Isabelle's birthday was that same weekend. I wanted to make sure there was no room for Mona to imply their wedding was a birthday party. They might as well have just jumped the broom because in the state of Illinois, Mona and I were still legally married. I shared my concerns with Judith. She said they were basically having an expensive party. The longer Mona was married to me, the more alimony she would have to pay.

I wondered who would inform me of the chaos that I had just set in motion. Would it be Judith or Mona? To my surprise, it was neither. It was my son.

"Mom!"

"What's wrong?"

"Mom is trying to reach you."

I chuckled. "I guess the fuck she is."

"She said if you don't drop this case then she can't be in my life anymore." I heard the hurt in his voice through the phone.

"What parent would say that to their child?"

"She said she has resources, and you don't."

"Well good, because she's going to need every fucking dime!"

On the first business day following that long weekend, I received a copy of the notification Judith emailed to Mona. The first two lines jumped off the page: "Dear Mona Hatchett, I have been retained by your wife, Nikki Blue, to represent her in the case to dissolve your marriage. Please contact me by close of business Friday to further discuss this matter." I read one line over and over: "I have been retained by your wife." She might as well have said, "Bitch, did you forget you're married? Call me!"

That night, I asked Ce to stop by Mom's house on her way home from work. She looked bewildered when she came in and kissed us both on the cheek.

"What's going on?"

I motioned for them to join me on the couch. "I know you've been worrying about me, but I had to grieve before anything else. Close your eyes, now open them, and read this." I watched as my sister's eyes widened.

"You better be glad Mommy is here and I can't cuss like I want to. But yes! Yes, Nikki! I was so tired of her being so mean to you when she was the one that cheated." She reached over and hugged me. "I'm so happy for you but you're nicer than me. Karma and the universe will handle the rest."

My mother looked confused. "What the hell is happening?"

My sister and I fell out laughing as she handed my mother the letter. "Sorry, mom," she said. "Read it."

"Good! You didn't deserve what she did or the way she did it. I'm going to go read my Bible."

Ce motioned me to the couch and peeked around the corner to see if my mother had shut her door.

"Mommy was so upset the day you called and told me Mona and Isabelle were getting married. She got here before me, but she called me and asked if I were close by. She didn't want to see you hurting like that by herself. She kept saying, 'That's my child. That's my child.'"

I knew that things would get uglier between me and Mona. The most important person I worried about was Karlos. At twenty-six years old, he had his own problems to deal with. Although both of his moms had told him not to move in with Kiya and Connor, Karlos had done the exact opposite. Mona never took to Kiya and Connor the way I did. Over time, Kiya and I grew extremely close. I had already fallen in love with Connor. But I wondered if Kiya would let me see him if she and Karlos broke up.

I had come to terms with the loss of a life I'd always wanted. There were days when I could barely get up. I felt like the walls were crashing down around me until Karlos and Kiya FaceTimed me one evening. They looked uncertain as they stared into the camera.

"Mom, you're going to be a grandmother."

I flew to Chicago a week after Karlos and Kiya gave me the good news. That trip coincided with Judith informing me that Mona had retained an attorney. I told her I was in Chicago visiting and I wanted to schedule a face-to-face meeting. It was important that she put my face to my name.

I couldn't wait to lay my eyes on my child. I scanned the crowd for his car outside the airport. He smiled when I started dancing and waving.

"Mom, you're turning into Grandma."

"I am Grandma!" We got to the apartment and I could barely get through the door before Connor ran to me.

"Miss Nikki! You're here!"

"I came just to see you. You are getting so tall." I hugged Kiya.

"And what have you been up to?"

She rubbed her stomach. "Obviously a lot, but Connor wants to ask you a question."

"Okay." Connor was such a gentle and precocious child. Whatever it was, I knew he had to be thinking about it for a long time.

"Miss Nikki, I want to ask you a question." He ran in front of me so he could see my face.

"You can ask me anything."

"What is my sister or brother going to call you?"

"I call both my grandmothers Nana. So, I'm sure the baby will call me Nana."

"What can I call you?"

"What do you want to call me?"

"I think I want to call you Nana, too."

"I would love for you to call me Nana." My heart melted. I had loved this child from the first day he came into my life. I no longer had to wonder how I would keep him and his mother in my life.

I wasn't sure what kind of space Karlos and Kiya were in, so I followed their lead. It had only been twenty-four hours before I noticed that Karlos wasn't emotionally present. It was on the third day of my weeklong visit when I felt the need to leave. I stayed out of their way as they fell into their routine of school and work. I was happy to have the apartment to myself.

I showered and got dressed for my meeting with Judith. I took my time getting ready and settled on a black top paired with black leggings. A black leather trench coat presented the textbook image of a grieving wife.

I pressed the buzzer for their nondescript office in Boystown. I reached the top of the steps and sat down when a tall redhead approached me.

"Nikki, it's a pleasure to meet you. Judith is wrapping up a call, but I'll let her know you're here." I looked around the office and was impressed with the LGBTQ awards the firm had received. I relaxed in the cushy chair, knowing I had made the right decision. Judith walked out about fifteen minutes later. She was at least five feet nine. Her jet-black mane framed a round face with red lips.

"Nikki, I'm so sorry. That call ran longer than I expected."

For the next hour, I briefed her on the status of my marriage to Mona. It was important that she knew the lifestyle I had before and with Mona. I inquired about what rights I had if we were still married and Mona had "married" someone else.

Judith ran her fingers through her hair. "Don't worry about that. She's spending money on a mistress using marital assets. They can't get married until your and Mona's civil union is dissolved."

The cab ride back to the Southside was surreal. It seemed like something out of a Lifetime movie. I had never wanted to be a member of the divorcée club. I was overwhelmed with sadness until I realized that in all the Lifetime movies, the wife always wins.

CHAPTER THIRTY-NINE

I was ready to get back to Virginia and move on with my new life. I ordered takeout from my favorite restaurant and got back to the apartment before Karlos and Kiya. I cleaned up the apartment and set the table. Kiya and Conner arrived before Karlos.

"What's all this?

"I wanted to treat you guys tonight since I'm leaving in the morning."

"Thank you. I'll call Karlos and see what time he'll be home."

I packed my bag while we waited for Karlos. He came in and dropped his keys on the table. I watched him walk over to Kiya and kiss her on the lips and tousle Connor's hair.

"Your mom treated us to dinner tonight."

"You don't have money for that, Mom. We were going to order pizza."

"Stay out my pockets. Oh, and I want all three of us to talk after Kiya puts Connor to bed."

I tried to lighten the mood by asking Connor to help me fix our plates. I was happy when Karlos and Kiya followed my lead and we laughed over dinner. Karlos helped me clear the table while Kiya gave Connor a bath. I was laying out my clothes when Connor shyly walked into the living room behind Kiya.

"Go give Nana a hug. She has to leave early in the morning."

"When are you coming back, Nana?"

"I don't know, honey, but it'll be soon." I sat on the couch and waited for Karlos and Kiya. Karlos was the first to join me.

"Kiya's putting Connor to bed, Mom."

"I'll wait."

"What do you want to talk to us about?"

"I said, I'll wait."

Kiya looked nervous as she sat next to Karlos.

"I wanted to talk to both of you before I left because I don't know when I'll be back. But what I do know is that you have to make some decisions before this baby is born."

I spent an hour listening to them attack each other.

"Listen! Either you leave each other alone and co-parent or grow up and work toward providing a family for Connor and this baby. Kiya, you've been a parent for three years. So, you know what sacrifices that requires. Karlos, you've been a father figure to Connor. Things are different now. If y'all decide to stay together, you'll be a father of two at the age of twenty-six. That's a lot of responsibility, but you made these decisions."

"But, Mom …"

"There is no but. It's not about you anymore. So, I suggest y'all have a heart-to-heart conversation. Karlos, you need to start looking for a higher-paying position. You gave Techworks two years. They keep promising you a promotion and it never happens. Get focused because this baby will be here before you know it."

They took turns kissing me. I waited until they shut their door before getting on my knees and praying they would make the right decisions.

It felt good being back in Virginia in the comfort of my mother's home. I was surprised when I got a call from Devon, informing me he'd secured my first book signing at Bound Books in in D.C. My sister was the first person I called.

"Hey hoes…I heard you was looking for me!" she said. We cackled as only sisters do. "Do you know how amazing this is? Congrats, Nikki."

"It hasn't hit me yet," I said. "The signing is in two weeks. Maybe your stylist can do my hair. I'll ask her if she knows a good makeup artist. Ugh… what am I going to wear? I gotta find a job because it's hard living off seven hundred and fifty dollars per month."

I had thirty days to transfer my disability benefits from Illinois to Virginia. I decided to visit the office in person when my messages went unanswered. Less than ten miles away from the office, my tire blew out. I put my hazard lights on when drivers began honking their horns. I contemplated stopping at a gas station, but that meant the line would be longer. I pulled into the Social Security parking lot and got out to view the damage. I'd cracked the rim on the front driver's side. Before I could get back into the car an attractive Black woman walked toward me.

"Are you okay?"

"My tire just blew out."

She looked at the tire. "Yeah, I saw you pull over."

"How'd you know something was wrong?"

"You had your hazards on. My husband is an FBI agent, so he taught me to be aware of my surroundings."

I extended my hand. "Thank you. I'm Nikki."

"I'm Tammy. I'm a manager for the call center. Come on, let me get one of the security guards." We were almost at the door when a guard walked out.

"Everything okay, Miss Tammy?" He was a burly brother with a kind smile.

"Hey, Bobby. Her tire just blew and she needs to call a tow. But I don't want the line to get too long." She looked at her watch.

"I can see the lot from my window. Park the car in that first space and I'll keep an eye on it until you call a tow company after you see someone."

"Thank you, Tammy."

I ran into the office, took a number, and waited. The office was packed. An hour had passed before my number was called. I explained that I needed to request the remaining balance of five thousand dollars from my disability award. The representative gave me another number and told me to wait for my name to be called. Another hour passed before I was called. I showed the representative, who was a Black woman, my determination letter. I explained the urgency given my blowout in the parking lot.

"What kind of car do you drive?"

"Excuse me?"

"What kind of car do you drive?"

"I drive a 500 SL Mercedes."

I had to maintain my composure when she said, "Maybe you should sell it to earn some cash until your balance is awarded."

"May I speak to your supervisor?"

"She's with another client."

"I got time." I waited until, as I suspected, a white woman motioned for me to approach her window. I explained my situation and asked who I could have my attorney contact. She excused herself and returned with a letter requesting my bank account information. She said the funds would be deposited into my account within seven business days. I smiled at the other representative as I left.

Just when I thought my day couldn't get worse, it did. I walked out to the car and sat in the passenger seat. I called our insurance company and requested a tow. I was shocked when the representative informed me the account had been canceled.

"How could that be? I've had this policy for years."

"I'm sorry, ma'am, but the account holder canceled the policy for the 2005 Mercedes as of yesterday."

"Who's the account holder?"

"I'm not at liberty to share that information, ma'am."

I called the first person who always calmed my nerves.

"Hey Ce." I recapped the situation.

"Wow, Mona."

"She's mad about me retaining an attorney, but I'm not backing down."

"You can't back down. Fuck her! But where are you?" I told her my location. She told me to call the insurance company and explain to them that I was going through a divorce and my wife canceled my policy of fifteen years. I called the insurance company closest to my mother's house and was relieved when I was immediately given my own policy.

I called my stepfather who told me to search for the closest Mercedes dealership. I did exactly what he said, and lo and behold, there was an auto shop that specialized in Mercedes ten miles away. He met me at the auto shop and within two hours I had a new tire and rim. He followed me back to my mother's house to make sure I got home safely.

"You know, this is just the beginning. She never expected you to fight back but don't give up. You didn't do anything wrong."

I kissed him through the window. "One day, I'm going to make you proud."

I told my mother what happened as soon as she got in from work.

"Continue to be the person God wants you to be. She will have to pay for how she's treating you."

"But Mom ..."

"Listen to what I'm telling you."

I remembered my mother's words when Judith instructed me to create a list of every item of value in both homes. The items would include everything Mona and I had purchased after our civil union was established. She also informed me that Mona had retained Jeffrey Talbert as her attorney. She mentioned that they once were colleagues. I called my sister.

"Let's research his firm and see what their reviews are." I waited as she feverishly tapped the keys. "Hold on, here are his reviews."

"My attorney is a partner with the top LGBTQ firm in Chicago, Judith Katz and Associates," I said.

"I just sent you a screenshot of her attorney's reviews. Your attorney has five stars while her attorney has two point five stars."

"He can't hold a candle to Judith. Besides, he's a man. He'll think differently than a woman. I hired an ole lesbian barracuda. She's not cheap, but she's worth every dime. I peeped her raised eyebrow when I told her my concerns about Mona's relationship with the mayor. She looked up the judge's docket we're on."

"What did she say?"

"She said Judge McClain's fair. She's not swayed by political affiliations."

"Good. She never thought it would go this far. Besides, these are public records. No one knows you guys are married and I'm sure she wants to keep it that way. At least for now."

I tried to focus on my first book signing. I had no idea what to expect. I called my sister's hairstylist, and she was happy to fit me in. Devon sent over a list of RSVPs for the reading. I was surprised that we were almost at capacity. I didn't have enough money to get my hair and makeup done and buy a new outfit, so I made the decision to prioritize my face and hair. I settled on an orange sleeveless accordion dress. I paired it with a pair of flat brown sandals with turquoise and orange beads. The makeup artist agreed to come to Morgan's house so we would be closer to the event.

"This is really happening. You've worked so hard in the face of so much adversity. How do you feel, best friend?"

"I don't think it will hit me until I'm on the stage."

My anxiety increased as Morgan zipped through D.C. rush hour traffic. I stole glances at myself in the side-view mirror. This was really happening.

Morgan dropped me off on a side street while she parked. I rounded the corner and saw a long line. I tried not to look shocked when someone yelled.

"Nikki Blue!"

Was I supposed to respond? Not knowing what to do, I simply looked in the direction of the voice and smiled. I was happy Devon was waiting for me at the entrance. He placed his hand on my elbow and guided me up a stairwell to the backstage area.

The dimming of the house lights was our cue. The curtain rose as Evelyn Ball, the publisher of *HER Magazine*, sat in a chair and introduced herself before reading my bio. I took a deep breath and stepped onto the stage. The audience applauded as I playfully bowed. I didn't relax until Evelyn asked the first question. The questions from the audience began to flow when I responded that I thought of myself as an accidental author. I only became an author to re-create myself after suffering a stroke. I became more comfortable as I read excerpts.

Devon was at the edge of the stage to guide me to a signing table. The first person in line was London. I stood up and we embraced. She still had the body of life.

"I love you, Nikki Blue," she said.

"You are wrecking nerves up in here. You know I love you. Thank you for coming." Toni leaned over and whispered in my ear.

"What character was London in the book? I know she was one of the strippers cause her body is evil!" I playfully pushed her away. I recognized a familiar face just when I thought I had signed the last book. Crystal from NSBA stepped up just as Devon moved toward me.

"We have a call with Rod at HueWeb," he said. Crystal's face fell.

"This is an old friend, give me five minutes." I hugged Crystal and shook the hand of the young woman standing beside her. "Hey lady. Thank you for coming out."

"Well haven't you become the successful author. This is my mentee, Kenyatta. She just came out to her family and they're having a rough time. I told her about you and the challenges you've overcome. I bought two books and hoped you would sign them."

I faced Kenyatta. Her eyes welled with tears.

"Aww sweetie, why are you so upset?" She wiped her eyes.

"I didn't think you would be so nice."

"Well, guess what? I am! I'm going to write my email address down if you ever need someone to talk to." She hugged me tightly.

"Thank you, Miss Nikki."

I was getting tired when Devon ushered me into a small office behind the stage.

"I didn't mean to rush you when you were talking to that young lady."

"That was me at one point in my life. It doesn't cost a thing to be kind to someone. You never know what someone is going through."

"Rod Barnes is a legend in the radio industry. He started out as a disc jockey at WBLK in New York. HueWeb is a social media platform for urban viewers. You will be the first out blogger. He gives me a hard time but he's really a teddy bear."

"Wow," I marveled, "you came out the box swinging with the media placements."

He smirked. "I pitched a monthly column, but Rod will give you the details."

I sat quietly while he dialed Rod.

"Rod Barnes, here."

"Rod, it's Devon and Nikki Blue."

"Yeah, yeah. I thought we were scheduled for three." His baritone voice was intimidating.

"We're on the East Coast. We're on time."

"Well, okay. So, what are you going to be writing about, Miss Nikki Blue?"

"Thank you for the opportunity to share my voice, Rod. There aren't enough African American LGBTQ voices in the mainstream. My articles will highlight those narratives from a lifestyle perspective. My first novel,

Little Girl Blue, is a number one international bestseller on Siren. I think the timing is right."

He chuckled. "International bestseller, huh? Well, good for you. That's a noble undertaking. You may face some pushback from some of our conservative viewers. But, if you're up to it, let's do it!"

"Thank you, Rod. I'm so excited."

"You're welcome." I waited for Devon to end the call.

"You are doing the damned thing!" He gave me a high-five.

"I couldn't have done it without you."

CHAPTER FORTY

The joy of my book release was short-lived when Karlos called me in a full panic attack.

"Mom! Why are you doing this?"

I sat up on the couch. "What are you talking about?"

"Why are you trying to take all of Mom's money? She said you need to find a job and take care of yourself."

"Why am I trying to take all her money?" I retorted. "I sold my house, left my family and friends so we could be a family. She doesn't get to leave me with nothing after fifteen years."

"She said she can't be in my life if you don't drop the case."

"I'm your birth mother. You're supposed to protect me."

"You brought her into my life. She's been my other parent for most of my life."

"Karlos, no one should ever come before me. I'm sorry that she hurt us, but you have to manage your own grief."

"I got laid off from Techworks. She's opening a café at CAPA and offered me a position to help get it started."

"I don't think that's a good idea, but you're grown. You have to make your own decisions. Moving forward, I'm asking that you don't mention her to me. I love you."

"I love you, Mom."

My heart ached for him. Since blocking her on my phone, the only way she could hurt me was by hurting my child. I took out my notebook and began to write my first article for my monthly column. My pen flowed across the paper until four o'clock that morning. I was exhausted yet exhilarated. My voice would finally be heard.

I began working on the sequel to *Little Girl Blue* when I received an email from Judith. Mona's attorney had declined our negotiated alimony amount of three thousand dollars per month for one year. Judith informed me that fifteen hundred per month was their final offer. In addition to their final offer, I would have to sign an affidavit taking my name off our house in Michigan.

"What recourse do I have?"

"As your counsel, I am required to inform you that we don't have to accept their final offer. I'm sure she doesn't want to drag this out."

"I don't have anything to lose. I've already lost everything."

Two days later, Judith informed me that Mona's attorney had not responded. She mentioned that Mona did not have as many resources as we thought she had. I informed her that was not my concern. I simply wanted what was fair.

I recalled my aunt Ros's voice: "About damned time. I was tired of you saying you didn't want to block your blessings. She's been horrible to you."

"With all due respect, Auntie. I don't care what anyone thinks. I can't do ugly things to her and ask God to bless me."

God continued to place people in my life that I would have never met on my own. My spirit was weary over fighting someone I once loved. I woke up one morning and found my first edited article from my editor. Her edits made my words and emotions jump off the page. My voice would finally be heard. I sat up and posted the article to the HueWeb platform.

I became more proficient in using social media. I was thrilled to learn that I could upload my articles to HueWeb where they could be shared to all my social media pages. Family and friends would be able to read and comment on my articles. I was surprised when Karlos and Kiya called to tell me how many people had commented on my article. They insisted that I create an Instagram page to gain more followers and support. They pushed back when I resisted.

"I don't have time to do all that. My life isn't that interesting."

"As an author, it is," Kiya chimed in. "I'll help you create a page with content, like pictures of your book cover or readings."

I exhaled. "Fine." Two days later, she called me early in the morning.

"Have you seen your IG page?"

"No, why?"

"The lesbians are after you!"

I clicked on my IG page and was shocked to see over two thousand followers.

"That's crazy! They're asking where they can buy my book."

"Right! So, send me your passwords and I'm going to put the Siren link to your book and bio up. They will be able to click on it and buy your book."

"Thank you. All this shit is new to me. I just want to write."

"You're a published author now. You gotta let people know your work is out there."

Like a rainbow after a storm, God sent me a sign that all was well. My phone pinged and there was a message from an unknown number. The woman said she read my article and she empathized with my story. I clicked on my page and read multiple comments from family and friends.

However, not everyone was happy about my editorial debut. I received an email from Judith informing me that Mona no longer had legal representation. She was adamant about not settling on the three-thousand-dollar monthly alimony. She was arrogant in her demands that I not write any future articles about my life with her. I heard the amusement in Judith's voice.

"I told her that our offer of two thousand dollars per month for two years was our final offer. As for your articles, she can't prohibit your livelihood."

Still, I hated that we were in this space. My spirit wouldn't allow me to gloat about being stuck in this hand-to-hand combat. I continued to pray, and God continued to bless me.

Early one morning, my phone pinged with a text. My eyebrows furrowed as I read the message: *I have been watching your journey. I read your book and may have a friend who is interested in your work. Are you available to talk later today? SDK.*

SDK? Who was SDK and how did they get my number? I wracked my brain until it hit me. I hadn't spoken to Siobhan Daniels-Kent since she represented Karlos during his brief acting career. She was highly respected in the entertainment industry. Her work included a vast body of movies that were classics in the African American community. I recalled her being a woman of few words.

What do I say? How do I say it? I felt like I was going to hyperventilate. I finally responded by thanking her for reading my book. I texted that I was available later that day. I assumed she was still based in Chicago. I was surprised when she asked if we could do three o'clock, given the time difference in Los Angeles. I couldn't concentrate as I watched the clock. I wanted to call my sister, but I didn't want to jinx anything. I was in a writing zone when my phone rang.

"Hello?"

"Hello, Nikki. It's Siobhan. Thank you for your flexibility. I had another call."

"No worries. I'm working on the sequel, and I needed a break anyway."

"Yes, keep writing! That's why I'm calling. I have a friend who may be interested in your work."

"What do you mean by interested in my work?"

"As in adapting your book into a film."

"I'm about to throw this phone down! What are you saying?"

"Finish the sequel and when I think you're ready, I'll make the connection. You're a great storyteller and I think the timing is right for a project like this. So, get to work and we'll keep in touch. I'm proud of you. Gotta go."

Siobhan Daniels-Kent had read my book? A producer is interested in my work? *Father God. I don't know what your plan is but if writing is my passion, show me my purpose.*

Siobhan was the guardian angel God sent to guide me. I wanted to nurture our relationship, so I decided to work in silence. I didn't want to let her or myself down. Kiya's call was the distraction I needed.

"Why haven't you called your other mother?" I asked.

"We did call you. You're so busy now that you're an author."

"I know, right? How are you feeling? How far along are you?"

"I'm five weeks but it feels like nine…" She hesitated.

"I'm sure. What's wrong?"

"Me and Karlos were talking and…we wanted to ask you if you would come and help us before the baby is born?"

"Of course. When would you want me to come?"

"We want you to be in the delivery room for the birth. It would be Karlos, you, and my mom."

"You're going to make me cry."

"Don't cry. We love you so much and we want you there."

"I would love to be there." I hung up the phone thinking about how love heals all wounds.

Karlos was excited that day when he called to share his news. "Mom, Mom hired me to work at the CAPA cafe."

"Are you sure you want to do that?"

"My experience at Techworks prepared me to create initiatives that will generate new revenue streams for CAPA."

I laughed. "You better talk that corporate shit!"

We soon realized that Mona wasn't finished hurting us. After Karlos was at the job for two months, Mona brought Isabelle in as a consultant for the CAPA café. I tried to soothe his heart.

"She has you reporting to Isabelle?"

"It's so weird, Mom. We were in a staff meeting and Isabelle was there, and Mona said, 'I don't care who has a problem with Isabelle working here.'" That was the first time I heard him refer to her as Mona and not Mom.

"Her staff was looking like, what's going on? It was so crazy. She lives with Mona now."

"You have to find another job. You can't work with the person your mother left our family for. I'm sure that's painful for you."

"It's just stupid, but Mom…"

"Yes, honey?"

"Are you still coming to help before the baby comes?"

"Of course, I am. I'll stay as long as you need me to."

Mona continued to show who she really was. I braced myself while listening to Karlos cry. I could barely understand him.

"What's wrong? Is the baby okay?"

He sobbed. "Why did she do this to us, Mom?"

"What happened?"

"Mona called me and started talking crazy shit. I'm sorry for cursing, Mom, but I've never talked to her that way. She's in denial, saying she never cheated on you and you're a gold digger who wants somebody to take care of you. I went crazy. I called Isabelle stupid and Mona said, 'I'm not Mom, I'm Mona to you.' I said, 'You're bat-shit crazy!'"

"Oh, honey. I'm so sorry you're going through this."

"Yeah, and I told her that I have to resign because I need to make more money before the baby comes. She said, 'Well, we'll find a way to get your ass out of here.' Then she had her CFO fire me. I can't believe this. Who the hell is she, Mom?"

"You needed to release all that hurt and anger. You've been holding it in for a long time. But now, you've got to find a career, not just a job. I know you're overwhelmed right now, but this is what I've prepared you for all your life. You found other people jobs when you worked for Techworks. Now, you have to do it for yourself."

"It's just a lot. We're going to have two kids now and…"

"You got this. Balls to the wall!"

He laughed. "I love you, Mom."

I couldn't sleep that night, worrying about him. My spirit was becoming more and more weary until I received an email from Judith. I was afraid to read it. I would fight to the end, but it felt like someone kept moving the finish line. I prayed before opening the email. Tears streamed down my face as I read the details of our settlement. Mona agreed to a lump sum of twenty thousand dollars, to be paid in two payments. I was also awarded two thousand dollars per month for two years. I would finally get what I deserved, to start my life over just as she had.

I immediately called my stepfather. "Good! What did she think was going to happen?"

I called my sister and got the response I expected. "She thought you didn't have a voice. Your silence was more powerful than anything you could ever say."

My mother's response was what I expected as well. "I told you. God will restore what was taken from you."

I thought about the settlement. Mona and Isabelle's relationship started two years before our separation. And there we were. She had to pay me alimony for the same amount of time she was unfaithful.

CHAPTER FORTY-ONE

I was relieved to tell Karlos the divorce was finalized.

"What are you going to do with all that money, Mom?"

"It's really not a lot of money. But I'm going to use it to start my life over. I'm just glad it's over."

"Me too, but guess what?"

"What?"

"I have an interview with Siren."

"What? How did you land that?"

"I posted my resume on a professional platform and a recruiter reached out to me."

"I told you. You've got to believe in yourself more. When's your interview?"

"It's a three-part interview process, but I'll let you know."

"You got this!"

"We got this, Mom."

Four days later, Karlos was contemplating a six-figure offer between Siren and its biggest competitor, Network. I lived for the excitement in his voice.

"Mom, what should I do? Siren offered me an IT recruiting position making one hundred thousand with full benefits. Then Network calls me for an interview. I have to make a decision by Friday. I can't accept Siren's offer and interview with Network."

"No, you can't," I agreed. "You don't want to tarnish your reputation in the recruiting industry. The ball is in your court. Let the recruiter from Network know that Siren made you an offer and ask her to counter. She wouldn't have called you if she didn't want you. Call her and be honest with her. She will want to beat Siren's offer. I'm so excited for you. Call me after you talk to her."

Our prayers were answered two days later when Karlos's interview was fast-tracked. Network countered with a package he couldn't turn down. My heart was full of pride and joy. He needed this win.

I prepared to return to Chicago for the birth of my second grandchild. Karlos and Kiya created a beautiful gender reveal video. I was over the moon to find out I was going to have a granddaughter. I called Kiya from the baggage claim.

"Nana is here!"

"Yay!" It was chilly in Chicago for the first week in April. I started dancing like my mother when I saw Kiya's Jeep. She pulled over and got out. I could see her huge belly under her jacket.

"You are so big!"

She rolled her eyes and reached to grab my bag. "Aht! Give me this damned bag."

I spent the first week cooking and cleaning so Kiya wouldn't have to. I tried to stay out of their way as they prepared for the addition to our family. Kiya's mother, JoAnne, popped up every now and then. Kiya let me know she was aware of the tension between us.

"I wished you liked my mom."

I continued to fold their clothes. "Your mom doesn't like me. It's been you, her, and Connor for so long that she's struggling with you having your own family. Connor is now my grandson as well. I've always loved him. Your children are blessed to have two grandmothers. Let's not talk about this right now. I don't want you stressed about anything."

The space in the apartment got smaller as we counted down the days for baby Kimora's arrival. The tension in the air was stifling. Karlos could do nothing right and Kiya let him know it. Late one night, I was jolted out of my sleep by loud voices in the foyer.

"What is going on?" I heard Kiya crying as Karlos threw his keys on the table.

"Shhh…be quiet before you wake Connor up," I said. "What happened?"

He shook his head. "She's crying over some damned tacos."

"What?"

"We were hanging with some friends up north and she wanted tacos from a place all the way south. I wasn't driving past our house to get tacos at midnight. I told her to order something else."

I patted the sofa motioning him to join me. "Honey, listen. Her body and mind are going haywire. Everything is magnified ten thousand times and she can't help it. She has a whole person inside of her. The baby requires more and more each day and she's not even here yet. I hate to tell you, but it's going to get worse before it gets better."

He covered his face with his hands. "I don't know if I can do this, Mom."

I chuckled. "Well, it's a little too late for that. But let me tell you a secret. Have you heard that saying, 'Happy wife, happy life?' You guys aren't married, but hopefully one day you will be. Until then, when Kiya is happy, you'll be happy."

"But what do I do?"

"Any and everything she wants. If she wants tacos at midnight, go get the damned tacos. Your life will change once Kimora gets here. There are so many things you'll have to learn, but you'll be fine. Now, go in there and apologize." I kissed him on the cheek and pushed him toward their bedroom.

We were on pins and needles as Kimora's due date came and went. JoAnne hovered over Kiya, but she also made sure I didn't have too much alone time with Connor. I knew we would have to have a come-to-Jesus conversation, but now was not the time. Everything was about Kiya and Kimora.

I heard them stirring during the early hours of April 13, 2018. Karlos rushed into the living room.

"Mom, Kiya is having contractions. The doctor wants us to go to the hospital. JoAnne will pick you up and bring you to the hospital." Kiya wobbled to the door as Karlos grabbed her bags. I was thankful Connor had spent the night with one of their friends in case Kimora came. I waited for Karlos to set the alarm before getting on my knees and praying for a safe delivery for both Kiya and Kimora. I got dressed and waited for JoAnne's call. I rushed out of the house and put on my best face.

JoAnne and I made small talk as she raced to the hospital. We rushed to the maternity ward and scrubbed in before entering the delivery room. I walked in and hugged Karlos.

"You okay?"

"It's really happening, Mom. Thank you for being here."

I sat on the couch in the corner. I watched as the nurse prepared Kiya for delivery. We all perked up when the doctor walked in and the nurses prepped him for delivery.

"We have a full house this morning. Who do we have here?" He looked at one of the nurses. She nodded toward me and JoAnne.

"Mom of dad and mom of mom." He clapped his hands.

"Wonderful! Let's meet this little lady."

I felt as though I'd been holding my breath for hours. I watched from afar as JoAnne paced around the room. I was proud of Karlos as he held Kiya's hand. He wiped her drenched mane while telling her how wonderfully she was doing.

"There's the crown. I'm going to count to three and I want you to take a deep breath before giving me a big push." I stood up and moved toward the foot of the bed.

"Okay, one...two...three...big push! Big push!" Kiya bore down hard and suddenly a little face appeared. JoAnne, Karlos, and I laughed through our tears when a little human looked around the room with open eyes.

"Oh, my goodness! Eyes wide open. I've never seen a newborn so alert," said the doctor. "One last push and she will be with Mommy and Daddy." I watched in awe as Kiya pushed. The doctor adjusted his stool and with one last push Kimora Calabrese came into the world. JoAnne and I instinctively hugged as Karlos cut the umbilical cord and the nurse placed Kimora on Kiya's chest.

"She's beautiful." Kiya kissed her forehead before a nurse motioned Karlos to a chair beside her bed. He removed his shirt and cradled Kimora in his arms before laying her on his chest. I watched my son become a man.

I was emotionally drained as JoAnne drove me back to their apartment. I was happy I had the place to myself. I closed my eyes and realized Kimora was born one day before my mother's birthday and the same birth date as Kiya's paternal grandmother. My mother and her great grandmother would always watch over her.

I remembered the clichés my grandmothers used to say: *When there's a death, there's a birth.* They never told me that the death didn't have to be in body. It could be in mind and spirit. I suffered the death of my marriage and the life I thought I would have. But God gave me new life with the birth of my granddaughter. I had to be strong for her. I had to show her what courage and resilience looked like. I loved Connor just as much, but this world was a different place for little Black girls.

I couldn't wait to get dressed that morning. I took a cab to the hospital to meet Miss Calabrese. I stopped in the gift shop and bought a bouquet of flowers for Kiya and a teddy bear for Kimora. I gently tapped on their door.

"Hi…" I whispered as Kimora nuzzled into Karlos's chest.

"Look at her, Mom."

"Oh, my God…but why does she look like you only carried her. Look at those Calabrese lips and those rosy cheeks. She's perfect."

Kiya sleepily opened her eyes.

"Do you want to hold her?"

"Let me wash my hands." I hurried to the bathroom and scrubbed my hands before returning to the couch. Kiya instructed me to place her baby blanket on my shoulder. I listened as she lovingly coached Karlos how to hand her to me.

"Babe, make sure you hold her head."

I cradled my arms as he gently handed her to me. "She smells so good, Kiya." I spent an hour gushing over my granddaughter before rushing to the airport. I had to find a job if I was going to be able to visit as often as I wanted to. Then I remembered I was supposed to receive my first alimony payment from Mona the month before. I had grown accustomed to doing so much with so little that I forgot about it.

I checked my account and the deposit had not been made. I voiced my concerns to Judith about Mona not making the deposits on time. She included a clause requiring Mona to pay a fifty dollar per day late fee. I appreciated Judith's effort, but I knew Mona Hatchett. She was going to make the deposit at the last minute, out of spite.

I was so wrapped up in my own world that I lost touch with what was going on with my family. My sister reminded me that we were supposed to drive home to New Jersey to visit our family.

"You need to get away," she said. "You don't do anything but stay in the house and write. A girl's trip with Mommy will be fun."

We rented an SUV for the weekend. We were outdone when we got to the rental site and our car wasn't available. My mother and I stepped back and let my sister to do what she does best…negotiate. Thirty minutes later, we pulled off the lot in a white, drop top Mustang.

We made a coffee run before heading up 95 North. My mother was in the back seat scrolling the Internet while me and my sister caught up.

"It hurts me that you're so sad."

"I know, Ce. I'm trying to regain my independence but it's so hard. I never thought I would be starting over at fifty."

"I know, but now you can finally live the life you've always wanted. You don't have to stand in anyone's shadow. You have your beautiful grandchildren, and you'll find someone who's courageous enough to love you openly."

"I don't know if I even believe in love anymore. Maybe I'll join a convent."

"Have you heard from…I will never say her name. What a fuckin' disappointment. Oops…sorry, Mom."

"She can't hear you," I said. "For some reason, she won't wear her hearing aids. But I blocked Mona. She can only communicate with me through my attorney. She's late on the first ten-thousand-dollar payment. She was supposed to wire it to my account last month. I gotta go through this shit for two years. She had the nerve to tell Karlos she has resources, and I don't. If you're all that, be a bad bitch, pay a lump sum and be done with it. As matter of fact, let me check my account. That bitch better give me my money."

The sun was shining as we drove over the Delaware Bridge. My jaw dropped when I accessed my account on my phone. I whispered to my sister, "Ce…"

"What?" She squealed when I placed my phone in her view.

"Eeeeee! Yes!" My mother sat up between the front seats.

"What happened?"

"Mommy, Nikki's first lump sum from the divorce settlement just hit her account."

"Woohoo! You deserve it." My sister started hunching her shoulders.

"Look at God! You're looking for an apartment, working on your second book, and you're going to be back and forth to Chicago with your babies. Okay…but you know I'm petty. We need a theme song to remember this day."

I thought for a minute.

"Oh, damn…wait." I scrolled through my playlist and the beat from Rihanna's "Bitch Betta Have My Money" blared through the speakers. We fell out laughing as we started singing at the top of our lungs and laughed until we cried.

My mother sat up and started singing. "Yeah…get my money, bitch! Better get me my money!" My sister and I laughed harder.

"Those are not the words, Mommy," I said.

We sang until we couldn't sing anymore. I sat back and transferred money to my accounts that were in arrears. That weekend was one of the best weekends I had in a long time. My spirit felt lighter as we drove to our favorite Jersey sub shops for the road trip home.

"I can drive some, Ce."

She looked at me. "We would never get home and I gotta work in the morning."

I playfully pinched her on the arm.

"I love you. Thank you for being such a wonderful little-big sister."

I feverishly looked for apartments upon returning to Virginia. My mother couldn't hide her sadness when I told her that I needed to regain my independence. I knew she worried about me living on my own, given my health issues. I couldn't convince her that I would be fine. I asked myself the same questions until I received a text from Siobhan early one May morning. Her text simply read, *Where are you with the sequel?* I texted that I was headed to Chicago and the sequel would be submitted to my publisher in two weeks. I put the phone down and continued packing when my phone pinged again: *My producer friend is in Chicago working on a project. I will make the connection. Talk soon.*

CHAPTER FORTY-TWO

I felt like a million dollars as I waited for Karlos outside the airport. I waved when I spotted his car. He jumped out and hugged me hard.

"Okay! You look amazing, Mom."

"Thank you, I feel amazing. How are my babies?"

He shook his head. "Oh, my goodness, Mom. Connor is such a helpful big brother. He's the only one who can make Kimora laugh. She's changing so much already."

"How are you and Kiya?"

"I don't know how you did all this by yourself, Mom. We are so tired all the time, but Kiya reminds me so much of you."

"Yeah, she's a good mother and you'll learn to become a good father. Don't be so hard on yourself. She's done this before, you haven't."

Connor ran to me as soon as I walked in the door.

"Nana! I thought you weren't coming back for a long time." I scooped him up in my arms.

"I told you I was coming back." I took off my shoes and winked at Kiya.

"Let me wash my hands." I walked back into the living room and kissed her on the cheek.

"Hi, sweetie." I peeked into the basinet.

"She just went to sleep. Isn't she perfect?" Kiya said.

I sat on the couch and watched Kimora sleep. "She really is. Is she everything you thought she'd be?"

"That and more."

I kicked into full Nana mode as I washed everyone's clothes while making a grocery list. It was nice to have alone time with Karlos while we grocery shopped. We were driving back to the house when he mentioned Mona.

"Mona sent a lot of stuff for Kimora."

I hesitated. "That was nice, but has she called to check on Kiya and Connor? She always kept them at a distance. Like she didn't want to get too close to them."

"Yeah, Mom, but you and Kiya became so close so quickly."

"I can't help who I love. I've loved Kiya and Connor from day one, but I love them even more now. You cannot allow Mona or anyone to separate Kimora from her mother and brother. She can't just check on you and not your family. Your relationship with her is your business, but I know one thing. My grandchildren will never have a relationship with either of them."

"But Mom, you're making me choose. She was my other mother."

"Like I said, that's your business. But they will never be around my grandchildren or we gonna have a problem."

I thought about our conversation while I fried chicken. Was I wrong? Why should she get to decide when or when she didn't want a family? She chose her family the day she walked out on us. The more I thought about it the more disgusted I became until Connor peeked his head around counter.

"Nana?"

"Yes, punkin?"

"I'm so happy you're here."

"Me too, honey. Me too."

CHAPTER FORTY-THREE

Siobhan texted me on my third day in Chicago. I thought she'd forgotten about me. She texted: *I gave Phil your number. Are you available for dinner tonight?* I texted back: *Sure, where and when?* She texted: *Expect a call from Phil.* My reply: *What should I wear? Should I take a draft of my manuscript?*

I realized that I never shared Siobhan's messages with Karlos and Kiya. They were seated on the couch while Kiya breastfed Kimora.

"Do you guys mind leftovers for tonight?"

"Those wings are gone, Mom, but we can order something. What's up?"

I started rummaging through my suitcase. "Remember Siobhan Daniels-Kent? Her agency represented you in high school?"

"Oh, man, yeah. She was scary. She was nice, but she didn't play."

"Right! Well, one day out of the blue she texts me that she read my book. She said I was a great storyteller and – drumroll –"

"Come on, Mom, tell us," he said.

"I'm meeting with a friend of hers, Phil, who may be interested in purchasing the option to turn my book into a movie."

Karlos jumped off the couch and hugged me. "Siobhan Daniels-Kent read your book? That's crazy! You've worked so hard, Mom."

"I don't know what I'm going to wear."

Kiya placed Kimora in her bassinet as I pulled clothes out of my suitcase. She began scrolling on her phone. "Oh, my God!"

"What?" I said.

"You're having dinner with Phyl Ford!"

"Who's Phyl Ford? I don't know him." She sat next to me on the floor and continued scrolling.

"Phyl as in Phyllis Ford. It says, 'Phyllis Ford, affectionately known as Phyl to the inner film circle, came out as she takes the helm at Webflix.' Look at the films she produced. She's a beast!" She pursed her lips dramatically and handed the phone to Karlos.

"Mom…"

"What?" He handed me the phone.

"She is bad!" I took the phone and looked at an image of Phyllis Ford. She was dark skinned with salt-and-pepper braids.

"Yeah, she's bad. I've seen pictures of her, but I've been grinding so hard that I never thought someone like her would notice my work. I'm what they call an indie author, or an independent author. It's harder to get noticed by big Hollywood executives."

Kiya took the phone from out of my hands and continued to read. "It says she's from the Low Country in Savannah, South Carolina…"

I tuned them out as I focused on an outfit. I settled on wide-legged black linen pants paired with a sheer black blouse. I pulled out my black peep-toe heels and lay down to take a nap.

My phone rang at twelve noon.

"Hello?"

"Nikki, it's Phyllis Ford."

"Hi, Phyllis. Siobhan said you'd be calling." Her southern accent was intoxicating.

"Yes, she thought it would be cool to connect since we both happen to be in Chicago. I know it's short notice, but are you available for dinner tonight?"

"Tonight? Yes, I'm free. What time works for you?"

"How about seven. I'll make reservations at the Landmark. It's a new American grill on the Gold Coast."

"Great! I'll see you soon."

"Looking forward to it." I felt Kiya's presence before I opened my eyes. I sat up as she gently laid Kimora on my chest.

"Look at Nana's punkin." I fell back asleep as our heart beats became one. Kimora woke me up by nuzzling my cheek.

"I think she's hungry," I said.

"You gotta get ready anyway. What time are you meeting her?"

"Ugh...seven. I'm so nervous."

"Don't be nervous. She's interested in your work. "

I meticulously applied my makeup. The air-conditioning felt cool against my skin when I opened the bathroom door. I walked into the living room and dabbed some perfume on my wrists.

"Okay!" Kiya sat up on the couch as Karlos patted Kimora's back.

"You are so silly," I said.

"You look good, Mom."

"Thank you. Say a prayer for me."

I called a Rider and waited in the foyer. Melancholy set in as the driver drove pass CAPA and turned onto Lake Shore Drive. The sparkling skyline of downtown Chicago reminded me that pressure makes diamonds.

I tried to calm my nerves as I walked into the Landmark. I followed the host through a dimly lit room decorated in burgundy and slate-grey tones. He sat me at corner booth with a magnificent view of Lake Michigan. I positioned myself so that I could see Phyl when she walked in. I wasn't prepared when she did. Heads turned as she sauntered through the restaurant. Her presence lit up the room. She was fuller than she appeared in print. Her shoulders were swathed in a black long-sleeved shirt that dipped into a small waistline. Her bell-hooped, African print skirt brightened the room.

"Please, forgive me. Have you been waiting long?"

"Not too long. The view is worth the wait." She slid into the booth and sat directly across from me.

"I'm trying not to fan out. I am meeting with Phyllis Ford."

She motioned to the waiter. "You are far too kind. I'm just a Geechee girl who likes to tell stories."

The waiter returned with our drinks, and she held up her glass.

"Congratulations on your bestseller, Nikki."

"Thank you, but it's not like it's *The New York Times*."

She sipped her drink and titled her head. "Never diminish your accomplishments. Being the first anything is an honor. You're an amazing storyteller, especially as an indie author in a genre that's not often celebrated. "

"I feel like a small fish in a big pond."

"Oh, but you're not. You are a superstar in the making, and you don't even know it."

"I'm just a little lesbian from Asbury Park who decided to tell my story."

"No, my dear, you are 'the' lesbian. To come out at the age of thirteen in the early eighties was quite courageous. The world had to catch up to you. And that's why I wanted to meet with you."

I sipped my drink. "My partner, Lars, and I would like to take you under our wings. There's a caveat to the proposition. But first, let me ask you a question. Why did you write *Little Girl Blue*?"

"I wanted to tell my story."

"I'm sure you've found that your story is often the story of many who feel they may not have a voice."

"How did you know that?"

"Your story is my story. I just never had the courage to tell it."

"My story?" My eyes widened.

"Why is that so hard to believe?"

"You're this larger-than-life, successful producer."

"What does my story mean if I can't tell it? If I don't have anyone to share it with? I recently lost my mother. She made me promise her to proudly love who I want to love. That brings us to the caveat. You can choose to do one of two things and I'll support either decision. First scenario, we can negotiate a deal for Lars to adapt your books into a film. Second, you can give me the opportunity to get to know you…personally."

I tried not to look as disappointed as I felt. "You're not interested in my work?"

She leaned in.

"I am but I am more interested in you. I cannot consciously pursue both."

I was speechless.

"I'm sorry if I've offended you, but I've adored you from afar for quite some time. At this stage in my life…Wait…How foolish of me. Do you have a significant other?"

I shifted in my seat.

"No, I don't. I don't even know if I believe in love anymore."

She casually waved the waiter away. "I've read your blogs. You once wrote that if there was a mutual interest, you wouldn't leave the other person standing alone. You said you would meet them in the middle."

"What are you asking me?" I watched as she drew an imaginary line on the table and extended her hand.

"I'm asking you to meet me in the middle. Allow me to get to know who Nikki is. One day at a time."

I'd only been divorced for a year, but I refused to give up on love. Never again would I stand in anyone's shadow. I deserved to be openly adored. In that moment, a movie reel of my life flashed before me…*Molestation. Trauma. Fear. Rape. Rejection. Bullying. Disappointment. Divorce. Hopes. Dreams. Love.*

I gazed into her eyes, took a deep breath, and placed my hand in hers.

www.ingramcontent.com/pod-product-compliance
Lightning Source LLC
Chambersburg PA
CBHW050702290626
47170CB00016B/2564